★ JORY ★

Milton Bass

A SIGNET BOOK

NEW AMERICAN LIBRARY

A DIVISION OF PENGUIN BOOKS USA INC.

PUBLISHER'S NOTE

This book is a work of fiction. Names, characters, places, and incidents either are the product of the author's imagination or are used fictitiously, and any resemblance to actual persons, living or dead, events, or locales is entirely coincidental.

Copyright © 1969 by Milton R. Bass

SIGNET TRADEMARK REG. U.S. PAT. OFF. AND FOREIGN COUNTRIES
REGISTERED TRADEMARK—MARCA REGISTRADA
HECHO EN DRESDEN, TN, U.S.A.

SIGNET, SIGNET CLASSIC, MENTOR, ONYX, PLUME, MERIDIAN and NAL BOOKS are published by New American Library, a division of Penguin Books USA Inc., 1633 Broadway, New York, New York 10019

First Signet Printing, August, 1987

3 4 5 6 7 8 9 10 11

PRINTED IN THE UNITED STATES OF AMERICA

For RUTHIE
Michael and Lissa

★ 1 ★

The gray clouds moved around the bed not quite making a sound, not quite looking like anything I knew, but being there, pushing, squeezing, coming at me so hard that I couldn't breathe, that my chest was pushing up and down to get some air, to let me live. And I was saying to myself come on now, get up, stand up, move, get them off, but it was like they was holding me flat to the bed, tied down tight without the strength to lift my finger or my head.

I could feel my body swelling against the squeezing, but it was only my hands that was able to grow until the fingers was like sausages and the things up over the bed was swirling around like a dust storm trying to tear the guns from my hands but the fingers were caught in the triggers and the bullets were coming out in a steady stream that tore into the line of men, ripping out bone and skin and knocking them down but they always stood up again with my pa in the front holding both hands to the sides of his head and I wanted to stop the bullets but the fingers was so big that I couldn't pull them loose.

They were all there in that line, every one of them, those whose names I knew and those whose names I didn't, with my pa in the front and the gray clouds pressing in, weighing down on my chest and my belly and the guns so hard, so hard against me while the bullets poured out, from the guns, from me, in a red wet stream that tore and tore and tore. . . . It went on forever, it went on forever and a day until all of a sudden I could feel the light breaking through my eyelids, the light from the outside shining pink through the skin, and as the light grew brighter I could feel the swelling going out of my hands and my belly and the pressure easing from the dark clouds pushing at me and I could tell that it was going to be all right, that they were going to let me be again this time just as the light flashed into my eyes quick like a mirror reflecting the sun and I grew soft all over because I knew from the times it had happened before that I was going to go into sleep, all soft and easy, just before it was time to be awake.

It was on the afternoon of my fourteenth birthday that Ab Evans kicked my pa to death in the Trail End saloon. There were seven men in the place and for some crazy reason George Tyler laughed out loud.

I had known right from the first peep of the sun that something was bound to go wrong. things just didn't feel right. First of all, Dr. Jimmy's mare, Frisky, kicked at me when I went to harness her up and that's a horse that never acts mean. And then I had a funny ache right in the pit of my stomach and I couldn't find no reason for it no matter how hard I put my mind to it.

Pa had put in a hard night, moaning and shaking and yelling all over his cot and once he fell out and I had to drag him back on it. The tremens, he called it. "I got the tremens real bad," he used to say whenever he'd been drinking a specially long time and he'd see things crawling all over the stable walls. Some folks might of got used to it what with all the times he went through it, but even today I shiver a little whenever I hear in my mind those terrible yells and I can see him shaking like he was dying of the cold. He was a sick man, my pa, a terrible sick man.

When he woke up in the morning I tried to get a little coffee down him but it kept coming up and spattering over his chin and finally we both gave it up.

"Can you get on alone for a while, son?" he asked, and like always, I told him sure I could get on alone. So he walked out very careful the way he always does and it was right then I got that ache in my gut and everything.

He didn't come back all morning and along about two o'clock I got worried because he usually used to drop back to see what I was having for lunch and maybe do one or two of the chores at the stable. Pa and Mr. Jordan, the owner of the livery stable, used to act like Pa did all the work, but Mr. Jordan knew how things were. He would give me two dollars a week extra to make sure we had food and he made me promise not to say anything about it. Pa used to buy food some times, but most often it was lucky we had the two dollars or we would have gone a mite hungry. Not that Pa ever ate much. He probably ate less than any man I ever saw, but I sure made up for him and twice over. Takes a lot of food to make you as big as I am and most people used to say all my food went to my hands because I could cover the fists of any boy in town.

Well, as I say, it got to be around two o'clock and all the chores had been finished and things were slow and I was tired of reading in Pa's old law books. No matter how under the weather he was, we always had an hour or two at those old law books of his and that was the only time he ever looked happy in that stable: when he'd close his eyes and smile and reel off that stuff and I'd follow along in the book. He must have been a big lawyer in the East before my ma died and he took me out here to live. That's what everybody used to say all the time, what a big lawyer he must of been back East.

Well, as I say, it got to be around two o'clock and I thought I'd better shack around the bars a little and see maybe he was too sick to come on home. I tried the Mexican's first; he said Pa had been and gone a long time ago. Pete Ruger said the same thing at his place and Gimpy Milder said I'd missed him by about an hour.

So finally I came up to the Trail End and walked in and sure enough there he was standing at the bar very close to Mr. Evans and saying something practically right in his ear. And Mr. Evans would grunt and push him away with his elbow and Pa would come in again and start talking fast and low and looking like he was going to cry about something.

I hung back because it looked like an important conversation and I didn't want to interfere with Pa's business. But finally Mr. Evans raised his voice real loud and yelled, "Get the hell out of here. I ain't going to buy you another drink."

"But you promised," my pa said. The way he said it I felt

so ashamed; it was shameful to hear my pa asking anybody anything in a voice like that.

"That's right, Ab," the bartender said. "You promised him another drink if he'd recite all that poetry stuff."

"You keep out of this," Mr. Evans yelled at the bartender and he shut up because everybody always said that Mr. Evans was no man to fool with drunk or sober, and he looked mean drunk to me. "He didn't recite good and I ain't going to waste no more whiskey on him. It's like pouring it down a dry well, anyway "

"But you promised," Pa said, and it was like seeing a man beg on the street, you feel all sick inside. "You promised you'd buy me another drink and you've got to keep your word."

Everybody had got awful quiet while this was going on and I thought maybe one of the men was going to speak up but nobody said anything, just sat there and watched kind of solemn-like. And I was so ashamed that I just stood there against the dark of the back wall near the door and I don't think anybody even knew I was there.

And Pa reached up and grabbed Mr. Evans by the arm and was going to say something, but he never got around to it because Mr. Evans swore something awful and whirled around and knocked my father right down on the floor. My pa he lay there in the sawdust and raised up on his elbow and Mr. Evans kicked him in the chest and knocked him down again.

"You hear what I tell you," Mr. Evans yelled. "I ain't going to buy you no more drinks, you drunken bum." Pa started to get up again and Mr. Evans pulled back his boot and Pa twisted his head and the point of the boot came forward awful fast and caught him right above his left eye and there was this horrible popping sound and my father fell back and stiffened up and just lay there with a trickle of blood coming down out of his nose. I ran toward my pa and a couple of men jumped out of their chairs and Mr. Evans just stood there a minute and then he stepped back. I got down on the floor and lifted my pa's head and it felt all wobbly and heavy and the men felt him over a couple of places and then they pulled me up off him.

"Cashed in," the smaller man said and right then the sick feeling I'd had all day won out and I threw up all over the sawdust and just missed splashing some on my father laying there.

"Christ, what a mess," the bigger man said and he turned and looked at Mr. Evans. And Mr. Evans was pale under his dark skin and he said he didn't mean to but what the hell was he supposed to do with an old lush who wouldn't leave him alone.

"Get Charlie Baker," he said, "and tell him I'll take care of the expenses." And he walked out of the place. Nobody said anything till after he left and then they all started gabbling and the bartender gave me some beer to drink and I got sick all over again. They lifted my father up from the floor and laid him across two tables they pushed together and then Charlie Baker the barber came in and he got some of the men to move my father over to the back of his place.

George Tyler walked over and said how sorry he was and how he wouldn't have laughed if he'd known my father was going to die. "That was a mean thing to do, Mr. Tyler," I told him, "that was a very mean thing to do." And he smiled the way he's always doing and said he didn't mean no harm and then he backed off quite a ways before he turned around and walked off.

Someone must have run off to spread the news because a lot of men came into the saloon, and pretty soon Mr. Jordan came along and took me over to his house behind the store and Mrs. Jordan cried all over me and she got me started up and it was just terrible. People all of a sudden started crowding into the store and Mr. Jordan had to keep running out to help his clerk. Mrs. Jordan made me sit down and kept shoving pie and milk into me until I thought I would plumb bust. She'd stand there watching me and after I'd finish she'd stare at me some more and bust out crying again and this would get her cutting into the pie and there I'd have another slab to deal with. It was funny because I felt this powerful hunger even though I was stuffed, and the more I ate the more I wanted. All of a sudden I was lifting a forkful to my mouth and it felt wobbly and heavy and I threw up all that pie and milk right back on the table and that's all I remembered until I woke up undressed in a big bed that had soft white sheets and smelled as clean as anything I ever smelled in my life.

Mr. Jordan was sitting in a rocking chair by the side of the bed looking me right in the eyes.

"How you feeling, boy?" he wanted to know.

"Fine, just fine," I told him. And I did, I really did. Somehow the heaviness was all gone and I felt just like I did the day before when things were going along as they always had been.

"Where's my pa?" I asked him.

"He's in the ground, boy," said Mr. Jordan. "You've been sleeping for two days now and we couldn't wait."

"Oh, no," I said. "I just had a little too much pie, but I feel all right now. I'll go in and help Mrs. Jordan clean up the mess and then we'll go over to see they done right for my pa."

"You been sick, boy," he told me. "You been laying here two days with a fever fit to burn you up. Me and the missus been sponging you and changing the bedclothes as fast as we know how. We put your pa in this morning and I saw to it that they done right."

And I knew if he said so that that was how things had happened and if Mr. Jordan said my pa was put down right I could bank that it was so. And I kept on feeling all right so I knew that things were going along as they should be.

"I'm much obliged to you, Mr. Jordan," I told him, "and I'll make up to you all the trouble you've been put to."

"I only did what I should have," he said. "You and your pa always gave me honest work for my money and I'm beholden to you for whatever livery business I've got."

"You paid us fair and square," I told him, "and I'll make up for the extra."

"You owe me nothing, boy," he said, "and I want you to stay on at the livery at the same wages and I'll get a Mexican boy to help you. You been running that place practically by yourself this past year and you got a man's wages coming to you."

"I thank you kindly," I told him. "Me and my pa—" and then for some reason tears started falling down my cheeks and there wasn't nothing I could do. I kept brushing them away and trying to push them back, but they just kept on rolling out and Mr. Jordan looked away and pretended he didn't see me. And the missus came running into the room and made a big fuss to see me awake and felt my head with her cool hands and went running out and came back with a big bowl of chicken soup.

"Drink up, Jory," she kept saying. "You've gone and dehydrated yourself with all that sweating." She seemed real proud of that word because she kept repeating it. She'd heard my pa explaining it to me once and I guess this was the first time she'd ever had a chance to take a real whack at it herself. It's nice how a simple thing like a word can bring happiness into a person's life.

Well, she finally decided I had enough and tucked in the covers and told me to go to sleep. so I did and I must have gone into that same kind of sleep because it was dark as pitch when I woke up again. There was a little bit of light coming from under the door so I slipped out of the bed to see what was going on. I opened the door into the kitchen and there was a lamp glowing soft on the table. The door to the Jordans' room was ajar and I could hear snoring fit to stampede the stable. The big clock Mr. Jordan had carted all the way from Chicago was ticking away almost as loud as the snoring and it was ten minutes past two o'clock.

I opened the door to my bedroom wide and there was enough light to see pretty well once you got used to it. My clothes were folded neat on a chair in the corner and it took me just a minute to skit into them. I held my brogans in my hand until I unhooked the window and dropped over the side onto the grass. It was black out there and there wasn't even any noise coming from the saloons. It was just one of those nights between trail herds when everybody decides to quit early.

I was still feeling a little wobbly so I walked pretty careful down the side of the road and once I got so dizzy that I had to sit down on a rock for a minute. But as soon as it passed I felt as strong as I ever did in my whole life and right then I knew I was going to do what had been in the back of my head all along. I don't even remember getting up from that rock, but next thing I knew I was standing on the southeast corner of the town and there in front of me was Ab Evans' cabin by his stock pen.

I felt around on the road until I found me a rock just a little bit bigger than my fist. I edged up to the door which wasn't quite closed and I pulled it toward me as slow as can be. It made some noise, but I could hear him inside all the time snoring like a pig and I kept pulling until the opening was big enough for me to slip through.

When I got inside, the stink of whiskey almost made me sick to my stomach. So I walked over to where I was standing over him on his log bunk and he was laying there grunting and snoring just like the pig that he was.

And I raised the rock up high and I said, "Mr. Evans." And he just kept on snoring away. "Mr. Evans," I called a little bit louder. "Mr. Evans, Mr. Evans."

And I kept saying it a little bit louder each time until finally he gave a big grunt and pulled up on his elbow and stared right in my face. His eyes glowed in the dark and he looked up at me and said, "What, what?" And I brought the rock down on him as hard as I could, but it glanced off his forehead and smashed into his nose and there was this crunching noise and he fell back with blood streaming down his face. And he got up on his elbow again and looked up at me with those eyes glowing and I brought the rock down again as hard as I could and this time hit him right square on the head and there was this hollow plunking sound and he fell back down flat, making a gurgling noise in his throat. And I brought the rock down again and again until finally all I could hear was me crying and swearing and saying all kinds of crazy dirty words. And then I stopped crying and I could hear the blood dripping on the sheaves in the bunk.

I walked out the cabin and closed the door behind me, and then I walked down to the creek behind our stable and threw the rock in the water and washed my hands which were covered with blood. And I noticed that the shirt had blood all over it, too, but there didn't seem to be any anywhere else except for a few spots on my shoes. So I took off the shirt and scrubbed it in the wet sand and scraped off the shoes and then I wrung out the shirt as hard as I could.

I walked back to the Jordan house fast as I was able because I was feeling chilly and light in the head, and I crawled back in the window and folded the shirt as carefully as I could over the back of the chair so the air could get to it, and slipped off the clothes and back into Mr. Jordan's nightshirt and got into bed again. It was cold at first, but it soon warmed up and I lay there awake. And I thought of Mr. Evans.

And then I fell asleep.

★ 2 ★

He was the biggest man I ever saw, maybe ten feet tall, and he was dressed all in black and his eyes glowed in his head so bright that they looked like diamonds in a bed of coal. He was so big you couldn't turn any way to get away from him and I kept walkiing closer and closer even though I wanted to turn around and run. But it wasn't no use because I just knew he was on the other side too, so I kept walking closer and closer, just waiting for him to reach out and squeeze and squeeze and squeeze. But the more I kept walking the more he stayed the same distance away so I started to walk a little faster and I could feel the sweat pouring down the groove in my back and then finally the two giant hands lifted out from all that black with the two eyes shining and they grabbed me by the shoulders and started to squeeze and I yelled, Pa, Pa, Pa . . .

And Mrs. Jordan was standing over me in the broad daylight shaking me by the shoulders and saying, "Jory, Jory, boy, wake up now!"

I stopped yelling and looked around and it was the same bedroom and I was soaking hot with my mouth so dry I couldn't have yelled no more if I wanted. Mrs. Jordan looked awful scared standing there and I wanted to say something to make her feel better but there just wasn't nothing to say. So we just looked at each other for a little while until finally I felt just too weak and I fell back on the bed and closed my eyes.

"Jory," she said, "the fever's come back something bad and you've got to drink some of this tea. You'll dehydrate yourself, Jory, if you don't drink some of this tea. Just lift your head a little while I spoon you some."

So I opened my eyes and lifted my head and she kept spooning that tea into me. Every once in a while my head would get too heavy and slip a little and the spoon would jounce and tea would splash on the bed, but she kept on spooning until that big glass was empty. And I fell back on the bed while she slipped the nightshirt off and sponged me with a damp cloth and put a soft, clean-smelling fresh one on me and then she let me be for a while.

I lay there thinking about Pa and Mr. Evans and the Jordans and the livery stable and what was going to become of me without Pa to take care of. I knew I could keep on working at the livery stable and the Jordans would look out for me, but I didn't want to live in that town anymore. Me and Pa had kept to ourselves and there wasn't nobody but the Jordans who cared one way or another about what happened to us. The best thing would be to get out and go find a gold mine and then go east and become a big lawyer like my pa had been. That was exactly what I would do once I had enough money for a horse and supplies, and I could feel the fever easing out of my body as I sank lower and lower into that nice easy feeling you get when the horse becomes part of your legs and you go loping along to the end of the world.

The next thing I knew Mr. Jordan came tearing into the bedroom trying to be awful quiet, and he looked down at me real anxious and asked how I was when he saw my eyes were open. "Pretty good," I told him, and he pulled up a chair and sat down right by the bed. I could hear Mrs. Jordan banging a few pots around now that she saw I was awake, and I knew that in about fifteen minutes I was going to be swimming in chicken soup.

"Jory," said Mr. Jordan, "some strange things been happening in this town." I didn't say anything or move my head or even blink.

"Someone got at Ab Evans last night and busted his head to little pieces. Didn't take nothing. Just finished him off and moved on. Town figures it was some Mexican who didn't like what Ab did to his woman."

I looked over to where my shirt was drying and it wasn't there.

Mr. Jordan looked over there, too. "That's what the town figures," he said. "And I figure I'm going to let them figure what they want to figure." And he got up and went into the kitchen.

Mrs. Jordan came bustling right in and slipped her hand under my nightshirt and clucked happily when I felt cool to her touch. "That was a fast fever," she said, and went tearing right out again. She was back in a minute with a big bowl of soup and a tiny little spoon and was about to feed me when I told her I could sit up and take my own nourishment. She watched me while I tried to work that little spoon and then went out and got me a real tool.

"I ironed your shirt for you," she said.

"Umm," I told her through the spoon.

"That damp night air just wilts the hell out of everything," she said. And she whisked the empty bowl out of my hand and went stomping out of there just like my jaw wasn't hanging all the way down to my knees.

★ 3 ★

There wasn't nothing to getting back into the work of the livery stable and nobody acted any different about anything. It was as if my pa had never been there. The Jordans wanted me to move in with them and have the Mexican sleep over at the stable, but I didn't trust nobody with the animals but myself and they agreed they would feel a lot safer about the stable with me there. I did take my supper with them every night and Mrs. Jordan collected my laundry every week, but mostly it was all just like before with horses going in and out all day and drunken cowboys half the night when they hit town. We did pretty well in that stable and I was putting by almost eight dollars a week out of my pay. And every night I'd sit there going through the law books like me and Pa used to except that I hardly knew what I was reading and didn't much care.

The weeks and the months went by and I just went on working steady and stopped thinking about goldfields and suchlike. The Jordans started talking about adopting me legal-like and me one day having the store and the stable. Mrs. Jordan taught me to do figures and got all excited about the down growing under my nose. "You'll be getting married on me one day," she kept saying, and truth to tell, I was beginning to think a bit on the girls walking down the street on a warm afternoon.

The day of my fifteenth birthday loomed pretty exciting to me because the Jordans had invited the Cooper family in from their ranch for dinner, and the Coopers had two girls, Laurie who was nine and Linda who was sixteen. I didn't know which one they were figuring on for my wife, but I was hoping it was Linda.

Well, I was standing there thinking about Linda and the way her dress pushed out here and there when these two cowboys came tearing into the barn on their horses and scared the bejeebers out of me and all the animals to boot. You could tell right off they were from the Texas bunch that had just driven a herd in because the tall one was as slim-hipped as a man could be without having his pants fall down, and the little one was the fanciest thing I had ever seen. His clothes weren't that gaudy, but he had two ivory-handled guns strapped low on his waist, and with his bandy legs and all, he looked like a man with a pair of stilts all ready to go.

They turned out to be nice fellows and kidded around quite a bit, and the little one showed me some fancy draws with his irons. He sure could make those things whirl in his hands; fast as I thought my eyes were, all I could make out was a blur when his hands started their motion. He could draw with one hand or two, throw them up in the air, behind his back, almost anything you could think of. It was just like seeing one of those shows when the medicine doctor came to town.

The tall one looked on kind of offhanded, like he had seen the tricks a good many times before, but he didn't say nothing till the little guy had worked out about fifteen minutes. The gunman's face started to sweat and he had a funny look on him with his eyes popping out a little.

"That's enough, Jocko," said the bigger one. "We got some dust to wash down."

They gave me an extra dollar to brush their horses extra special and went on to wash their dust down. The little one asked me where the best-looking women hung out and I told him the Golden Spur, and there was one girl there named Dora who looked just like a real, live doll.

"You ever have her?" the big one asked. "Does she move around or just lay there like a dead elk?" I didn't know what he was talking about so I just stared at him to see if he was going to add any more details. "Is she good or bad?" he finally said.

"Good," I told him. "She's real good."

"That's good enough for me," he said. "Come on, Jocko."

I did a real fine job brushing down their horses, gave them an extra measure of feed and carried in just enough water to balance them out. Everybody got good service at my stable.

The Mexican boy was late so I had to run all the way to the Jordans, but the Coopers were already there when I got there. Mr. Cooper said he had done the chores double quick so they could get a nice start into town. It took five hours to ride in from the Cooper spread, and they all looked a mite dragged out. But the womenfolk were so glad to get into town for a day that they would have run all the way with no fuss.

Mrs. Jordan had every pot on the stove steaming, and she told me the tub was all set up in the shed for me to take a bath. I allowed as how I didn't really need one, but she said she could stand only so much horse smell at the dinner table and I better hurry along. So I lugged several buckets from the stove to the tub, cooled it just right from the trough, slipped off my shirt and pants and went in. I was splashing around in the soap when I happened to notice two pair of eyes looking straight at me through a chink. "Who's that there?" I yelled, and I heard Laurie giggle as the eyes disappeared. Mr. Jordan came running out to find out what all the yelling was about, but I told him I had just shouted a dog off.

When I came into the supper table, I gave Linda a real sharp look and she got a little bit red, but she looked me right in the eye and never blinked a bit. The squirt was all giggles, but she was like that all the time and nobody paid her no mind.

That was a dinner I'll never forget even if I live to be a hundred. We did in three whole chickens and gravy and mashed potatoes and beans and carrots and two kinds of pie and two kinds of cake and some sugar candy that Linda had made up special. I got me a new pair of pants and a shirt from the Jordans, and the Coopers had fetched me in another shirt that Mrs. Cooper had decorated all fancy, and Laurie had sewed me up a fancy handkerchief and Linda had made me a fancy neckerchief. Mr. Jordan and Mr. Cooper had taken something out of the jug in the shed before supper, and Mr. Jordan got up and made a speech about how happy they were to have me a member of the family and all that, and Mrs. Jordan started crying and it got me all watery, and everybody laughed at how red my face was. Not that many nice things happen to you so that you ever forget a night like that.

The Coopers were sleeping in the room I used sometimes and Laurie was on a pallet on the floor in there and Linda was to sleep on the settee in the parlor and I was going to bed down in the barn. Everybody had eaten so much that they started yawning right after supper and I sat in the parlor with Mr. Jordan and Mr. Cooper mumbling to each other while the women cleaned up the dishes and suchlike and then they started laying out beds.

I just about had enough strength in me to drag off my clothes and slip between the blankets on the pile of hay. I had hung the lantern on a post and I lay there thinking I ought to get up and blow it out but I never did make it.

When I'm sleeping in the livery stable, the footsteps of a strange mouse are enough to get me jumping, but all that excitement and food had tuckered me to nothing, and Linda must have been shaking me a good bit before I come to. I figured she'd been shaking awhile because her face was all red and she had a funny look on her and she was squeezing my shoulder enough to pinch a bit.

"What's goin' on?" I asked her, feeling snug and cozy on my straw pallet.

"I want to talk to you, silly," she said, still red in the face and still shaking.

"Well, let my shoulder be," I told her. "It ain't a chicken leg."

"Silly," she said. "I just want to give you your special birthday present." And she hauled up her nightgown almost over her head and there were those two big things pointing right at me and her belly button and everything else.

"You already gave me a neckerchief," I told her.

"I know it, silly," she said, "but this is what our hired hand had me do for him on his birthday and I'm doing it for you too."

"You go on back in the house," I told her, and just then Mr. Jordan and Mr. Cooper walked in the barn and stopped right there staring at us. Mr. Jordan was carrying a shotgun and Mr. Cooper had a piece of firewood in his hand, and they both stood there looking at that crazy Linda who was still holding her damn nightgown up to her ears.

Mr. Cooper walked right up and whacked her on her big rear end with the piece of firewood. He hit her so hard that she didn't even yell, just stared at him a minute and then run on into the house. I was laying there all wrapped up in my blanket and I knew right then I was a dead duck. So did Mr. Jordan 'cause I saw him raise the shotgun like he was going to blast Mr. Cooper as he lifted the piece of wood.

"Boy," said Mr. Cooper, looking down at me kind of baleful while he weighed the wood in his hand. "Boy, I'm giving you the benefit of the doubt because this isn't the first time missy has pulled a trick like that. But, boy, if ever word of this comes back to me in the saloon or the store or the field, I'll know who spoke of it, and you better look out, boy." And he turned and walked out of the barn.

Mr. Jordan came over and got down on one knee beside me.

"You invite that girl out here, Jory?" he wanted to know.

"No, sir," I told him. "First I knew about it was when she shook me awake."

"I'd heard one or two things about her," said Mr. Jordan, "but it's the kind of story you pay no mind until it's too late. You better walk easy around Mr. Cooper from now on."

"Yes, sir," I told him, and he got up and walked out.

He wasn't hardly out of the barn before I fell asleep again, but as I was going off I thought how I better turn the lantern off this time and what in the world was wrong with that Linda Cooper in the first place. I also had a funny feeling in the pit of my stomach and I figured I better stop at three pieces of pie and one piece of cake the next time we had a special supper.

★ 4 ★

The Coopers were gone when I came in the house next morning, and Mrs. Jordan said Mr. Cooper had packed them all up in the middle of the night and headed for home. She never said a word to me about what a crazy coot that Linda was, and although there was a lot of questions I wanted to ask her, I figured I better not say anything that might get back to Mr. Cooper.

I got to the stable later than usual but Juan had really cleaned the place out nice and there wasn't much for me to do but sit around and talk to the horses. My stomach was just about telling me it was time to look into the sack Mrs. Jordan had fixed up for my lunch when all of a sudden those two Texans came staggering into the stable. The little one's face and clothes looked like he had slept on a barroom floor and the big one had dried puke all over his shirt. They smelled worse than any pile I'd ever had to fork out, and the big one was mad clean through.

"I been looking for you," he gritted right through what teeth he had in the front of his mouth. "Oh, how I been looking for you."

"Well, here I am," I told him, looking around for where my pitchfork was. Juan had stuck it off somewhere and I didn't have nothing but my two feet to defend myself with. That big Texan looked like he was going to do me in proper.

But just then his whole face changed and he sat down right in the middle of the floor and started to cry. The little one just leaned against the wall like maybe he was dizzy.

24

"You told me she was good," sobbed the big one. "You told me she was real good, and all she did was lay there like a dead elk and then pinch me off."

I had no idea what he was talking about, and I wasn't going to get near no bawling calf that would butt me in the stomach when I didn't expect it. So I just let him sit there and cry himself out. He wasn't the first Texan I'd seen bawling like a baby, and the bigger they were the more they cried when they were full of dead whiskey.

The little one pushed away from the wall and braced me. His hands hung low by his guns and he stared at me like I was dead already. I didn't dare move a muscle because I knew he was ready to go off at the slightest sound.

"You told him she was good," he said staring right through me like I wasn't even there. "You told him she was good, and she wasn't no good."

His hands were steady like rocks, like they were made out of stone, but I could see his eyes move a little and I knew he was going to pull. But before I could jump out of the way, his hands moved in a blur, the guns came out, leveled at me, flipped in the air and were back in the holsters before you could even sneeze. I'd seen some of the fancy artists showing off in the saloon, but I had never in my life seen anything like that. And then he walked over to one of the empty stalls, lay down in the straw and went fast to sleep. The other one got up off the floor, went into the same stall, lay down and passed right out too.

I figured I'd curry them out when they came to, so I sat down in the sun near the door and polished off all that chicken Mrs. Jordan had laid in for my lunch. It tasted as good as it had the night before, and I got to thinking that it was just as well that Linda had acted as she had or else Mrs. Jordan would have packed up this chicken for them to eat on the way back to the ranch. It was just as Juan always said: "Everything happens for the best."

About two o'clock I heard a groan from the Texas stall, and I went over to see what was doing. The big one was laying on his back, snoring so gently that you could just see his lips go in and out every time his air went through him. The little one was sitting up against the wall, holding his head in his hands and groaning just as softly as his friend was breathing.

I brought him a dipper of water but he didn't see it with his eyes closed, so I nudged it against him and he jumped a bit but still kept his eyes closed. I jiggled him again and he opened his eyes and saw the dipper. He reached for it awful slowlike and took it careful in both hands. Then he started to gulp it down with the water running out of the sides of his mouth and getting his shirt and pants all wet and I don't know when I've seen a sorrier sight. He emptied that whole dipper, more over than in him, and then he tried to get up off the floor. He wouldn't have made it if I hadn't of helped him, but I finally got him out to where he could stagger around a bit.

He finally settled down again on my chair near the door and spent awhile just staring at the dipper which he still held in his hand. I finally took it away from him and asked if he wanted some more water. He shook his head and just stared down at the floor for a while. Then all of a sudden his hand flashed and there I was staring at a gun muzzle again. This man was making me nervous.

He slipped the gun back in and then did the same thing with his left hand. He was just as flashy with the left hand as with the right, and I figured this little Texan must have killed nine hundred men in his time to get this fast with the irons.

"Man, oh, man," he said. "That was a night. That was sure a night."

"If you felt as good last night as you feel bad today," I told him, "that sure must have been some night."

"Yeah," he said, and he laughed a little. "That was sure some night. Old Slim turned down every piece in the place because he wanted to try that special dolly of yours and then she went and dry-gulched him." And he laughed a little bit more and he started laughing harder and then he just started rolling around on the chair until finally he fell down on the floor. And he looked up at me and the smile went right off his face like somebody blew a lantern out.

I realized he really wasn't looking right at me and I turned around and there was the big fellow standing just outside the stall and he had his gun in his hand and he looked like Mr. Devil himself come to exact payment for every tort and libel ever committed by man.

He didn't even know I was there. All he saw was that little guy sitting there on the floor, and when he cocked his gun, even the horses in the stalls stopped moving around.

"You laughin' at me, Jocko?" he said. "You gettin' some merriment from my dire problems?" His drawl got so heavy I couldn't hardly understand him, but the little guy did. He didn't twitch a muscle.

"Get up, little man," said the big one. "Get up and show us your famous draw. You want to do some tricks with me, Jocko? You want to find anything out one way or another?"

The little one very carefully shook his head from side to side, not moving it too fast or too slow, just showing very definitely that he wasn't laughing anymore, that he didn't want to do any tricks, that he didn't want to find anything out.

"All right," said the big one, slipping his gun back in the holster and straightening up till he looked about ten feet tall. "Let's pick up a couple of bottles and get cleaned up and ride back to camp to see how things are doing."

I ran to the stalls and started slapping blankets and saddles on, and by the time I got back they were standing in the middle of the stable laughing about something and as friendly as two Texans could ever be. They slid into their saddles and the big one leaned down and asked how much they owed me. I told him they had paid the night before, but he reached in his saddlebag and threw me another dollar.

"You did a good job with the horses," he said, "and that damn whore never thought to come over here and look in the saddlebags." And they both laughed out loud, turned in the stable and whirled out of there like every Texan thinks he has to. I'd seen about everything in my years in the stable, but those two were a caution, a living caution.

After supper that night Mr. Jordan took me aside and started to ask me about what had happened in the barn the night before. I told him everything, including the part about when I was taking a bath, and he seemed mighty disturbed about it all.

"That Cooper's a brooding man," he kept saying, "and I don't like it, I just don't like it."

I could hear him and Mrs. Jordan talking about it in the kitchen after supper, and I couldn't understand what they were all so upset about. I hadn't done nothing, and I couldn't help what that crazy Linda went ahead and did, sticking her bare things out at me like they were flapjacks or something.

That night I dreamt I was in a field of mushmelons and they all had big brown eyes that kept staring at me until I thought I was going loco and I woke up with this awful pain in my stomach and I made up my mind right there that two pieces of cake were my limit the rest of my life no matter how good it tasted. A boy my age had to start using some common sense.

★ 5 ★

I was just finishing rubbing Old Black down the next morning when I felt a pair of eyes sitting on my back. Don't laugh none about that. I can feel people coming around corners and going into rooms and suchlike, and my pa told me I had a sixth sense I had inherited from my ma. He said she could tell when a man was going to take a drink even before he thought about it himself.

Well, I felt these eyes resting on my back and I turned around real slow because the first thing you learn working with animals is to move easy till you find out how fast you really have to move, and my pa used to say that man is the most skittish animal of all.

There was the big Texan leaning against the wall and smiling at me kind of quiet. Texans have two kinds of smiles. One is a crazy kind that means he's about to take something apart and the other is a kind of quiet one that means maybe he's going to take something apart and maybe he isn't.

"Howdy, boy," he said. "You're real good with those horses, boy," he said.

"I like horses," I told him, "and I like to do a job right."

"Not many people left in the world with that kind of attitude," he said. "It's real refreshing to meet one."

And he walked over and stuck out his hand like we were meeting for the first time. I wiped off my hand and then shook his real formallike.

"Boy," he said, "two of my hands have took off on me and I need help to get my remuda back to Texas. How'd

29

you like to hire on for the trip? I'll pay you man's wages and if we get on together I'll see Mr. Barron takes you on regular when we get back home."

Well, it's a right nice feeling to have a grown man offer you a grown man's job just like you was a grown man yourself. I almost said yes before I had time to think about anything, but just then Old Black turned around and nipped me on the shoulder like I was being disloyal. And I thought on how the Jordans didn't have nobody to run the stable and all they'd done for me and I was sure wishing I could just forget everything and tell him yes I want to take care of your horses and ride three months with you to Texas and see the world and work as a hand and find some gold and go east to law school and then come back and be governor.

But I had responsibilities and I told him, "Thank you kindly but I can't leave here right now."

And he just smiled a little more and said, "Well, think it over. We'll be here a couple more days. I gotta see if I can make that elk move." And he flipped his hand at me and strolled on out of there.

While I was finishing rubbing Old Black down I couldn't help but think how much pleasure it would be to go off riding all day and sit around the campfire at night and jaw about the world and such.

Just then the little Texan came stomping into the stable asking if his friend had been there. He was wearing a different pair of guns, not as fancy as the ones the day before, but all worn down in the handles like they had seen a lot of use. I told him his friend had gone and he figured he was already at the saloon. While he was talking to me, he kept pulling his guns and whirling them, like they was part of him like breathing.

"You any good with the draw, kid?" he asked me.

"I never even held a gun in my hand," I told him.

He looked at me like I had just told him I could fly in the sky like a bird.

"Everybody ought to know how to protect himself," he said very seriously.

"My pa didn't take to guns," I told him, and I thought how wrong my pa had been. Nobody would have kicked at him if he'd been good with some kind of weapon, even his fists.

"But I'd sure like to learn," I said.

That was all this little man needed to set him off. He pulled loose the thongs around his legs and unbuckled the belt. Then he buckled it around my waist. I was two notches bigger than he was, and he was mighty particular about how the belt settled on my hips.

"The grip has to set about halfway between your elbow and your fingers," he said, and he fussed around me like the dressmaker lady did around Mrs. Jordan when she was having one of her fittings. I felt peculiar the way he was pulling at me here and tugging at me there and lifting my hand and letting it fall and swinging it so that the fingers brushed against the handles of the guns.

"How does it feel?" he kept asking. "How does it feel?"

"Feels fine," I kept telling him. "Feels fine." But he'd go right on fussing some more. It got so I was hoping somebody would come in the stable, but it was one of those days when the world let me be.

Finally he was satisfied that they were hanging right where he wanted them and he tied the thongs around my thighs. "Not too tight, not too light, but just right," he sort of sang to himself, and that's just how they felt. The guns were heavy, heavier than I ever thought about when I saw them hanging from somebody else, but the belt and the thongs snugged them to me like they'd been there awhile.

He stepped back and looked me over real careful, like he wanted to buy the horse but had heard rumors about one of the legs.

"Take hold of the guns," he said. "Don't pull them, don't do nothin'. Just take hold of them."

I reached down and grabbed the handles. Well, I didn't grab them because you couldn't grab them. My hands slid onto them and the fingers curled around those butts like I had nothing to do with them. They slid right around like they'd been there before and were going to stay forever and I felt my thumb touch the top piece that stuck out the back. The cool of the handles went right up my arms into my head and made things look a mite hazy for a minute.

"They're loaded," he said. "Those guns are loaded. Remember that those guns are loaded."

I hadn't thought about that before and they all of a sudden felt heavier than I thought they was. My fingers hadn't moved one bit from where they had first curled around, and I wanted to pull out those guns and shoot off all the bullets to make them lighter than they was hanging on my waist.

"Pull them out and point them straight ahead," said the little man, and I had done it before he finished saying it. I mean, I started to pull and then all of a sudden they were out there pointing straight ahead. They seemed to come up as if the holsters weren't there, like they'd been hanging in the air by my side. I tried to think back on how I cleared the leather but it was like that part had never happened. The guns didn't feel as heavy in my hands as they did on my waist, and I held them steady and even, straight on.

"Don't move none," he said. "I'm goin' to take them out of your hands."

He put his hands around mine from the back and lifted them clear. One he stuck in his waistband. I heard two clicks and saw him pull out a piece of metal from the side and push back a rod under the barrel. All the bullets fell out into his hand. He shifted the guns and did the same with the second one. He stuck the bullets in his pocket and handed the guns back to me.

"Slip 'em back in and we'll get down to work," he said.

And for the next two hours that's exactly what we did. "All we're goin' to do," he said, "is learn how to clear leather." And over and over and over again I'd stick those guns back in the holsters, hang my arms loose at my sides and grab when he yelled at me. That is, I grabbed at them at first, but he didn't want me to grab, he wanted them to spring out natural, and that's what we worked on.

He never got tired of showing me the motions and he was just as eager at the end of the two hours as he was at the beginning. My palms were hurting right through the calluses on them and I was looking for a way to end the lesson, but every time I made a move in that direction he pulled me right back to what he was showing me, and I don't know but what we might be there yet if Mr. Jordan hadn't come into the place.

He stopped real short when he saw me standing there with a gun belt on and the weapons hanging dangerous there from my side.

"What's going on here?" he wanted to know.

I looked at him real quiet for a minute and I couldn't think of anything to say. And then all of a sudden I don't know what came over me, but I made the motion and had the guns out and leveled at him, spun them in my hands twice and had them back in the holsters before he had finished his second blink. I don't know who was surprised the most in the whole bunch—me, the little Texan or Mr. Jordan. And I don't know why I went and did a crazy thing like that unless it's like my pa said, that men use guns when they can't think of anything to say.

"Boy," said the Texan, and he wasn't talking about me being any fifteen years old, "you sure fooled me about not handling irons before."

"Who are you?" Mr. Jordan asked him, and I could tell he was plenty upset about something.

"Well, sir," said the Texan, suddenly remembering he was a Texan and stretching his words out a bit, "my name is Jocko Reedy and I'm an old friend of the gunslinger here."

"You're a friend of nobody here," said Mr. Jordan, "and I'll thank you to get out of my livery stable."

"He is a friend of mine, Mr. Jordan," I said, "and he was just teaching me a few things about guns and such."

"Well, we've got other things to worry about," said Mr. Jordan, "and guns aren't going to help anything at all."

The little fellow swaggered over to me and held out his hands. I looked at his hands a second and then it dawned on me that he wanted his guns back. I had trouble with the buckle and then the damn things slid down on the floor and the left handgun fell out on the floor. We both bent down together and I cracked my head a good one against his, good enough to make me see darkness for a while and he fell down on one knee while he was trying to grab the gun and I could hear Mr. Jordan snorting somewhere in the background. There are good days and bad days, and I was getting a hearty sample of both at the same time.

Jocko finally grabbed his gear off the floor and buckled it on to his satisfaction, clearing leather two or three times to make sure he could kill any bears that jumped him outside the door, and he left after giving the same kind of wave his partner had. He had forgot his bullets were in his pocket. Sometimes I get the feeling that Texans are dipped out like candles.

"What's all this gun business?" Mr. Jordan wanted to know as soon as Jocko had cleared the door.

"Nothing special," I told him. "These fellows have been coming around a couple of days, and this one decided to show me how to handle an iron."

"That kind of thing will just get you into trouble," said Mr. Jordan. "You know your pa didn't take to guns." We just stared at each other, thinking the same thing.

"My pa—" I started, but Mr. Jordan cut me off.

"We've got other things to think about," he said. "Cooper was in to see me just now and he said Linda told him you asked her to come out to the barn and asked her to lift her nightie for you and you were going to do bad things to her."

"I never did no such thing," I told him. "I never said one word to her about that, and the first thing I knew about it was when she was shaking my shoulder."

"I believe you," said Mr. Jordan, "but I think Cooper is going a little crazy over the way that girl is acting and he needs to pin the blame on somebody. He's drinking quite a bit in town and he might take it into his head to do something rash."

"Well, I never did nothing," I said, "and I'll go right over to Mr. Cooper's and make that Linda tell the truth."

"It's gone beyond that, I'm afraid," said Mr. Jordan, "and I think caution would be the better course in this matter until the whole thing blows down. It's best you get out of town for a spell. Ma and I have decided you should go to my brother in St. Louis for a while until things straighten out here. We can put you on tomorrow's stage and you can probably come back at the end of the summer."

I had never met Mr. Jordan's brother and from what I had heard Mrs. Jordan say about him I didn't want to meet Mr. Jordan's brother, let alone live with him for six months or so. Mrs. Jordan said he was the meanest, cheapest man in St. Louis, and he grudged his own wife and kids the food they ate. Mr. Jordan was always saying to her that she was too hard on the man, but she would just roll her eyes at the ceiling and wonder how the Lord could have made two men so different in the same family. Things must be pretty rough if Mrs. Jordan had decided I could go stay with that man for a spell.

"You scoot on home as soon as Juan shows up," said Mr. Jordan, "and come by the back alleys."

"Yes, sir," I told him, and the plan was already working in my mind. I wasn't going to any old St. Louis with any skinflint, I said silently to Mr. Jordan's back as he walked out of the stable, and as soon as Juan showed up I hightailed it for the saloons.

They were just starting to light the lamps inside, and I could see pretty good through the windows but neither of the Texans was in any of them. Then I thought of the Golden Spur. The Golden Spur isn't really a saloon but a lot of drinking goes on there and I guess you would call it a saloon because I can't think of anything else you might call it. I don't even know why they call it the Golden Spur because there isn't any sign over it. It's a good-sized house on the edge of town and there's seven women and two men living there and a lot of drinking goes on and they whoop it up till all hours. Only one of the girls is pretty and that was the one I told the Texans about, and I figured maybe they were out seeing her.

I ran all the way out there, but by the time I reached it the dark had set down good and they had all the curtains drawn. I could hear the women laughing and once in a while a man would give a hoot but I couldn't tell what all was going on and who all was going on about it. I waited around a few minutes and while I waited I got to thinking about St. Louis and Mr. Jordan's brother and the next thing I knew I was up there at the front door knocking away. The laughing kept on as loud as ever so I knocked louder.

Just like that the door jerked open and this old lady in a beaded gown was looking right at me.

"Come on in," she yelled, "and join the party."

I walked in and stood in the hallway. All the noise was

coming from a room on my left, but it was dim in there and I couldn't see much through the beaded curtains. Those people sure went in for beads.

The old lady looked me over for a minute. She had one of those cheroots hanging down from her lips and the smoke curled up in her eyes so she had to blink a lot, and she looked like she was trying to decide something.

"You're a pretty young kid to be coming here, aren't you, bucko?" she said.

I didn't know what my age had to do with it. I'd been in saloons plenty of times before this one.

"I mean," she said, "have you got the money, kid? Have you got the money?"

"I got some money," I told her, "but I didn't come to buy any whiskey."

"Whiskey," she yelled. "Whiskey!" and she looked real mad. "I never sold a kid a drop of whiskey in my life," she said. "We'll take care of your ashes, kid," she said, "because that's our bounden duty in life. But you'll never get a drop of whiskey in here. Whiskey, indeed," she said, and turned and stalked out of the hall into the room behind the beaded curtains.

I stood there all alone. The noise and laughing had been going on all the while the old lady and me had been talking, and I figured I better get out of there while the getting was good. But that hall was less lonely than St. Louis was going to be, so I turned left and walked through the beaded curtain. And saw a sight I'll never forget if I live to be fifty.

The two Texans were there all right, the big one drunk as a skunk and weaving around like a blind man. The little one was off in a chair in the corner with a big fat girl sitting in his lap and they was kissing something awful. The old lady wasn't in the room at all, and she must have gone out the door at the back of it. There were three other ladies in the room. One of them was about as big and ugly as a lady can get and she was all dressed up in a beaded dress that ended just above her knees. Her legs were wide as fence posts and looked about the same except she had a lot of sores and scabs all over them. She was laughing like crazy at the way the big Texan was weaving around the room and since half her front teeth were gone her mouth looked as dark and dangerous as the inside of a well.

The other lady had only a sort of nightgown on and you could see through it and she was wearing nothing at all under it. She was a little bit better-looking than the one with the dress on, but it was strange to see her in a nightgown around suppertime. She was drinking out of a bottle of whiskey, tipping it up every now and again and taking long pulls on it. The whiskey would run right down her face onto her nightgown and it made the stuff stick to her body in an interesting way. This nightgown wasn't at all like the ones Mrs. Jordan wore.

The third lady was the pretty one that I had always admired when she walked down the street shading her face from the sun with her pink parasol and looking so trim and neat compared to the ranchers' women who all looked alike. I saw her first when I had come into the room but I didn't mention her because of the way she was dressed. Or rather the way she wasn't dressed. She didn't have a stitch on. So help me, not a stitch.

She was prancing around the Texan like an Indian at a rain dance and she wasn't wearing nothing at all. You could see her tits hanging down just like Linda's and between her legs there was all this hair and everything on her seemed to bounce around like a bag of jelly. She had quite a pottbelly on her and I wondered how she could look so trim and neat in her clothes and so puffy without them. And when she laughed I could see that she was missing a couple of teeth on the side and she had this big scar running down the side of her belly. But I knew it was her all the same even though she didn't look quite the same.

I walked over to the big Texan who had taken the bottle of hooch away from the lady in the nightgown and was guzzling it while the lady without any clothes was trying to take it away from him. They were all laughing and pushing each other and nobody noticed me for nothing. I grabbed hold of the Texan's arm, but he shook me off without even looking. So I grabbed hold again and I said, "Mister, mister," I said, and he turned around fast and stared me straight in the face. He looked at me for a little bit, long enough for everybody else to stop what they were doing and look at me too.

"It's the boy," he said. "It's the boy." And he grabbed hold of my arms and lifted me right up toward the ceiling. I'm big for my age and I carry a lot of weight, but he lifted me right up in the air like I was Laurie Cooper or something.

"What are you doing here, boy?" he wanted to know.

The naked lady reached up in the air and grabbbed me by the leg.

"What do you think he's doing here?" she said. "He came here to do what everybody does here," and she squeezed me so hard right on my pisser that I thought I was going to faint. I'd never been squeezed there by anybody, let alone squeezed hard, and it was the peculiarest feeling you ever could have. I'll tell you the truth. Much as it hurt, I wouldn't have ninded if she had squeezed me again.

I got dropped to the floor mighty abrupt, and the Texan swung me in close to him. Out of the corner of my eye I could see the little feller still sitting in the chair with the fat lady, and he was sticking his hands inside her dress and she was shrieking laughter something awful.

"What you doing here, boy?" I was asked again. But before I could say anything the naked lady put her arms around me and started kissing me all over the face. She smelled like sweat and her breath stunk a great deal. She was covering me with some kind of goo that was all over her and I thought surely that this was the purgatory my pa was always talking about and that I was going to spend the rest of my days here being stunk up by this woman I had once surely thought to be the most beautiful thing I had ever seen in the world. I knew now why the big Texan had been so mad at me for telling him about her in the first place.

Except that now he seemed to get mad that she was kissing me and he dropped my arm and grabbed her away and started kissing her on the face and rubbing her big things with his hands. I started thinking that maybe St. Louis wouldn't be so bad when all of a sudden the naked lady just folded up into a blob and lay hanging there in the Texan's arms. And he looked down at her for a minute and said, "Jesus Christ," and dropped her plunk on the floor like she was a sack of potatoes. She hit kind of solid and just lay there, breathing heavy through her mouth. I started to bend down to help pick her up, but he grabbed my arm and pulled me over to the side.

"Leave her rest, boy, leave her rest," he said. "She's had a busy afternoon." He pulled me off to the side of the room and asked me again what I was doing there. His eyes were still red as fire but he didn't look drunk anymore.

"I want to go away with you," I told him.

"Why?" he wanted to know.

I told him the whole crazy story right from when those silly girls peeked at me in the bath and how Mr. Cooper was talking wild and the Jordans wanting to send me to St. Louis. He nodded his head a few times during the recounting and then thought about it a minute.

"If you don't want to leave this town," he said, "we can fix it so that this Mr. Cooper don't cause nobody no trouble."

I knew right away what he meant but I didn't want any part of that kind of thing. The Coopers had given me all those nice presents and it wouldn't be right if I was responsible for something happening to their pa. I'd lost my own pa and I knew what it was like to be without one. I'd rather go to St. Louis than to cause anything like that to happen.

"No," I told him, "I aim to leave town one way or another. If it isn't to Texas with you, then it's going to be St. Louis."

"Settled then," he said. "Texas it is."

I grinned up at him and he grinned down at me. He stuck out his hand and I shook it solemnly the way Pa and I used to do when we agreed on something we had been debating about.

"You want me to come out and talk to your folks?" he asked.

"I better tell them myself," I said.

"We'll be leaving first light," he said. "We'll spend the rest of the night here and then head out for camp. You got a horse?"

"No," I said, "all I have is my clothes and my pa's books. But I aim to leave the books behind."

"You ain't going to need any books out there," he said. "We'll stop by the livery stable first light and you and Jocko can ride double out to the camp. Then we'll mount you out in style."

"Thank you," I said, and we shook hands again. He turned and reached down and picked up the naked lady on the floor.

"I'll go see if I can wake her up," he said and carried her out through the door in the back.

Jocko and his friend were down on the floor and she had her dress off all rumpled up beside her. He was crawling all over her and she was just laying there like she was dead or something.

"Good-bye, Mr. Jocko," I said. "I'll see you in the morning."

He didn't seem to hear me so I just turned and went out in the hall. The ugly old lady was sitting there in a chair with a bottle of whiskey in one hand and a full glass in the other. She looked like she might fall off the chair any minute.

"Did you get taken care of, kid?" she wanted to know.

"I sure did, ma'am," I told her. "Real fine."

"They're good girls," she said. "They work hard. No complaints about those girls."

"Yes, ma'am," I told her. "They sure are nice."

There wasn't any sense in getting into an argument with a drunken old lady.

★ 6 ★

Mrs. Jordan was sitting at the kitchen table with her head in her hands when I came in. The supper pots were all on the table, but I could see that nobody had touched the food and that it was cold. Mr. Jordan was nowhere around.

I'd been late for supper before but this was no ordinary late. She was holding her head because of me, and Mr. Jordan was out seeing that Mr. Cooper wasn't beating my head in with a piece of wood.

"Mrs. Jordan," I said, soft as I could. It was too soft. "Mrs. Jordan," I said, and this time it was too loud because she jumped a foot out of her chair and stared around with a wild look.

"Jory," she said, "where on earth you been? Mr. Jordan's tearing the town upside down."

I was just about to tell her when Mr. Jordan himself came striding in, saying, "I been everywhere and he ain't—" when he caught sight of me.

"You all right, Jory?" he said, looking me over real careful.

"Right as rain," I told him. "I got held up—" and right there I told the Jordans the first lie I had ever told anybody in my life. It came real easy. "Because a fellow gave me a dollar to deliver a message down over at the pens."

"I didn't think of the pens," said Mr. Jordan. "Didn't think anybody'd be there without any herds in town. Let's eat."

Mrs. Jordan bustled around getting things back on the stove and whipping up new biscuits and I ate till I near bust.

Everytime I get nervous I work up an appetite something awful.

After we finished I went in my room for something and there were my bags all packed. Mrs. Jordan came in and started to give me all kinds of instructions on what to do as soon as I reached St. Louis and about maybe going to school and of keeping clean and of writing every week and she'd cry a little and go out and get me a piece of pie and she'd tell me to never mind what Mr. Jordan's brother was like because I would be coming home soon and she'd go out and get me a piece of cake and then she'd start all over again from the beginning.

Finally Mr. Jordan came in with a letter he said I was to give to his brother, and then he made me go over what I was to do when the stage hit St. Louis.

"My brother knows about you from the letters I have written him," he said, "but he has no idea you are coming to stay awhile, and St. Louis is a big city. Therefore, you'll have to hire someone with a wagon to carry you and your belongings to his store. I told him to enter you in a school and under no circumstances are you to work full time in the store. He will be paid for your board and lodging and you'll be under no obligation to him on that score. Anyway, we hope it will only be for a few months and then you'll be back here and working in the store with me."

I'd only been listening to him with half a mind, but I looked up at him when he said store instead of stable. He'd been waiting for the look.

"That's right," he said. "When you come back, you're coming in the store full time with me and we'll hire somebody else to run the stable."

Mrs. Jordan stood there through all this, beaming one minute and crying the next, and it got so it was hard for me to tell which parts she was happy and which she was sad about. I wasn't too happy about any of it, and I was unhappier that they were making all these plans and I was about to dust off on them. A dozen times I wanted to say whoa there, Mr. Jordan, no use talking about all this St. Louis and the store and all that. I'm going to Texas with a couple of crazy fellers and maybe find some gold along the way and come back rich. But I just couldn't ttell them. I just couldn't.

As soon as I heard the two of them snoring, which didn't seem to take any more time that night than any other night, I hopped out of bed and started taking the trunk and satchels apart to pick out what I could take along with me. I knew there wasn't much you could carry on a horse, especially with the horse lugging double, so I just gathered in an extra pair of pants and some shirts and stockings and underwear. I hadn't realized how much clothes and things the Jordans had given me in the past year, and it was hard to leave a lot of that stuff. But my pa always used to say that you had to travel lean and light, and it looked to me that the Texans were of that school, too.

The day had been a long, rough one and I was tempted to lie down and nap for a while, but I was afraid I'd oversleep and then I'd be St. Louis bound for sure. I rolled my clothes into a bundle and slipped up the window as soft as I could. All of a sudden I remembered the last time I had gone out this window and my stomach gave a big jump. I thought of all the Jordans had done for me since that bad day, and I knew I just couldn't leave without some kind of explanation. So I set down my bundle and found me a piece of paper and a charcoal stick. The moon wasn't that bright but there was enough for my business, and I started to write down how I couldn't go to St. Louis and the Texans seemed like nice fellows and I had always wanted to be a ranch hand and I was going to find gold and it kept coming out all wrong. I kept crossing out everything I had written and starting over but it never came any easier the second or third or fourth or fifth time. I ruined three sheets of paper trying to tell them why I was doing what I was doing, and finally I knew I'd never be able to get it across.

I took me a clean sheet and moved around so that the moonlight was square on the paper. I found me a new piece of charcoal and I honed down the end with my knife. And then careful as all get out I wrote in big letters across the sheet: I LOVE YOU.

I tiptoed out to the kitchen and put it under Mrs. Jordan's breakfast coffee cup. They were snoring loud enough so that I had no trouble getting back into my room. And then I tiptoed back into the kitchen and put Mr. Jordan's coffee cup over half the piece of paper too.

I slipped out the window into the moonlight night. The next-door dog came up and sniffed me a couple of times and then went back on his porch. I walked down to the stable and listened inside the door. I could hear Juan breathing soft on his straw bed, and Old Black stamped a time or two to show me he knew I was out there.

Then I hunkered down on the outside wall and waited for first light.

★ 7 ★

Just because you work in a livery stable doesn't mean you're good at riding a horse. Oh, I could get around all right, but brushing them down and feeding and watering was more my specialty.

Those cow ponies sure were different from the old plugs Mr. Jordan had for hire. He kept a live pair for the young bucks who wanted to show off for their girls, but they kept running away from everybody and when Daisy Turner got her arm busted the time she went out with Bud Morton and the wagon got turned over, Mr. Jordan decided enough was enough and sold the pair to Ab Evans who killed one of them somehow and sold the other one to somebody passing through.

It didn't take those Texans long to see I wasn't too at home in the saddle. By the time I got to their camp from the livery stable that first morning my rump was as sore as a spring boil. The Mexicans watching the remuda were the first to notice the way I slid off Jocko's horse and started limping with my pack to the chuck wagon. They were jabbering away in Spanish and laughing fit to bust and imitating the way I was creeping along.

The two Texans hadn't said a word when they picked me up at the stable, and the way they looked I knew better than to start any conversation. Whiskey sure does wear a man out. One night when my pa passed out before he finished his last bottle, I drunk down the whole third that was left. It burned so bad going down that I thought I was going to die

45

but I had made up my mind and I kept swallowing till it was all gone. My eyes were so full of tears that I couldn't see nothing and the more I rubbed the blinder I got. So I just sat there and waited, waited to see what was so all-fire great about this stuff that my pa couldn't live without it and the cowboys came whanging into town fit to bust until they had themselves a mouthful.

I sat there quietlike with the tears running down my face and then boom I fell off the stool right onto the stable floor. And I wanted to get up and yell my head was floating off but I couldn't move even my little finger. I could feel the spit running out the side of my mouth onto the floor, and I had the crazy feeling it was my blood running out and I was dying. My head was trying to float away from my neck up to the sky and I started crying because I couldn't move and couldn't go back and not drink the whiskey.

I lay there a long, long time and I think I slept a little because I had these dreams about my dead mother and I dreamed my father was dead too.

I started moving again in the middle of the night some time and managed to crawl up on my bunk where I slept without dreams until the horses started stomping around about daybreak. I woke up before my pa and had put some coffee on when he finally got around to stirring. He got up real slow like he always did and started rummaging around in the empty bottles looking for a little bit to get his day started. I felt so guilty watching him that I almost cried. Here he needed it so bad and I had drunk it up and hadn't even liked it. So I pulled two dollars out of my hoard underneath the floorboard and ran all the way to the Trail End where I bought him a bottle from the sweeper.

The look on his face when he put the first belt down in the morning was one of the saddest things I ever had to see, and I was glad right then and forever since that whiskey didn't agree with me.

And that's how I knew how the Texans felt and why I didn't even say good morning when they came to get me.

But the big fellow had ridden off his bad feeling on the way from town and he grinned a little at what the Mexes were jabbering about.

"You got a sore ass, boy?" he asked me.

"It's a mite tight," I told him.

"A mite tight," he repeated to himself. "I'll bet it's a mite tight. No time to rub it for you now, though. We got to get moving."

And move we did. He gave a big holler to the Mexicans and there was such a hurrying and a scurrying as I never did see. Jocko caught up a nice-looking little pony for me from the herd, but when I went to get up on him, he bucked me off in two shakes. So one of the Mexicans jumped on and rode the meanness off him. And when I got back on he was nice as a lamb.

There must have been about close to a hundred horses in that herd, and besides me and the two Texans there were twelve Mexes, including the cook and his helper. The helper was a couple of years older than me but he was nowhere near as big. Come to think of it, the boss Texan was the only one bigger than me in the whole bunch. My pa was a big man before he got so flabby and hunched over, and he said my ma was a tall woman, taller than most and maybe even a little bit taller than him. Anyhow, that's why I'm so big for my age according to my pa, and he knew the answer to everything. Most everything anyway.

We started moving real easy that day because the big Texan said everybody had got fat and sassy sitting around and he didn't want nobody fainting on him. I thought he was making fun but a couple of times in that sun with the dust blinding me awful I got all dizzy and thought I was going to fall right out of that saddle. I think the only thing that kept me from going out cold was the fire in my rear end. I tell you I didn't know what hurting was until that day. I asked the Texan what he wanted me to do and all he answered was, "Keep up." So I just jogged along as best I could, knowing there wasn't going to be any relief till that sun went down in that sky. You never saw sun move so slow in your born days. There were times when I felt I just had to reach up in that sky and push that lazy bugger on his way. I was sitting on a great big boil just like the one I had on my neck last year, that when Mr. Jordan finally popped it the stuff squirted clear across the room and my pa turned green and disappeared for the rest of the night.

I think I had said to myself for about the fourteenth time that if we didn't stop after the next rise I was going to just get off and die where I was when we came over the next rise and there was the chuck wagon all unhitched and a nice fire burning and the cook and his helper scurrying around the pots and suchlike.

The Texan made a signal with his hand and the Mexes spread out in a circle and turned the horses to milling around and next thing you knew they were roped off in a section near a stream that was running out of nowhere into a little grove of trees. Four of the Mexes sat their horses while the rest of them came galloping up hooting and hollering and jumping off their horses like they was a circus or something.

The Texan and Jocko had already unsaddled their mounts and one of the Mexes led them off to the fenced-in section. I gritted my teeth hard and slid careful off the pony. I knew if I fell down there would be hell to pay from the crowd, and I also knew that if I fell down, nobody there would come over to pick me up. I made it and started to reach under to uncinch the pony when I felt a nudge on my shoulder. I looked up and there was the Mex who had first imitated me when we had rode into camp that morning. He nudged me again toward the chuck wagon and took hold of the cinch. I just stood there wondering what was up. He unhooked the saddle and slipped it off, threw it over his shoulder with the blanket, grabbed the reins and moved off toward the fence. Nobody paid any attention to what was going on so I limped over to the wagon and helped myself to one of the tins there.

That was a right nice thing for that fellow to do. I've always liked Mexicans because they've always been so nice and friendly, and me and Juan worked right nice together at the livery stable. A lot of people don't like Mexicans. I don't know why. I suppose it's like whiskey. I sure don't like whiskey. But I do like Mexicans.

Now that some of the pain had been removed from my rear end I realized how hungry I was. The cook had a big pot of stew cooking away and a pan of biscuits and a giant pot of coffee going. He filled up my plate with the stew and

I grabbed me three biscuits and a cup of coffee. I knew better than to try and hunker down like the rest of them so I took the food to the tail of the wagon and set my stuff down there.

I dug my spoon in real deep and shoveled it in. That was absolutely the worst mess I ever tasted. There was a sour, stale flavor to the gravy and the meat was really just a mess of slimy fat. I took a big bite of a biscuit to shove it down and it was like chewing a chunk of sticky sand. So I grabbed a mouthful of coffee to wash it all down and that was the end. It was so hot that at first I couldn't taste anything, but when the taste came through finally I knew it was about as close to dirty dishwater as you could humanly get.

Everybody else was shoveling theirs down as fast as they could go and some of them were already passing through for seconds. There wasn't no decent place for me to dump the stuff, and I knew I had to live a long while with that cook. So I took it slow and easy as the grease thickened in the pan and the biscuits turned to stone and the fat rose in the coffee cup. And spoon by spoon and bite by bite and swallow by swallow I got that whole mess down. And you know something? The weight felt pretty good in my belly when it got there.

The cook smiled at me as I walked back with the empty tin and made a motion toward his pot, but I just smiled a big smile in return, rubbed my belly three times and washed out the pan.

Jocko was hunkering down on his heels smoking a cigarette and I walked over in his direction. When I came close, he said without stirring, "Drop your pants and let me look at your ass."

Everybody stopped talking and though nobody turned to look they were all watching.

"I ain't in no mood to josh about my ass, Mr. Jocko," I told him.

"I ain't joshing, boy," he said. "I aim to ease your pain a mite."

I think if the devil himself had come up to me with any kind of optimistic suggestion, I would have paid heed, and Jocko had been real friendly up to then. So without another thought I unbuckled my belt, slid my pants down careful and bent over north with my south going straight at Jocko. I heard the low whistle he gave, but the cool air felt so good on the hurts that I just stayed there leaned over for a while and enjoyed the pleasure. By the time I got around to turning my head to check his face the whole crew, including the big Texan, were standing there staring at my butt. The only time I ever saw faces like that before was when I went to Mr. Kelly's funeral with the Jordans and the widow Kelly had plunked down dead beside him at the grave. There was shock as well as sorrow in those faces, and I began to think of ways I might get to St. Louis.

I reached down to pull the trousers back up.

"Hold it, boy," said Jocko. "We aim to give you some relief with a magic Mexican potion."

The cook went to the chuck wagon and came right back with a pan of brown-looking liquid. He handed Jocko the pan and a dirty rag and Jocko dipped the rag in the pan and then rubbed it slowly over my rear. Oh, that felt good. He kept dipping the rag and squeezing the stuff over my rump till all the liquid was gone and my pants down below had soaked it all up. It sure felt cool and nice and I bet I would have stood there forever if he hadn't ran out of the magical stuff.

"There," he said, "that ought to do it."

My pants were too soggy to pull up and my boots were too wet to pull off to get my pants off, and I guess I would have been there till kingdom come if a couple of the Mexicans hadn't come over to help me get out of the predicament. So there I was wandering around camp with my tail in the breeze, and I hung the pants over a couple of spokes on the chuck wagon wheel and put the boots near the fire to dry.

It was then that the tired hit me and I just about managed to pull a blanket over me before I went out. There was some kind of stone pushing into my belly, but I just didn't have the strength to move my hand under the tarp and pull it out. And when somebody gave me a passing kick in the dark to let me know dawn was on the way, the second thing I felt was that stone still sticking in my belly.

The cookfire was going strong in the dark and some of the Mexicans were already passing through the line. It was real cold and I was shivering before I was able to dig another pair of pants out of my sack in the chuck wagon. I slipped them on real slow but there wasn't even a twinge in my rear. I had a lot of trouble getting my boots back on because they had been near the fire too long, but it just hurt a little bit when I finally had to sit down to do it. Breakfast was biscuits and beans and bacon and coffee, but that was like no biscuits and beans and bacon and coffee that Mrs. Jordan had ever made. It went down fairly good in the dark, however, and the light was just about starting to peek through when I was washing my tin.

Jocko came riding over leading a pony, and he handed me the reins and galloped off before I could say anything. The big Texan came over and said I could ride easy again today, but starting tomorrow I would have to earn my own keep. I told him I was ready today, but he just grinned a little bit and galloped off.

So I stuck my foot in the stirrup and vaulted right up on that horse. And he bucked me right off. I'd forgotten about that. Nobody came over to help and nobody paid much attention. The pony just stood there waiting so I got up and went on him again. And he threw me off again. This time I hit the ground real hard and my nose started bleeding a little. Nobody was paying no mind to me at all. So I caught hold of that pony again and went up real slow on him. He gave one buck which I was ready for and then he just quit. Texas horses are like Texas men. They've just got to prove something even if it don't mean a damn thing in the first place.

I settled easy in the saddle and it felt pretty good. Everybody had moved off by then so I spurred the pony a bit to catch up. He set into that nice easy roll and I leaned back to enjoy myself. Except that my rear end started to hurt, and by the time I had caught up with the herd the blamed butt was smarting and burning just as bad as the day before, if not worse. I had to grit my teeth to keep from yelling and here it was just first light.

I saw old Jocko up ahead and much as it hurt I spurred the pony to catch up with him.

"Jocko," I yelled, "what the blame devil was in that magic Mexican potion?"

"That was coffee, boy," he said. "That was leftover coffee. The Mexicans say the important thing is to believe."

And he galloped off ahead. And left me there in the dust with what I believed to be the sorest ass in the world.

★ 8 ★

I never really got mad at Jocko for the trick he played on me because every time I thought on what he done I couldn't help remembering how cool that old coffee had felt on my hot butt. And secondly, he was the only one who spent much time with me. The big Texan kept apart from everybody most of the time, popping up everywhere while we were on the move and sitting just outside the firelight at night while everybody jabbered away or listened to one of the Mexes sing with the guitars. I didn't go near him too much because every time I did he thought of some piece of work he wanted me to do.

The Mexicans stuck pretty much to themselves. They were friendly enough all right, but not one of them spoke enough English to tell you where the fire was and I had spoken Mexican to Juan by waving my hands one way or another and kind of slurring a grunt.

The big Texan didn't need to tell Jocko what to do because it looked like they had been together a long time, but they didn't seem too anxious to jaw about anything except work either day or night. So when they didn't have horses or campsites to talk about, they just didn't do much talking to each other. Both of them knew enough Spanish to talk to the Mexes, but neither side seemed too anxious to try much of that.

My rear end started feeling better the third night out, and when Jocko dropped down beside me after chow to ask how it was, I answered him real civil. Maybe old coffee does have some special healing power on burning blisters.

53

Jocko was wearing his set of guns that he had worn in the stable that day he had showed me how they worked. He never went around without a set of irons on. The big Texan wore a single gun, and at night he sometimes walked around without it. Some of the Mexicans didn't even have guns and those that had them didn't wear them all the time, either rolling them in their blanket roll or keeping them in a box in the chuck wagon.

But Jocko always had both his guns on, and it was real funny to see him squatting at his constitutional with his chaps off and his pants pulled down and those two guns hanging by his side. The Mexicans had made up a dirty saying about Jocko and his guns which the cook translated for me but I didn't think it was so funny.

"Well," said Jocko, "now we each played a trick on the other."

"What do you mean, Mr. Jocko?" I said. "I never played no mean trick on you."

"Well, you lied to me," he said, "and that's the same as a mean trick."

"I never did so lie to you," I told him, and right then I thought of the lie I had told the Jordans and wondered how they were and whether they missed me or were mad because I had skedaddled off instead of going to St. Louis.

"You certainly did so lie to me," he said, "when you went and told me you never handled guns before."

"Well, I never did so handle guns before," I told him.

"Do you mean to sit there and tell me again that you never handled guns before," he said, "when I saw with my own eyes what you can do with the devils?"

"I only did what you showed me," I told him, "and nobody had ever showed me before."

"I'll be ding-danged," he said. "I do believe you are being sincere and honest."

"I'm no liar, Mr. Jocko," I told him, and right there I thought again of the lie I had told the Jordans and I vowed I would never tell another lie again in my life no matter how many St. Louises I had to go to.

"Well, then, boy," said Jocko, "you are a natural. A natural-born natural and I do envy you."

He stood up and unbuckled his gun belt. Then he reached

down a hand and pulled me up to my feet. He handed me the gun belt and I strapped it around my waist. Jocko kept his guns cinched tight, but the belt just about made it around my belly. He reached down and tied the rawhide around my thighs and stepped back to look me over.

"Draw," he yelled, and next thing I knew my hands were full of guns. I didn't even remember reaching down and pulling them out. They were just there. I didn't know what to do, so I flipped them around twice before putting them back. The first flip went fine but on the second one my left hand missed and the gun fell down on the ground and went off.

You never saw action like went on in that camp in the next few minutes. People started hollering and horses galloped around the rope ring and the big Texan came out of nowhere and grabbed Jocko by the arm.

"What the hell's going on?" he wanted to know.

Just then two Mexicans on horses galloped up and slid off right by us. They were going just as fast when they lit on their feet as they had been when they were on the horses, and they went right past us and disappeared into the dark.

"What the hell's going on?" the Texan yelled again.

I didn't know what to say and Jocko seemed uncertain as to how to explain the whole miserable business. The cook came running by yelling, "Indians! Is it Indians? I think it is Indians."

"Ain't no goddamn Indians," the big Texan snorted. "It's just some goddamn fool and I want to know which one it is."

"It's me," me and Jocko said at the same time.

"It's who?" the boss bellowed.

"It's me," we both said again.

By this time things had quieted down a bit and a circle of men was forming around us. They knew that whatever it was that was wrong was wrong right where we were standing.

"I dropped the gun," I said, loud enough for everybody to hear.

"The kid didn't do nothing wrong," said Jocko.

"Show me what the hell you did do," said the foreman.

I picked the gun up out of the grass and slipped it back in the holster. Then I made the move, covering the foreman with both guns, flipped them twice and slipped them back into the holsters. The Texan looked at me kind of strange.

"I dropped the left-hand gun on the second flip," I told him.

"Where'd you learn to draw like that, boy?" he said.

"Mr. Jocko taught me," I said.

"I only showed him the motion a few times," said Jocko. "He says he never handled irons before that."

"Where'd you learn to draw like that?" the foreman asked again.

"Mr. Jocko showed me how back in the stable," I said.

"You mean to say you never handled irons before Jocko showed you the move last week?" he said.

"My pa and the Jordans didn't hold with guns," I told him, "and nobody ever let me come near any."

"Well, boy," said the big one, "God help the world if you ever decide to go into the business."

He turned around to the crowd and said, "Get your sleep, *muchachos*, tomorrow the land gets mean."

And he turned to Jocko and said, "Don't teach him too well, *hombre*, or he might bite your head off." He and Jocko laughed at each other for a minute and then everybody went away.

Jocko waited till they were all gone and then he gave me a long look, tilting his head on the side and smiling a little bit.

"You think you'll ever bite my head off, boy?" he wanted to know.

"No, sir, Mr. Jocko," I told him. "I don't bite my friends."

"Well, then," he said, "in that case I think we can indulge in a little gun instruction each day and we might as well start tomorrow."

"I'd like that," I told him. "I'd like to be good with a gun."

"You're not going to be good, boy," he said. "You already are good. You're going to be great."

★ 9 ★

Jocko Reedy had what my pa would call an obsession with guns. He owned seven handguns but no rifle. He kept five of his guns in a locked chest in the chuck wagon, and the first time he showed them to me he took them out of the chest like they were jewels and rubbed each one with an oiled cloth before he put them back in their special cases. The holsters for the guns were kept in a separate sack and they were carefully worked each week with a special soap he had bought in Mexico.

He loved guns like my pa loved whiskey, and I guess he was just as sick in his way as my pa was in his. Three of his guns were real fancy, with pearl handles and all kinds of doodads, but the other four were plain work guns that were in perfect shape but not anything special for looks.

It took him a long time to make up his mind as to which guns he wanted me to learn on. I thought he was going to talk me to death before I even touched one again. He spread them all out on a blanket near the chuck wagon lantern and gave a speech on each one of them, telling me what it was and where he got it and how it behaved. I sat there and listened best I could. His two favorites were .41 Colt Thunderers that had just come out that year and he'd bought off a drummer for a mess of money. They had special bone handles on them and the thing that made Jocko so excited was that they were double-action self-cockers that you just kept pulling the trigger on and they went bang,

bang, bang, bang, bang, bang, until all the bullets were gone. He never even offered to let me hold those guns and I didn't dare ask.

The other gun he seemed to favor most was a Colt .45 Peacemaker that also had a bone handle with the head of a steer on it. Jocko favored the weapons made by Sam Colt. He talked about him like he was a close friend but I somehow got the idea he'd never met him. "God created men," Jocko would say time and again, "but Colonel Colt made them equal." He was always referring to his guns as his equalizers, patting them with his hands or dusting them with his cloth or rubbing them with some oil. "You be good to your equalizers," he would say, "and they will take care of you."

He finally decided that I would practice with the two Navy Colts in the bunch. The other two guns were 32-20 Colts that he used for long-range target shooting, but he figured the .36-caliber Navy was the right weight for me. I told him I could handle any weight he had, and he said, "If Bill Hickok don't think they're too light for him, then I reckon they won't be too light for you." I didn't know who he was talking about, but I didn't want to argue with him neither, so I just nodded my head and took the guns.

The minute I put my hands around the butts I forgot all the talking Jocko had done before and spent my time listening to the talk he was doing now. Because it was different with the guns right there in my hands; everything had a meaning and made sense. He showed me the click for safety and half cock and full cock and how to load and how to unload. He went over each thing like I was three years old, but as long as I was able to work with the pieces while he was talking, I didn't mind at all. It wasn't that much different than when me and Pa read law books together. Jocko had the same easy way with the guns, serious but easy, that my pa did, and it was comforting to listen to him out there all alone away from everything I'd ever known.

We spent two nights just going over how you took the guns apart and put them together again. He had me do that to every one but his Thunderers; I never did get to touch them. Once he tied my kerchief around my eyes while he had me break down the guns, scatter the pieces and then whip them back up again.

Once he even got out a screwdriver and undid the six screws on the Colt to show me how to clean and oil the whole business. "Never fool with the barrel on the frame," he said, " 'cause if you change the head space just this much"—and he put his thumb and finger till they were about touching—"you ain't got yourself a gun no more. Just a bunch of metal."

Every time we finished fooling with the guns I had to clean them out and oil them down and work some soap into the holsters. By this time I was pretty tired and ready to dump the whole thing, but Jocko was right there like a hawk and I never pushed him on it. I could tell he was going crazy watching me, waiting to grab them and do it all himself, but he was like my pa when it came to that, he worried about me first. So I held my fretting down to even it off with his worry.

I felt pretty funny riding around with two six-guns strapped on during the day but nobody kidded me about them. The Mexicans stood off from me a little since the night I dropped the gun, and I figured they figured I was a crazy kid who might hurt somebody by dropping a gun on his foot or something. They were still friendly but they were definitely standoffish.

After Jocko was satisfied that I could tear the guns down and put them together again, he started me off on practicing drawing and aiming. He showed me how he had filed off some of the cocking piece so that the thumb could slap it into full cock when the hand hit the butt. He spent hours watching my thumb as it hit the gun, and he would take his file and work off a little bit here and a little bit there until he was satisfied that my thumbs and those two cocking pieces were mates.

I was surprised at how little holster there was when you got it all tied down just right on your leg. Seemed like nothing at all was there in the way when my hands slapped down, and the guns would be pointing straight out at full cock while I was thinking, Slap! "Go!" Jocko would yell and there they would be, ready to go.

There was a lot of monkeying you could do with the guns, like filing off the sear or not using the trigger at all, but Jocko, he liked his shooting pure and clean. "Most people with handguns," he said, "it's just pure luck they hit anything at all. It's only the people with the born feelings who can pull and shoot and hit anything." And he'd give a long look every time he said that. "You got the born feeling, boy," he'd say, "and it's your duty to use it."

There were times when the duty was more than I cared for, when the damn drilling and drawing and cleaning up was more work than I wanted after a day when the horses didn't do nothing but what was mean. It got awful dull, too, the same thing over and over and over, but as I said, there wasn't nothing else to do in the first place.

Jocko had me drawing from all sorts of positions—standing, crouching, sitting, laying down, running and falling and drawing, rolling and drawing and anything else you might think of. He showed me how to change hands from one gun to another and a thing he called the border shift, which is a throwing of the gun from one hand to the other.

"Ain't maybe one or two men in the world can shoot accurate with two hands," he said, "and you never can be sure. And just 'cause you do it once don't mean you can do it again. You just have to practice in the hopes that if the time ever does arise, you will arise with it."

Jocko was always full of stories about what happened to this gunfighter or that gunfighter in this town or other, but he never mentioned any of his own doings with the gun. I made up my mind that if I ever had any occasions, I would copy Jocko and be closemouthed about it as befits a man. A couple of times I almost asked him about some of the stuff he'd done, but I never did.

It wasn't until Jocko was satisfied with my stand-up draws, the falling and the rolling and the shifting, that we started riding away from the herd each day to have me practice shooting at targets.

Shooting at targets is a lot of fun when you are hitting the targets, but it isn't so much fun when you are not hitting the targets. Jocko made a deal with me in which he would pay for the bullets when I hit the targets and I would have to pay for the misses. I had quite a wad of money on me from my savings, but I didn't take no pleasure in handing any over to Jocko. I suppose I should have paid for all the bullets, but Jocko seemed more anxious than I was that I should shoot so much so I didn't feel too guilty about that.

Jocko had a big metal chest in the chuck wagon that was just loaded with bullets, and he did just as much shooting as I did each day. I could draw a lot faster than he could, but I couldn't come near him on the target shooting. I would throw a rock up in the air and just about two times out of five he could hit that rock with a bullet. I was lucky if I could do it one out of ten times. I was a lot better at standing targets than I was at fast-moving ones, but he was just about perfect in that department. I got better as time went on but I sure paid for a lot of bullets out of my own pocket.

One time the big Texan rode out after us and got in on the shooting spree. He couldn't touch Jocko or me in the draw or even in the target shooting, but he handled a gun like he was born with it. He watched us working out the different draws and then tossed rocks for us while we banged away.

I had a real lucky streak and hit three out of three of the rocks he tossed, and he put both hands in the air and said, "I surrender. You two are just the living limit. Don't neither of you ever get mad at me 'cause I'm just liable to mess my pants at the thought of it."

"This boy's got it," said Jocko. "I'd just like to match him up against one of them fancy boys in Dodge."

The Texan stopped smiling and looked a little mad.

"Look, Jocko," he said. "I've told you never to start taking this gun business too serious. It's one thing to practice and shoot at stones and suchlike, but it's quite another to play for keeps. Don't go filling the boy's head with all kinds of wild ideas."

"I'm not filling him with anything," said Jocko. "Just showing him how to take care of himself if he ever needs be. Every man needs to know how to take care of himself."

"A man has to be serious about a gun," said the foreman.

"It's no toy you fool around with. You've seen too many carried out of saloons over some crazy little thing that never should have been taken serious in the first place. A man with a gun by his side has to be careful how far he pushes things."

"You telling me I ain't got sense enough to walk around with irons?" said Jocko, and his eyes got a red look like when a man has been drinking too much.

"I'm telling you not to fill the kid's head with a lot of foolishness," said the big Texasn. "Those people in Dodge eat people like us for breakfast. They don't care whether a man lives or dies, and they don't much care if they live or die themselves."

"I'm not going to do anything foolish," I said. "Jocko's doing me a favor showing me how all this works. My pa didn't hold with guns and people didn't hold much with him. A man without a gun out here doesn't seem to be much of a man the way people talk, and I don't aim to let anybody ever do to me what people did to my pa."

"Well, you just take care, you hear?" the foreman said and walked away.

"Don't you pay him no mind," said Jocko. "All we're doing is getting some exercise."

Holding a gun don't seem like much exercise, but in the beginning there were times when I thought my old hands would drop right off. I didn't enjoy those first days, what with doing the same thing over and over and over again until Jocko felt I had it right. But after a while I began to enjoy the workouts, trying each time to do a little better than the time before.

It got so I would spend the whole day practicing drawing while riding the lead, the wing or the drag. I'd keep imagining situations and suit the draw to the right minute. I killed all kinds of rocks and bushes and little animals that scampered away like they weren't dead at all. I'd fall off my horse and come up with the gun, having it clear by the time I hit and rolled and dead on something by the time I lit. A couple of times the Mexicans caught sight of me doing my act and came tearing over to see what was wrong. There was much shaking of heads. The Mexicans didn't seem to mind

Jocko playing around with guns all the time and drawing on them and banging away at targets and such. But they always looked at me funny after that night I dropped the gun, and I couldn't get real friendly with any of them no matter how hard I tried. The cook was the only one who spoke any real English and he would talk to me about things once in a while, but even he looked funny at me whenever I slipped the guns out of the holster. Once when I was doing spins and crossovers by myself in back of the chuck wagon, the cook's helper went by and as he passed he crossed himself, which I considered a mighty strange thing to do no matter how religious a person is.

And so the days went by with me riding and practicing all day and practicing with Jocko at night. It got so I felt off-balance without the weight of the guns on me, and once I even found myself having a constitutional with my pants pulled down and my guns still hanging beside me.

Jory, boy, I said to myself, the times have sure changed. Here you are with a butt so calloused you can't even feel the breeze and a gun habit so bad you can't even take a constitutional without their protection.

And I was squatting there making my pile and laughing away when I looked up to see the big Texan standing there watching me. He shook his head from side to side real slow three or four times, turned around and walked away. I wanted to say something to stop him but I couldn't think of anything.

I liked that big Texan. He worked me real hard but he was teaching me all the time he was working me. Sometimes he wouldn't say anything and I would find out that I was learning something just by doing it, and other times he would spell out for me what the problem was and how I should go about doing it. He taught me how to rope and he taught me how to handle horses, and all the time I had worked in that stable hadn't taught me one hundredth of the things the Texan showed me about horses. The Texan felt about horses the way Jocko felt about guns, but the Texan didn't act all crazy about it. Every morning I had to take the lumps out of four or five horses to make them saddle easy, and soon I took it for granted like my morning coffee. The

Mexicans whose horses I gentled got a big kick out of my chore and would stand there like big *patrons*, as they used to say, and make comments about my style. It was pretty rough the first couple of weeks, but it became so easy after a while that they just stood there quietly and took the horse when I rode him over. Once in a while a pony would catch me by surprise and toss me, and then the jabbering would start again for a couple of days, but it got so they hardly had no pleasure out of my riding at all.

★ 10 ★

One night after Jocko and me had been working out near the chuck wagon I was feeling too restless to roll in so I walked over to the campfire to see what was doing around here. Most of the Mexes had already gone to their blankets, but there were three of them sitting near the Texan and asking him questions about something or other.

I had no sooner plunked down near them when five men rode right into the light circle and looked down at us. That was a strange thing to begin with. First of all, the night riders hadn't given us no warning that anybody was coming, and second of all we hadn't heard nobody riding in. I still can't figure how five men could have rode all the way in here without none of us hearing them. Horses make noise and five horses make a lot of noise.

But there they were, up there looking down at us. They all had beards on them, wild beards that went every which way on their faces. And they were dressed for cold weather with long coats and sheep coats and two with fur hats. They were about as dirty-looking men as I have ever seen, and once I got a whiff of them I wondered how I hadn't smelled them coming, let alone heard.

They looked all around the camp in all directions, their heads cocked on a side and their noses raised up high, like they were looking or listening or smelling something that they couldn't quite be sure of. There was a darkness about them that reminded me of Ab Evans.

Two of the Mexicans stood up and slipped off into the dark without saying anything, but the Texan, the cook and I just sat there looking up at the men. Their heads dropped back down to us and all together they slid off their horses and stood in front of us. We just sat there.

I didn't know but maybe I should stand up in front of the grown men, but there was something told me to sit still till the Texan told me what to do. He didn't say nothing and the five of them spread out in front of us. They were carrying and wearing about as many weapons as I have ever seen in my life. They had shotguns and rifles and handguns and two of them had knives showing, and I could see more rifles and shotguns hanging from their saddles. There were belts of shells wrapped all around them, big shotgun shells and rifle shells and cartridges of different sizes to fit some of the strange-looking handguns they were wearing. I had never seen such a hairy bunch in my whole life, and a lot of strange people had gone through my livery stable.

"Howdy," said one of them, who I thought was a young-looking fellow till I saw he didn't have a tooth in his head. He looked young when his mouth was closed and old when it was open. I think maybe he was more young than old.

'Howdy," said the Texan, and he stood up. I stood up as soon as he did and two of the men turned a little bit in my direction but they didn't say nothing. The cook just sat there, looking straight ahead, just like the men hadn't been there.

"We've had a long ride," said the man, "and we saw your fire and thought maybe you might have a little extra grub from your supper."

The Texan looked down at the cook and said, "Pedro?" He asked it real soft, like someone was sleeping and he didn't want to wake them up.

The cook didn't look up at all, and in the same quiet voice he said, "There is some biscuit, that is all."

"You go get it, son, and bring it back here," said the Texan, and I thought that was real peculiar because the cook was a lot older than the Texan, and he'd called him son like he did me when he was feeling good. The cook took right off for the chuck wagon.

"Coffee's hot," said the Texan, nodding at the big pot at the side of the fire. There were four cups draining around it, and four of the men gave the reins of their horses to the other one and stepped over to the fire to pour themselves cupfuls. I know how hot that coffee was because I'd burned myself often enough, but they drank that scalding stuff down like it was springwater. They filled right up again and sipped the second cup, except for the one who had talked in the first place. He brought his over to the man holding the horses and came back just as the cook arrived with the biscuits we were supposed to be dunking in our coffee the next morning.

Those men took turns shoving biscuits through their mouths and in their pockets at about the same time. The talking one took a handful over to the man holding the horses and came back with his cup, which he filled again. One of the men took out a bottle of whiskey and they passed it all around their circle till it was gone. Then they dug another one out and passed that around till it was drunk up. It sounds awful fast but you never saw whiskey, coffee or biscuits go down like that crew put them away. I stood there amazed as they crammed and swoggled and grunted their way through everything, sounding worse than a herd of goats.

The Texan just stood there watching them, and they were watching him and me and looking around everywhere in the dark. The cook had disappeared somewhere and there was just me and the Texan standing there. I noticed out of the side of my eye that the lantern had gone out over by the chuck wagon, and I saw that one of the men had seen it too.

"How big a string you running here?" asked the talker.

"Quite a few," said the Texan.

"What's your brand?" he wanted to know.

"This is the Barron spread," said the Texan.

"Heard of it, heard of it," said the man.

"How many hands you got on here?" asked the man.

"Enough," said the Texan. "We got enough to take care of anything that comes along."

"Mostly Mexes?" asked the man.

"Some," said the Texan, "some."

"We could use some fresh horses," said the man.

"Got none to spare," said the Texan.

"Could trade off," said the man.

"No," said the Texan, "no trading."

"We need horses," said the man, and he stood up from the fire and dropped his cup on the ground. The others stood up too, and they all faced towards me and the Texan. The Texan didn't say anything.

"Hey, boy," said the talker, "you wear them guns like a real slinger. You real good with them guns?"

I was about to tell them that I was taking lessons from Jocko, but I realized they didn't know who Jocko was and probably didn't care about my lessons and all so I didn't say anything. I wondered where Jocko was.

"You real good with them guns, boy?" he asked again and took a step towards me. The Texan stepped right in front of him so that he was between me and the man.

"That's enough," he said, and there was something in his voice that made me feel fear. He wasn't feared but I was feared and I didn't know what had set me off. It was strange being there all alone with the Texan. I knew that Jocko and the Mexes were out there, but I couldn't feel them anywhere, and I felt all alone.

"You've had your coffee and your biscuits," said the Texan, "and now you best be on your way."

"We need horses," said the man.

"No horses," said the Texan. "No more coffee, no more biscuits and no more time. On your way."

"You and the boy figuring to send us on our way?" said the man.

"They're all around here," said the Texan, "twenty-four of 'em, and they got the bead right now."

"Mexes," said the man, and he spit on the ground. "Mexes! Their asses is five miles away by now."

"Not my Mexes," said the Texan. "You try them."

The men looked all around in the dark, cocking their heads and pointing their noses like they did before.

"Call him, Alf," said one of the men.

The talker looked at the Texan for a long time, and you could see from his eyes that things were going through his head. I couldn't see him all the time because the Texan was between me and him, but I swayed a little to the side and could tell that man was thinking hard.

"We thank ya for the coffee and the biscuits," he said. He turned and walked over to his horse. The others turned practically with him and got right on their horses without saying a word. When they was all mounted up, they looked down on us for a minute just like they had when they came in, wheeled and galloped off straight opposite the way they had come in. They went out just as noisy as they had come in quiet, and you could hear them for a long ways off.

The Texan and me stood there listening until we couldn't hear them no more. Then he turned and looked at me for a bit. "You did good, boy," he said, "real good."

Then in a loud voice he called, "Jocko?"

"Right here," said Jocko, from out by the chuck wagon. "I'm over by the wagon."

"I knowed you was somewhere," said the Texan. "Don't come in. Take Juan and Carlos and Sanchez and cruise the horses all night. I'll be right here."

Then he went over to the fire and threw some more wood on it. It blazed up from the ashes.

"Cook," he said, "hey, cook."

The cook came out of the dark over by the chuck wagon.

"You gonna need coffee and biscuits for breakfast," said the Texan.

"*Si,*" said the cook. "I think I make the biscuits now."

"Make the coffee, too," said the Texan. "I could use me a cup." He turned to me and said, "You want a cup of coffee, boy?"

"No," I told him, "I'm too tired. I'm going to crawl right in."

"You're a good boy," he said, "a real good boy. It ain't easy to just stand there sometimes."

"Mr. Jocko could have shown them some tricks with the guns if they was so all-fired anxious," I said. "I got me a lot more to learn."

"Tricks can be a sight easier than just standing still," he said. "You seem to have a knack for both."

The cook was over by the wagon getting all his stuff together and nobody had come back into the firelight. There was just the two of us standing there talking, and I felt me a kinship with this man that was like he was my pa or maybe even a brother which I'd never had. Or a sister neither. And I got a homesick feeling in my stomach. But I didn't want to be any place but where I was, standing there beside him. So I didn't say nothing else and just went and bedded down.

★ 11 ★

We made the trip in easy stages because the Texan said the horses were still tired from the drive up and he wanted them in good shape by the time we got back to the ranch. Jocko told me the ranch was so big that you could ride for days in all directions and not come to the end of it, and the Barrons lived in a house that had twenty rooms and an inside toilet for the menfolk and an inside toilet for the women. Well, not really inside, but there was a wooden tunnel from the house to where you took your constitutional.

Things went pretty quiet all in all. One day we came on this family of Indians traveling in the opposite direction, and they were about the filthiest bunch of buggers I ever did see. There was a pa and a ma and five little kids running around. They had one horse and one of these bunches of branches tied together that the horse was dragging and they had all kinds of things piled up on it.

The man didn't look too bad but the ma was about the fattest, greasiest old thing you ever saw. She was wearing a buckskin thing that I suppose you could call a dress, but I could just see Mrs. Jordan getting one sight of it, let alone a whiff.

Anyways they stopped and the man jabbered away at us. The cook could speak a few words of Indian and he palavered awhile, slipping in some English and some Spanish and some I don't know what. He turned to the Texan and said, "He wants some food and a horse."

"What's he got to trade?" the Texan asked.

The cook jabbered away and the Indian jabbered back at

him and ended up by pointing at the woman who was standing there like she was made out of stone. The kids had shut up completely and were hiding behind their horse.

"We can all use the woman once," said the cook. He translated in Spanish for the others.

"Tell him he can have the food but not the horse," said the Texan.

The cook jabbered away and the Indian jabbered back and the cook jabbered again and finally the Indian nodded.

"How much should I give him?" asked the cook.

"Give him a sack of flour and a side of bacon and some beans," said the Texan. "He's got a lot of mouths to feed."

The cook and his helper went to the wagon and hauled out the stuff the Texan had okayed. They put it down in front of the Indian who turned to his wife and barked something at her. She walked out into the field about a hundred feet, stood there a minute and quick as a wink flopped down on her back. She reached down and pulled her skirt up over her belly and then just laid there.

The Texan slipped off his horse and walked out to her. He unbuckled his gun and laid it on the ground. Then he slipped down his pants and there was his pisser sticking out like it was hurting something awful. I'd been having trouble with mine the last few months in town and I could tell how bad his was hurting him. Then he plunked right down on top of that Indian woman and thrashed around for a couple of seconds. She just lay there, never moving nothing. The Texan stood up and I couldn't see his problem anymore. He pulled up his pants, buckled on his gun, spat on the ground near where the Indian woman laid and walked back to his horse.

We had all been standing there—me, Jocko, the Mexicans, the Indian and the kids—all watching the Texan do what he was doing. When the Texan walked back, Jocko slipped off his horse and went over and did the same thing the Texan had done, including the spitting on the ground. Only I noticed his problem was nowhere as big as the Texan's. When Jocko was finished, the Mexicans took their turn, starting with the cook and ending up with the cook's helper. They all did the same thing except that some of them didn't have guns to take off and none of them spit.

When they had all finished, the Texan turned to me and said, "You want a turn, boy?"

"No, thank you, sir," I said, and somehow the sir came out harder than I meant and he looked at me funny.

"Don't blame you none, boy," he said. "She sure is the rottenest, foulest-smelling pig I ever stabbed."

"Amen to that," said Jocko.

"Ask him if he wants some more flour and bacon," said the Texan to the cook.

The Mexican jabbered away at the Indian and the Indian jabbered back at him.

"He says same around again of everything and one more for everybody," said the cook.

The Texan nodded and the cook and his helper went to the wagon and got the stuff and laid it before the Indian. The Indian woman was still laying on the ground, not even blinking as far as I could see. It almost seemed like she knew she wasn't through with her chore.

The Texan slipped off his horse, walked over to the woman and repeated the whole business, right down to the spitting. Then Jocko and then the Mexicans.

When they were all through, the Texan looked at me and said, "Last chance, boy." I just shook my head. He wheeled his horse and rode off to round up some of the horses that had grazed away from the herd. The Mexicans galloped off after him and got things moving again.

The Indian yelled out something and the Indian woman got off the ground and pulled her dress down. It took her quite a while to do it and it seemed to me she was a little stiff in the joints what with laying still all that time while a bunch of crazy men jumped all over her.

She walked over to the food and started piling it on the branches, tying it down with pieces of rawhide. The Indian stood there watching and the kids started running around again, laughing and shoving each other and plain full of fun.

The woman finished packing everything down and went to the head of the horse and grabbed the rope that was strung around his head. She hadn't said a word the whole time right from the beginning. The man looked up at me and stared me right in the eyes. He was a good-looking fellow when you checked him real close. He kept looking at me and finally he raised his right hand in the air with his elbow bent. He just stood there staring at me and holding his arm up. I looked right back at him, trying to figure out what he wanted. And then, I don't know why I did it, I held my right hand up in the same way he was doing. He nodded and it looked for a minute like there was a little smile on his face. Then he turned and started off and she pulled the horse's head and started after and the kids went running after them.

I stood there watching them for a long time while they dwindled in the distance. Then I whirled the pony and went galloping after the herd.

★ 12 ★

The days were long on the trail, and I guess I practiced pulling guns so much because there wasn't hardly much of anything else to do. The work was mostly sitting on your butt and jogging on ahead or aside or behind that crazy bunch of horses. They kept coming up with all sorts of ailments or busted hooves or even legs and we had to shoot two by the time we had gone four weeks.

Mrs. Jordan had made me take a bath every Saturday night and on special occasions, and to tell the truth I had got used to it. That's why I began to feel so crawly in the skin and slimy in the clothes after a while. We sweat all day and froze all night and the dust got into everything, until it hurt like the devil trying to clean yourself up a bit after your constitutional. Jocko claimed he hadn't pissed water in four years, just fine grains of sand running out of him like an egg timer.

Even the guitar-playing and the singing by the Mexicans became more of a pain than a pleasure after a couple of weeks. They only knew a few songs and they didn't play them too good if you listened close. Jocko never got tired of playing with his guns but with me helping to clean them and keep them in shape, even that didn't take too long a time.

Both the men and the horses were getting awful skittish and fights broke out in equal amounts. One horse took such a bite out of another one's flank that we had to do away with the beast. And one of the Mexicans sliced a nice chunk out of another one's arm in an argument over who was to put his bedroll where. The big Texan patched up the arm of

74

the hurt one and then took the other one out in the field and beat him unconscious. Nobody seemed to think twice about what was going on, but I was getting a mite unhappy with the cowboy's life, and I spent a lot of my time thinking back on all the people I'd meet each day at the livery stable and how Mrs. Jordan's cooking would smell when I'd get home at night. You never realize how good things are until things get worse. Not that the work or the people were so bad on the trail. It was just that I had nobody to talk to, and I even missed my readings out of my pa's law books.

The big Texan was always funning me on the big words I used sometimes and kept asking me what college I had graduated from. I told him I had never been to school in my life, but that my pa had studied with me nearly every day. The Texan would just grin and say, "You don't fool me none, perfesser. You're ninety years old and you been to college." I didn't think much of his funning me all the time on how I talked, but I wasn't going to challenge him about it neither.

Well, this is how things were the day we bedded down near a town called Travis. Jocko had started talking about this town about three days before we came near it, telling about a wild time he had had there some three years before. He said there was a dance hall girl there who could do more tricks than a medicine show magician, and he still had the marks on his body to prove it.

"That sure is a wild town, that Travis," he kept saying. "You and me ought to take a little jaunt in there."

"I'm ready," I told him, "just lead the way."

The foreman had been steering clear of towns because he said he didn't want to lose the crew for a week once they got the taste of whiskey in them. A couple of times we had bedded down near towns, but he had promised a dusting to anybody who slipped out for the night, and nobody was anxious to take him up on the offer.

The cook's helper had been down with a fever for three or four days and seemed to be getting worse even with all the powders the cook had made him swallow. The cook had made a bed in the wagon and the boy lay in there day and night, and sometimes I'd wake up in the dark of night to hear him moaning away. He hadn't been able to keep nothing down for three days and he was looking mighty frail the one time I peeked in on him. The cook was worried because it turned out the boy was his nephew and he kept talking about what his sister would do to him if anything happened to the boy.

It got so the boy couldn't take the pounding of the wagon all day, and the cook announced he wasn't moving another foot until the boy was well enough to travel. So we set down outside Travis and waited out the boy to see if he was goin' to live or die on us.

Jocko got all excited when the foreman said we would wait around a day or two to try to break the boy's fever and bring him back to working condition.

"We're going to go have us a little fun," Jocko said every time he came near me.

He and the foreman had rode into town to pick up some supplies and see if they could find some medicine for the Mexican, and they came back the next morning pretty drunk and mean-looking. The foreman had bought some powder off a man who said it was good for the fever, and they managed to get a little down the boy's throat. The foreman went around all day saying that Travis was the same stinkhole it had always been and nobody was going back there on this trip and maybe never if the dirty no-gooders didn't know how to treat customers better than that. It seemed like both dance hall girls had been killed off the week before by some crazy guy who had hired them for the night and then strangled them after cutting them up something awful. He had gone out a window and nobody had known nothing until the bartender went to see what was keeping them from eating their noon meal.

I was disappointed because I had wanted to buy a new shirt, but Jocko just winked at me and told me not to worry about nothing.

There must have been something real good in that powder the Texan had bought in town because all of a sudden the boy's fever broke and he was able to keep down some broth the cook had boiled out of old shoe leather or something.

"We'll be leaving soon as the sun drops," Jocko whispered in my ear.

"He's going to be mighty rough on us, Jocko," I told him. "He's not going to like us one bit, and he's going to whomp me good."

"He'll never know we're gone," said Jocko. "He'll think we're off practicing somewhere, and we'll be back before first light."

"All right," I told him, "but I got a feeling, a bad feeling."

It happened to be one of those nights when the foreman pulled into himself and didn't seem to see nobody else. I think he had brought a bottle or two back from town and was anxious to get off and drink himself quietly to sleep.

Jocko already had our horses saddled and tied behind some trees when he came to get me.

"What you so all-fired eager to get into town for?" I asked him. "That girl ain't there no more. There ain't no girls there no more after what that man did."

"The bartender told me there were two new ones due in today," said Jocko, "and one of them is supposed to be a lulu."

"Gee, that's great, Jocko," I told him, and I was hoping that the store had a shirt to fit me real good. I could almost feel the cool new clean cloth on my back and I figured that was lulu enough for me. I'd washed a couple of my shirts while we were laying over, but they still had a gritty feel to them. Sand ain't nowhere as good as soap for washing things with.

It took us a solid hour to ride into town and it was real black by the time we reached there. The place was nowhere as big as my town, but then again there wasn't no railroad siding there, and the place had no call to be as big. We passed the store on the way through but all the lights were out and whoever ran it didn't live in the back like the Jordans did. I'd had the feeling right along that nothing good was to come of this trip and here it was just like I felt.

We passed a small saloon on the street and then we came up on this big one. There was a sign in front that said Mike's and there were quite a few horses tied up outside. We slid off and started to tie up when Jocko said, "Where are your guns, boy?"

I looked over and he was wearing his fanciest pair, with the white stocks and the gold and silver trimming.

"Didn't figure I'd need guns in town," I told him, "and I got a sore spot on my side where they been rubbing."

"Where'd you leave them?" he wanted to know.

"They're rolled up in my pack," I told him.

"You know you can't leave nothing around them Mexes," he said.

"They ain't going noplace," I said, "and the guns can't go noplace if the Mexes can't go noplace."

"You should take better care of them anyway," he said. "They ain't your property, only a loan."

"I'll be careful," I told him, "and if something happens, you'll get your money."

"It ain't that," he said. "It's just that you have to take care of your guns."

He turned to walk into the bar, and I could tell he was real upset.

To tell the truth, I was getting more than a mite sick of those guns and all guns. Didn't make much sense to be always taking them apart and putting them together and oiling them and practicing all the time for someting that wasn't going to be any of my business. But Jocko had been real friendly to teach me and let me use his equipment and I wasn't going to make any fuss at this stage of the game. Once we reached Texas there'd be a whole lot of new things to do and I could forget about all this gun business.

Mike's place was sure a lively one and a lot more fancy than the Trail End or any of the others I had ever seen. There were maybe thirty people in the place and some of them were really dressed in fancy clothes. There were three card games going and quite a few people standing at the bar and some just gathered around in different spots, drinking and yelling and whooping it up.

It felt real good to be in a place lighted up all nice after those weeks on the trail, and I was glad I had come even if I wasn't going to get a new shirt out of it.

Jocko headed straight for the bar, and I trailed along behind him. The bartender said, "What'll it be, gents?" and then smiled as Jocko asked, "The girls here yet, Mike?"

"Oh, it's you, is it?" he said. "I never thought you'd make it back today after what you put away. No, the girls didn't come in on the stage, and I don't know where they're or when they'll be here. If they ever come at all."

Jocko looked so disappointed that Mike said, "But there's all the whiskey and beer you might want, and if you're so inclined, I'll dig you up a Mexican girl somewhere later."

"Well," said Jocko, "whiskey it is then."

"Same for your friend?" asked the bartender.

"I'll have a beer," I said fast. I didn't want none of his stinking whiskey and I'd never gotten around to drinking beer. My pa always said it raised hell with your insides sloshing around in there.

Jocko tossed down his shot with a flip of his head and just stood there for a minute, looking at nothing. He sure liked his whiskey, that man. The bartender was standing there looking at Jocko and looking at me for some reason. Jocko picked up his beer and drained half the glass in a long swallow. Then he stared down at the bar again for another minute. Whiskey is a good companion, my pa used to say. When you have your friend whiskey with you, you don't need anybody else. Jocko didn't even know I was there anymore. He was talking to his friend.

The bartender was still looking at me, so I picked the beer glass off the bar. The glass was dirty and there were things floating in the beer. It looked almost green in the lamplight, but the bartender was still staring at me for some reason, so I tilted the glass at me and took a swallow. I tasted green, not the glass green but the color green. It didn't taste good at all but I swallowed it down and turned around with my back to the bar and my glass in my hand. I could hear the bartender moving away and I felt a lot better about it all. Jocko had poured himself another drink from the bottle and was staring down at it.

Everybody was sure having himself a good time in there. One group was having the best time of all. They were a bunch of young fellows and one of them was telling a story. He'd say about two words and they'd all bust out yelling and laughing and stamping their feet. He'd stand there grinning a bit and when they calmed down a little, he'd let them have three more words and off they'd go again. I wished I could get in the middle of a bunch like that and just let myself go free and easy.

The card tables were the quietest spots in the room. Most of the fancy dressers were sitting there, puffing on long cigars and moving just about as much as they had to. If you got to tell somebody a secret, my pa used to say, tell it to a professional gambler. He don't care if people live or die and he don't figure any story is worth passing on. There was a gambler used to come to the livery stable all the time, and once in a while he'd give me an extra dollar for no reason at all. I asked him once why he did it, and he smiled and said, "For luck, just for luck." And he'd always rub my head after he said that. He got killed in the Trail End one afternoon when a herder charged him with cheating and his derringer caught in his sleeve. Me and my pa were the only ones at his funeral. My pa went along because he said any friend of mine was a friend of his.

I heard Jocko pour himself another glass, and I figured it was time I took another pull on the beer. But I just couldn't do it. I was mighty glad the girls weren't there because I'm sure old Jocko would have gone off with them and left me alone, and people would have noticed I didn't particularly care for the beer. It was sure hard to understand grown people. The things they pleasured themselves in I wouldn't have made a mule try.

The funny fellow in the corner was still telling his story but his friends weren't laughing much now. One of them walked away from the bunch and joined two men at the bar. The funny fellow started laughing louder at his own words, but I noticed all the time the others were laughing softer. He gave one big laugh and walked over to the bar to stand beside the one who had left the bunch and the other two fellows.

"Gimme some whiskey," he yelled, pounding his hands on the bar.

"Easy, Jack, easy," Mike said, as he came hurrying over with a bottle.

"When I'm thirsty, I'm thirsty," said the man, "and that's when I want a drink. And when I want a drink, I want a drink right now."

He took the glass of beer that was put down beside the whiskey glass and spilled it on the floor. Then he filled the beer glass brim full of whiskey.

"Watch this, everybody," he said, and drained that whiskey down in one swallow.

"Now where's my beer?" he said, picking up the whiskey glass.

Mike came over and took the whiskey glass, filled it full of beer and handed it back. Old Jack, he took that beer glass and sipped it and made believe he was gagging and choking and falling down. Everybody in the place was watching him and laughing like crazy.

"Man," he said, "that stuff is too strong for me. I better stick to whiskey."

And he filled that beer glass brim full of whiskey again and drained it with a long swallow. Now one thing my pa could do was drink whiskey. And following my pa around I also saw a lot of other men who could drink whiskey. But I never saw anybody drink whiskey like I saw that fellow drink whiskey. I don't think I ever saw anybody drink water like that. He was really something.

He stood at the bar with both hands spread along the top and he looked into the mirror. I saw his eyes in the mirror and that man was about as drunk as anybody could ever get without falling down. He should have been falling down. Those two glasses of whiskey weren't the first ones he'd had that night. But he was standing there easy, both hands spread to steady himself, and his mind going steady ahead, working away at something.

He was a nice looking fellow, tall and slim with corn-colored hair and a lot of wrinkles around his eyes even though he wasn't too old. He was wearing nice-looking clothes with real expensive Mexican boots and silver spurs and his gun hung low. It was a Navy and it looked like it had taken a lot of use. The holster was well oiled and looked real soft. He wore the gun like he knew how to use it, and I thought to myself what if one of the Mexicans steals the guns I left in my roll and won't old Jocko be mad at me.

Jack was looking at Jocko in the mirror and I turned all the way back around to see what old Jocko was doing. The bottle was half gone and while I'd been daydreaming away old Jocko had been working at his second favorite trade. He was still staring down into his glass, and I could tell by his face that he was real happy now, happy to be in where it was bright and noisy and where there was another bottle c whiskey when this one was gone and then maybe a couple t take home with us. The old foreman is sure going to be sor at us when we drop back there, I was telling myself. And had begun to wish we were back there because it was a col dark ride tonight and there was a lot of hard riding tomorrow

"Hey, there," said Jack, talking to Jocko in the mirro "You going to drink that big bottle all by yourself, littl man?"

Jocko didn't even hear him. But everybody else in th place did. Mike came moving over in the space betwee Jack and Jocko, polishing the bar with about the dirtiest ra you ever saw.

Jack turned sideways at the bar, facing Jocko and me. H looked Jocko up and down, his eyes resting a small time o the fancy guns.

"Those are fancy-looking pieces you got there, little man," he said. "They look too heavy for a little feller like you."

The three men who had been standing beside Jack ha somehow edged down the bar a little and the one furthes away carefully walked across the room. There was troubl here all right, but I didn't know what to do about it.

"Little man," Jack yelled, and his hand slapped down o the bar with a crack that made a glass jump.

Jocko's head snapped up and he looked around wildly not sure what was going on.

"That's better, little man," said Jack. "You pay attentio or something else is going to get slapped around here."

"You talking to me?" Jocko asked him.

Jack gave a big howl of a laugh. He turned to everybod in the room.

"Did you hear that?" he asked. "Did you hear that? practically bust my throat trying to get the gentleman' attention and he asks if I'm talking to him."

"Come on, Jack," said the bartender, "why don't you take it easy for a change?"

Jack turned his full attention on the bartender. He raise his hand and pointed his forefinger right at him.

"Mike," he said, "I'm getting a little tired of you. An I'm getting a little tired of this place. And you know what' All of a sudden this place might not be no more. And you might be no more. You're here for one thing. To bring me a drink."

He turned once more to Jocko.

"Ain't that right, little man? When we big fellers want to drink, it's his job to bring us a drink."

"That's right," said Jocko. "When we want drink, he brings us drink."

Jack laughed so he almost split. He walked over and hit Jocko so hard on the back that dust flew for a good minute.

"That's right, friend," he said. "You know what's what around here. Have a drink on me."

He put his arm around Jocko and squeezed the dust right out of him. Jocko was a little loose from the whiskey he had in him and his eyes bulged out while the big guy was hugging him. I'd been watching it all so careful that first thing I knew my pants were all wet from the glass of beer tipping in my hand.

Mike rushed over with a fresh bottle and started to pour glasses of whiskey for Jack and Jocko.

"Wait a minute," Jack yelled. "What the hell you trying to pull here? I said me and my friend was going to have a drink."

He picked up the whiskey glasses and threw them right at the wall where they busted into a million pieces.

"Now bring us a couple of real glasses," he said.

Mike came right back with two beer glasses and filled them up to the top.

"Here we go, little man," said Jack and tipped his glass right down his throat. Jocko tried to do the same but couldn't do it. He gagged once, started choking and went into a coughing fit that I was sure was going to kill him right there dead. Jack stood there roaring with laughter while Jocko staggered around all red and I could see that everybody else in the place thought it was pretty funny too. Except that old Jocko was in real trouble and I was feared for his life. He staggered back against the bar and stood there heaving and retching and carrying on something fierce while Jack was yelling right into his ear about ride 'em bronco, and things like that. Finally, Jack took a full glass of beer and poured it right over Jocko's face. He didn't mean him no good by it, but it seemed to help and Jocko stood there with his eyes closed, breathing hard and deep but alive and going to make it. Mike went over and filled a glass with beer and as soon as Jocko was able to see where he was, Mike handed him the glass. Jocko took a deep swig, then a deep breath and he was all right. All right as far as the shape he was in, I mean. He wasn't really all right by a long shot.

Everybody started to talk and go about his own business again, and I started to think of ways to getting us back to camp before the foreman came looking for us. The foreman and Jack wouldn't have gotten along cold sober, and I know for sure they wouldn't have gotten along with Jack drunk and the foreman sober.

I thought for a minute that Jack was going to go along his business along with everybody else, but just as he was about to turn off, Jocko had to pick that time to see if his guns were riding smooth in the holsters. He didn't shift them an inch, just enough to know they were slippery and ready, but it was enough to catch Jack's eye.

"Hey, there, bucko," he said, "you sure got a fancy pair of guns there."

"They're my best," said Jocko, and he slipped them again a little bit. I'd seen him do that a thousand times and never thought about it, but I sure felt nervous about him doing it now.

"You must be a deadly man down there in Texas," said Jack. "I'll bet you've left bones moldering all along the trail."

"I don't go looking for trouble," said Jocko, "but it if comes, it don't find me wanting."

He said the words real slow and heavy, like I'd never heard him use before. It didn't sound right.

"I can see you wouldn't want to spoil a pretty pair like that by notching them," said Jack, "but I'll bet those handles would be whittled away if you did."

"They've earned their keep," said Jocko, in that same peculiar voice. "They've earned their keep."

"Oh, you've got fancy hands," said Jack. "I can see you've got fancy hands. I'll bet you can make those things twinkle."

Jocko pushed himself away from the bar, and I could tell by the way his shoulders drooped that he was going to make a move. Jack knew that something was coming and he wasn't quite sure what it was. He dropped his hand to his butt and kept it there while he figured out which way the play was going.

One thing about a bar. The people in it know when something out of the regular routine is going to happen. My pa used to say that they could smell it, that there was this thing in the air like you smell when a bolt of lightning hits close by. "You watch," he used to say. "Even those with their backs turned to the action know right away when things are amiss."

Well, that's what happened right there. Everybody in that place stopped what he was doing at almost the same second and turned to look at Jocko.

Jocko, he didn't know who was watching or even where he was, I think. All he knew was that he had the feeling for the game and he was about to go through his motions. When he made his first move, you could hear a hum of wind from that crowd, sort of a sucking in of breath all of a sudden. Those guns had cleared the holsters and were going into the first whirl before the sound of the breaths had stopped, and I don't think anybody did much breathing the rest of that ten minutes.

Jocko gave them the full treatment, the whirls, the spins, the shifts, the crossovers, the behind the back, the under the legs, the over the shoulder, all the stand-up stuff. I'd seen him do it for four weeks solid and I still got a little shiver each time, so you can imagine how it was with those cow-pokes and gamblers in that saloon.

When he finally finished with his double flip and the zip into the holsters, they let out a yell that sounded like one man who was a hundred feet tall. They came clamoring around him and beat him on the back and yelled and if I had a dollar for every time somebody said son of a bitch, I would be the richest man in the world today.

Jocko was sweating like a Mexican cook and his face was gray under his color. He was done in from the whiskey and the exultation, as my pa used to say, of the zenith of his accomplishment, whatever that meant. Except that my pa was rarely wrong. Well, he could be wrong. He was dead, wasn't he?

Jack had been shoved out by the crowd and had stood silent while all the shouting and slapping was going on. Then when everybody was trying to buy Jocko another drink, Jack elbowed his way back into the center.

"Hey, there, bucko," he said, grabbing Jocko by the elbow. "I told you I knew a pair of hands when I seen one."

Jocko just stood there smiling a little at everybody, and I don't even think he knew it was his old buddy Jack come back to him. I was still trying to figure out a way to get us out of there somehow, but I knew it was pretty hopeless now. This crowd was bent and determined they were going to kill Jocko with free whiskey, and he wasn't going to be mine until I could claim the body. I felt a little better now that we had gone into this part of the business. So many nights I had stood in corners of saloons or just outside the door waiting for my father to have that one big one that would make him slump to the floor or fall over face flat to the table that I had become sort of numb to the business. I would drive everything out of my mind and not think of anything at all. I leaned against the bar and started to push everything out of my mind—the foreman, getting back, the Jordans—but through the mist I could hear Jack say, "I'll bet you shoot as good as you draw," and I came right back to trouble.

"Come on, everybody," Jack yelled, "give us some room. Come on, everybody, get out of the way." And he pushed and shoved people until there was some space around him and Jocko.

"My friend here," said Jack, "is not one of those fancy Dans who carries a sporty pair of weapons and doesn't know how to use them. He's a marksman."

The crowd started to edge in again, and Jack held up his hand.

"Stand back," he yelled, "and see what we are about to do."

He walked over to the bar and picked up a beer glass. It was half full of beer so he dumped the beer on the bar. He didn't spill it on the floor in front of the bar or the floor behind the bar. He dumped it right on the bar. Then he walked back to where the circle was and pushed his way through. He walked to the far side of the room, turned and faced where Jocko was. He threw off his sombrero and put the empty glass on top of his head. He didn't feel his way with it, just slapped it on top of the middle of his head and there it stayed.

"Come on, old friend," he said, "shoot it off."

The men faded right back out of the path between Jocko and Jack. Quick as a wink there wasn't a soul between them or a man close enough to get hit by a slight miscalculation.

"That's enough of that, Jack," somebody said, but he said it half-hearted, and nobody echoed him. They all wanted to see that glass shot off. I don't know if Jack had any close friends with him, but right then I knew that close friends or not there wasn't a man in that place who cared one whit whether or not Jocko made a slight miscalculation up or down. They could almost taste it.

Jocko stood there with his eyelids drooped just a bit, his body half turned away from Jack. His hands hung loose by his sides, and he was about as dangerous a looking man as you would hope to ever see. You knew right then and there that he could pull those two guns and blast that glass right into the air and pick off the pieces before they hit the sawdust. I found myself breathing a little quicker, and I hoped to hell Jocko didn't have too much booze in him to miss the shot. It was the kind of mark he would ordinarily have a pretty good chance of making, but the light was uncertain and the whiskey was surely certain.

"I can't do it," said Jocko.

"It's all right, old friend," said Jack, standing there like one of those Philadelphia statues my pa told me about. "I ain't got no fear at all in me. You just plunk this old glass off my head."

"Go ahead," somebody yelled, and they all started yelling for him to go ahead and shoot.

"I can't do it," Jocko said.

"Why can't you do it?" they wanted to know.

" 'Cause I ain't got no bullets in my guns," Jocko said.

There was a bad silence in the place. I stood there feeling ashamed for Jocko and sick to my stomach and wanting to be away from there. You could sense the change in the crowd. What kind of man went around with a pair of fancy guns and didn't have no bullets in them? What kind of man did all that fancy stuff with the irons and didn't keep no bullets ready for business? I don't know why Jocko didn't have bullets in that night. As far as I knew he always had bullets in the guns he was wearing. But that crowd didn't know that he usually had bullets in his guns. All they knew what that when the time came to use the fancy guns, there weren't any bullets in them.

Jack tipped his head forward and the beer glass fell on the floor and bounced a couple of times on the sawdust without breaking. He walked over to Jocko and pulled both guns out of the holsters and held them kind of loose in his hands. Jocko looked like he was going to say something but then he didn't. Jack stuck one of the guns in his waistband and then reached over to Jocko's gun belt and started pulling bullets out of it. He loaded Jocko's gun and then changed it with the other one and loaded that. Then he stuck them both back in Jocko's belt. He walked over to the bar and picked up two beer glasses and brought them back. He flicked Jocko's hat off his head with the back of his hand and put the beer glass on top of Jocko's head. Then he walked back to the other side of the room, turned and put the beer glass on his own head.

"Old friend," he said, "you and me are going to play a little game. When I say, 'Pull,' we're both going to clear leather and shoot these beer glasses off each other's heads. If you beat me, I'm going to give you my gun and one hundred dollars. If I win, I get your fancy guns."

I smelled blood and so did everybody else in that place. We all knew that Jack wasn't talking about shooting no beer glasses off people's heads. Jocko knew all right. I could tell by his face that he knew. But he didn't have much time to think about it because right then Jack yelled, "Pull!" and his hand flashed to his iron.

Jack was pretty good, but pretty good wasn't good enough where Jocko was ordinarily concerned. Jocko was great. Every time I had seen him in the past four weeks he had cleared his leather like a man possessed and he wasn't even thinking about it anymore. He was natural.

Only this wasn't a natural circumstance. This was a man pulling to kill you and not just to beat the drop of a rock or the throw of a can. This was forever and I knew right then that Jocko had never faced forever before and he went for his guns like he was dead already and that's what he was before the weapons had cleared leather. Jack's slug took him right in the throat and ripped his whole neck apart. He fell down on the floor like a sack of potatoes and the blood gushed onto the sawdust and the red spread out and out and out.

I wasn't surprised much because I had known Jocko was dead about ten seconds before he was. I was scared. I'll tell you right now I was scared. And I was mad. How was I going to tell the Texan about what happened to Jocko? How could you explain about that crazy Jack, and me wanting a new shirt, and why we were there, and how was I going to get out of there? And what would I do with Jocko? I couldn't leave him in a strange town without any friends and I stood there watching the blood drain on the floor and my hope with it.

Jack had walked right over to where Jocko was lying, still holding his gun in his hand and looking the same as he had before he had killed a man.

"That kind of shooting don't win no prizes, does it?" he said to the men who had drawn around the body. "If anything," he said, "I thought I was aiming a little high."

"Sure, Jack," one of the men said, "you always aim a little high or low or sideways maybe."

"You questioning me on anything, man?" Jack said, and he lifted his gun just a fraction in his hand.

"No, Jack," said the man, "I am not questioning you on anything."

"I wasn't sure," said Jack, "and I like to be sure about everything."

He walked over to where I was standing by the bar. By the time he reached me he had slipped his gun back into the holster.

"I'm sorry about your friend," he said, "but you can't blame nobody for an accident. You don't hold it against me, do you?"

I didn't know what to say so I didn't say anything.

"No hard feelings, are there?" he wanted to know.

I couldn't of talked if he'd hit me with a stick.

"You questioning me on anything, boy?" he said and

stepped back a pace. He looked down at my waist and checked again that I had no weapons.

" 'Course not," he said. "Ain't no feud between us. Where's your outfit, boy?"

"Ten miles to the east," I told him.

"I'll help you pack him up," he said.

Mike had brought in a lot of gunnysacks from the back, and while Jack was talking to me, one of the sweepers had wrapped Jocko's head and shoulders in the gunnysacks and they had tied ropes around the sacks. Jack and two of the men lifted Jocko up and carried him outside. It was sure dark out there. The one lantern hanging under the sign gave off hardly any light at all, but we found our horses in the pack and I showed them which was Jocko's. The horse was mighty skittish with the smell of blood, but they finally got Jocko on and tied him down with his own rope. The other men went inside but Jack stayed. He unbuckled Jocko's guns and took them off.

"A bet's a bet," he said to me like an afterthought. "You better not come back around here, boy, or anybody from your outfit. This town seems to be bad luck to you."

And he turned and went inside. Leaving me out there in the dark and cold with a dead man and two frightened horses.

I slid up in the saddle and turned the mounts to the east. I wasn't sure I could find my way back to camp. And I wasn't sure I wanted to.

★ 13 ★

That was a lonesome trail. My pa used to tell me stories about the Greeks or the Romans or somebody who went across a black river when they died, and I'll bet they hadn't a worse trip than I did that night.

I couldn't see my horse's head in front of me, but the wind was from the east so I just poked his nose in that direction and let him pick his own way along at his own pace. Jocko wasn't any trouble. I held the rein and his horse followed along as nice as pie. I was glad I hadn't stayed around the Jordans too long. Anybody who was too nice to me ended up dead. First my pa and now Jocko. Each one had his big weakness, my pa his whiskey and Jocko his guns. You can't have no weakness in this world, I told the old horse, or they'll kill you for it. He just kept on going slow and easy. Every once in a while he'd stop for a little while and graze on grass or something, but I didn't push him any. I didn't know if he knew where he was going, but he sure as blazes knew that I didn't know and that was good enough for me.

I don't know how long it took us, but it was really light by the time we reached the little knoll overlooking the camp. I came up expecting to see some worked-over grass and a lot of empty field, but there they all were, just as we had left them. The horses were still staked out with a couple of Mexicans lazing around them, and I could see all sorts of people sitting around the chuck wagon and drinking coffee.

I rode down real slow, not sure what I was going to do or say. By the time I had reached the fire, they were all standing up, but no one moved out to meet me. Finally, the big Texan came over to my horse's head. He stood there a bit and then stepped back.

"He go fast or slow?" he asked.

" 'Fore he hit the floor," I told him.

"How many?"

"Just one."

"Was he"—and it was like he didn't want to use his name—" on the prod?"

"Nope. Other fella."

"Fair fight?"

"Wasn't really a fight."

"Hungry?"

And I was. All of a sudden I realized I was as hungry as I'd ever been in my life. I couldn't think of a time . . . and all of a sudden I remembered Mrs. Jordan stuffing all that pie into me when my pa was done in. So I was real careful. I spooned those beans into my mouth slow and easy and chewed them three times over before I swallowed and drank my coffee like it was dangerous. And when the cook asked if I wanted more, I told him no even though my stomach was screaming to let it come, let it come. One of the Mexicans took my tin and walked off to scrape it clean. They were all sitting there watching me and nobody saying a word. I didn't know where they had taken old Jocko off to, but I was sure these people would take care of him. It felt really good just to sit there among them. It was like that sometimes at the Jordan house after supper when it was still too light to go to bed and we'd sit there on the porch and Mrs. Jordan would be knitting and Mr. Jordan would be smoking his pipe and I would just sit and rock, sit and rock, sit and rock, until I could hardly keep my eyes open to stumble off to the stable for the night.

The Texan had sat there rolling cigarettes and smoking them one after the other while I finished my chow. He looked real quiet and patient but I could tell he was upset with me and I wondered what I was going to be paid for my night's work. When he saw I was finished, he mashed out his smoke and threw the dust into the breeze.

"Tell me about it. Tell me all about it," he said.

"Well, there was this fellow Jack," I started, but he cut me right off.

"Tell me about it from the beginning, from the very beginning," he said. "Why did you leave camp?"

So I told him about it from the very beginning, about how I wanted a shirt and Jocko had wanted whiskey and women, and how there was plenty of whiskey but no women, and how Jack started fooling around and how Jocko was all of a sudden dead.

"I know of this Jack," said the Texan. "I've heard tell of him."

"I didn't even have my guns on me," I said.

His face got so red it looked almost black.

"What the hell you think this is?" he yelled. "Some kind of fun game you play in school? Luckiest day in the world you didn't have your guns on or you'd be lying somewhere in a hole with Jocko."

I don't know why I felt I had to tell him, but I figured it was important.

"I never went to school," I said.

"Nobody ever said you went to school," he yelled. "What makes you think you got the brains to go to school?"

I don't know what I would have felt I had to tell him then, but just then one of the Mexicans came up with a shovel on his shoulder and said something fast in Spanish.

"Come on," said the foreman, turning around. "He's ready."

They all walked out beyond the trees and I followed after. They had dug a grave out there, not too far from the trees, and it was a pretty spot. I never knew how Jocko felt about trees and such, but a man could do worse than to turn to dust in a place like that.

I walked over to the hole and peeked in. They had added some of our gunnysacks and you couldn't see Jocko at all underneath, but I knew he was there all right. I turned around to the cook.

"Has he got a gun down there with him?" I asked.

The cook looked at me kind of strangelike and shook his head.

"Wait a minute," I said. "Don't do nothing till I come back."

I walked back to the chuck wagon and fished out the key from where Jocko had kept it hid. I opened the box and looked down at his treasures. I finally decided on the Peacemaker that had been fancied up with all the trim. I opened the other box and filled the chambers with bullets. Nobody was going to catch old Jocko again as far as I was concerned.

I walked back to the grave and looked down in it. They were all standing around waiting on me, and I couldn't see any other way to do it. So I jumped right down in the grave. I had jumped into the leg section hoping to find a hole, but I landed on a bit of him anyway. I leaned down and pushed the sacks away until I could see a hand. I tried to open the fingers to get them around the gun handle, but they were frozen tight. So I finally just laid the gun under the hand and covered it all over with gunnysack. I looked up and there were about six hands waiting to pull me out.

By the time I had dusted myself off, the Mexicans had already started to throw dirt in the hole. They have a strange custom, and each one took a handful of dirt and threw it in on top of Jocko. When they had all taken a turn, they looked at me so I walked over and threw in a handful too. Then they looked at the Texan, and he stood there a minute and then walked over to the graveside. He started to lean over to pick up some dirt and then stood up straight again. He tried it again and stood up again. His face was getting redder and redder and finally he started cursing and kicking dirt in the grave with his boot, cursing and kicking and cursing and kicking, and I'll swear if he wasn't a grown man, I would have thought he had tears in his eyes. The cook went over and squeezed his arm and he stopped his yelling and kicking and turned around and walked back through the trees. Two of the Mexicans had shovels and they started to fill in the hole. They had already made a cross out of some boards they had nailed together from one of the packing cases.

It was like Jocko had never been. My pa had been. But here Jocko had spent some four weeks with me day and night and now I was having trouble remembering what he looked like. I could almost tell you exactly how many hairs my pa had on his face, but I couldn't tell you what color

Jocko's eyes had been or what he really was like. I wonder why that should be.

When I came back through the trees, the Texan was hunkering by the chuck wagon having a cup of coffee. My belly felt awful cold so I grabbed a cup off the back of the wagon and held it for the cook's helper to fill. The boy still looked a mite puny, but the gray was gone from under his brown and it seemed sure he was going to be around for a while.

I chunked down near enough for the Texan to know I was there but far away enough so he didn't have to bother with me if he wasn't in the mood. It looked like he wasn't going to bother with me so I sipped on the coffee which was hotter than blue hell. Mrs. Jordan said that in front of me without thinking once and then she turned redder than blue hell and told me never to say things like that. I wondered how she was doing.

"I can't get moving," the Texan said. "I just can't seem to get moving."

"You going to do something about that Jack?" I asked him.

"Nothing to do," he said. "This is his country. He may not be too popular, but he's more popular than a bunch of trail herders riding through. We'd face a hundred guns if we ever tried to go through there."

"It don't seem right, him killing old Jocko just like that," I said. "I keep feeling he gunned him down just to get those fancy guns."

"Don't make no difference why he did it," said the foreman. "It has been done."

"But he shouldn't ought to have those guns," I said, and right then I knew what I was going to do.

"Nothing we can do about it," said the foreman. "We'll set here the rest of the day and move out at sunup. I'm getting lonesome for Texas."

I didn't have to wait long after supper for things to settle down. Nobody seemed to have the strength even to throw wood on the fire, and as it died down, the hands drifted off to their blankets like they were going to sleep their troubles away.

I had staked my horse at the edge of the line, and I led

him off quite a ways before I saddled him up. He kept jawing away at the bridle like he was trying to tell me something, but I wasn't going to let no horse run my business. It weren't right for Jack to have those guns.

The breeze on the back of my head kept pushing me in the right direction, and it seemed no time at all before the couple of lights in the town stood out in the distance. I'd been thinking and thinking all the way in about how I was going to handle the situation, but when I reached the outskirts I was no closer to what I was going to do than when I had left the camp. I knew he would be there because he had to be there, and I knew I would do what I had to do because I had to do it, but what was going to come in between all that was something I didn't know. "He will take care of it," Mrs. Jordan used to say, and I was hoping He would help me out a little, too.

I tied my horse up behind a building on the edge of town and drifted towards Mike's through the shadows. There were only a few horses tied up outside, and I figured it was a slow night after a big night, which was how it had been back home. There weren't any windows to look through so I finally took a chance and peeked in through the swinging doors.

There he was at the bar all right, standing alone. I looked at the back of his head, then down to his back, then down to his hips. He was wearing them, wearing them like he'd had them all his life. A gun don't care who he hangs on. You can oil him and clean him and give him loving care, but he don't give a hoot and a holler whether you live or die. I knew that Jocko was just as disturbed at those blamed guns as he was at Jack for taking them away from him. Those Mexicans are always singing about women who are unfaithful to their lovers, but guns make a woman look like nothing when it comes to that.

There were only three other men in the place, two standing at the bar far down from Jack and one gambler sitting at a table and playing some game with himself. Mike didn't even have any extra bartender that night, and he was standing between Jack and the two men, swishing out glasses in a bucket of water. He had a glass of whiskey in front of him, and every once in a while he'd take a small swallow.

I pulled back in the shadows for a minute and then walked over across the street to where there was a general store. There was a single chair set up on mud boards and I sat right down in it because all of a sudden I felt too tired to stand. If I'd stayed in camp I would have crawled into my sack as fast as any of those other fellows.

It was too dark for anybody to see me sitting there, and the chill was enough to keep me from falling off. By the time the two men came out of the saloon and got on their horses, I was wishing I had brought my sheepskin jacket.

Jack came soon after. He stepped out of the door, moved to the side and stood there a minute to let his eyes grow accustomed to the dark. Jocko told me once this was what real gunmen did, one of their tricks. They never walked into a situation where their eyes would play tricks on them.

I didn't want him hurrying off before I had a chance to talk to him so I scrambled off the chair and ran over to him.

"Who's there?" he said, and I could see his hand on the butt of his gun.

"It's me, Mr. Jack," I said. "Jocko's friend."

"Who's that?" he said. "Whose friend?"

"Jocko's," I said. "The man you killed last night."

"The boy," he said. "It's the boy. What do you want?" And he kept his hand on his gun.

"I want to talk to you, Mr. Jack," I said. "It's mighty important."

"Walk before me over to the side, boy," he said, "and we'll have that talk."

I turned and walked over to the side of the saloon where there was a long alley stretching between the two buildings. I walked down in that alley a way and turned. Jack had followed me a bit but had stopped quite a few paces away. I could see him outlined fine in the light that was coming from the lantern on the sign over the saloon.

"Where you going?" he wanted to know. "Why you going way down there?"

"I want a favor, Mr. Jack," I told him. "I want you should give me back Jocko's guns. Those were his favorites and it don't seem right you should kill him for his guns."

"I didn't kill him for his guns," he said. "It was an accident. But a bet's a bet, even when it's an accident."

"It's not right, Mr. Jack," I said. "I want those guns."

"Then come take them," he said, and he was making his move.

I watched him fall backwards into the dirt, and it was afterwards I remembered the noise and the feel of the gun bucking in my hand. The gun was back in my holster, but I decided I better be careful so I pulled it out and walked towards Jack real careful. He was lying on his back with his legs sprawled out in different ways. I leaned over him and blood was bubbling out of three holes in his shirt, three real close holes. A nice pattern. His eyes were wide open but I could only see white in the little light there was.

Mike and the gambler fellow came tearing out of the saloon, yelling to find out what was going on. They were running up and down the street shouting, "Who fired those shots?" and, "What's going on out here?" But they never thought to look in the alley.

I unbuckled the gun belt from Jack but had the devil of a time pulling the thing out from under him. One gun was still in its holster, but the other one was on the ground somewhere, and it took me most of five minutes on my hands and knees feeling around for it. It was underneath Jack and I never would have come across it if I hadn't turned him over to get those white eyes away from me.

Mr. Evans' eyes had glowed red in the dark but Jack's were white, dead white. All of a sudden I didn't have no legs no more and I was sitting there in the dirt right next to Jack. He looked all soft lying there, like there was no bones in his body. He was never going to stand up again, drink those glasses of whiskey or stare anybody down. Eyes that didn't have nothing but white in them didn't put the fear in nobody. I had taken the man's eyes away from him. And now he had to give up the guns.

Meanwhile, Mike and the gambler were yelling away in the street, and not one other person came up to find out what all the shouting was about. You're better off to mind your own business, Mrs. Jordan used to say all the time, and I think most folks lived by that rule. It sure saved me a lot of bother that night.

I worked my way back to the outskirts and picked up my horse. He was making all kinds of snorts and grunts so I jumped right up and we took off out of there. I knew that trail pretty well by then so we moved along at a fairly good clip even in the pitch black. Finally we came to the bluff on the river about three miles above our camp. When Jocko and I had passed the spot going into town the day before, he had stopped to piss from the bluff into the water and then said the foreman would be drinking it in his coffee next morning.

It was too dark to be awful sure of the footing so I got off the horse and felt my way to the edge. There was enough moon to see the reflection of the water down below. I heaved one of the fancy guns as far as I could. Then I heaved the other. I took the bullets out of the belt and then I threw the belt in. I thought about it for a minute and then I threw the bullets too. And I was crying, crying real hard, just like when I was hitting Mr. Evans with that rock. I was crying and cursing and throwing those guns and the belt and the bullets as hard as I could and I wanted to throw myself too, throw myself out into that dark water and let everything disappear. My pa was dead and Jocko was dead and Mr. Evans was dead and Jack was dead, too, nothing left but that white in his eyes that looked like the piece of boiled egg that almost made you puke when you spooned it into your mouth by mistake.

But I didn't throw myself in. You don't do things like that even though you think of them. I did take my gun out of the holster and was about to throw that, but then I remembered it was Jocko's gun, not mine, and I had no business throwing his property away. But I wasn't sorry I had thrown those others away. I'd pay for them to whoever should get the money, but I wasn't sorry I had thrown those fancy guns away.

I rode the rest of the trail real careful and got off to walk a good quarter of a mile away from the camp. I rubbed the horse down with grass and tethered him on the edge of the herd while the night rider was on the far end. I started to slip over to my blankets when I saw that someone had built the fire up again. I was cold, real cold, cold enough to shiver through my sweat. I felt all greasy like my clothes were a snakeskin that could slip off and I needed to bake a bit in that heat.

The Texan was sitting there smoking and with a cup of coffee in his hand. I walked over and sat down near him. I was so cold that I would have sat down by that fire if I was going to die the next minute.

"You too restless to sleep, too, boy?" he wanted to know.

"Yes, sir," I told him.

"You and Jocko were good friends," he said.

"Yes, sir," I said. If I'd said any more, my teeth would have chattered to bits.

"You can't always stand by your friends like you'd like to," he said. "A man can only do so much."

I didn't know what he was talking about and the fire had thawed me alive again. So I said good night and crawled into my blankets. It seemed I had hardly got my eyes closed before it was time to get up and be moving again.

★ 14 ★

The horses were pretty frisky with the rest and good grazing, and we made quite a few miles the next day over pretty rough territory. We really had to hustle to keep them from busting out all over the place, and a dozen times I had to go swinging out wide over all kinds of snarls and thickets to drive some mangy cuss back in line.

By the time we finally started to get set for the night, I was so hungry and tired that I couldn't make up my mind if I was too tired to eat or too hungry to sleep. I was doing both at once by dozing over my beans when I felt a body jolt down beside me. The big Texan leaned back against the trunk of the tree and breathed out a cyclone of wind.

"Long day, eh?" he said.

"I got me blisters on my calluses," I told him, "and I wish somebody would splash cold coffee over my butt."

I almost started to laugh before I remembered it was Jocko who had splashed cold coffee over my butt. The Texan was remembering too because he didn't say nothing for quite a while.

"That was a good boy, that Jocko," he said.

I was spooning cold beans into my mouth and washing them down with warm coffee so I didn't say nothing.

"How come you're not wearing your gun?" he asked.

"Wasn't my gun," I told him. "Was Jocko's."

"What did you do with it?"

"I put it in the box with the rest of his guns."

"Jocko didn't have no kin," said the foreman. "You

seemed to be about as much kin as anybody could be. You keep his gear."

"You were his friend long before me," I said.

"No," he said. "I got the guilt feeling about his dying. I know I didn't do nothing wrong, but I got the guilt feeling, a real bad feeling. I don't want none of his gear, none of it at all. And I ain't going to give it to any of the Mexes. You take the gear."

He pulled his hat down over his eyes and settled down for a little snooze before bedtime. I sat there thinking about my inheritance. I was now the owner of five guns. My pa had left me a set of law books which were too heavy to lug on my travels and now I had five guns to add to the collection. I could see me walking around with five guns strapped all over me and it was quite a sight.

I also had a metal box with about two hundred rounds of ammunition and a pretty good saddle and a blanket roll with some odds and ends of clothes that I would never put on. Even if his duds had fit me, Jocko wasn't the cleanest man in the world and I didn't think any amount of washing would ever take the itch out of his wearables.

I went over to the chuck wagon before I crawled in for the night and got out the old dependable Jocko had given me the borrow of. I tied it down tight and it felt comfortable nestled there. I took it off and sat down in the dark and cleaned it real good, oiled the holster and put it on again.

Then I went through the whole practice routine—draws, spins, shifts and all. Jocko had been pretty fast at all that. Faster than Jack ever was. Funny that Jack should have outdrawn him by so much. The gun kept going round and round in my hands. I got out the double pair and strapped them on. I kept drawing and drawing, working harder and harder until it felt that the guns were part of my hands, that I couldn't ever leave them and for the rest of my life I would stand there whirling and shifting and drawing and sliding them back in.

"What you doing, boy?" asked the Texan, and before I thought about it I was diving to the side and rolling and covering him with both guns. It had taken all of my power just to cover because at the first sound of his voice I had almost pulled, pulled and pulled again.

I let the guns drop down almost to the dirt, I had wanted to just let go of them, but you can't let guns get mixed in the dirt and I stopped just short. I felt like I'd been riding broncos all day and then running miles and miles on my feet and then going up a mountain and carrying big trees and wrestling with grown men and swimming a river so wide you couldn't see the other side. I lay there as dead as Jocko, and I couldn't help but wish I was back in my bed at the Jordans' and tomorrow morning I would go to the livery stable and nothing was changed. But my pa was dead. Nothing would change that. Mr. Evans was dead. And I looked around in the dark for those eyes. Jocko was dead. Nothing would change that. And Jack was dead. I had killed a man named Jack, turned his eyes upside down. And I owned five guns. They were mine. If I wanted I could throw them in the black river and nobody would care and I could go back to being me again. If I wanted.

"Just practicing a mite," I said, getting to my feet as fast as I could but slow enough not to fall down again.

"I'm gonna start practicing with my guns again," he said. "I fear I'm getting a bit rusty. Tomorrow we'll drift off to the side of the herd and shoot some stones up."

And that's what we did for the next day and every day after that. We'd go out a ways and throw stones and shoot at them or set rocks up far away and try to pop them off. It got so I could hardly miss on the sitting target and did better than worse on the thrown rocks.

The foreman tried real hard but his aim was off somewhere else. He'd get so blessed mad he'd start shooting away without really aiming at anything and waste up all our ammunition. We ran out of Jocko's bullets the second week of our practicing and out of his the third. We bought some off the Mexicans, but they wouldn't sell us any more when they ran low, and we had to quit when we were down to the bullets left in our gun belts.

Meanwhile, I kept practicing my draws and shifts every night before I crawled in. Somehow I had the urge again and it kept me from thinking about anything or anybody. When I just stayed hunkered down by the fire I kept brooding on things that had happened and I didn't like that, I didn't care for it at all. So I concentrated on the horses and practicing draws during the day and just the guns at night. I'd break them down and clean them just like Jocko was still looking over my shoulder, and then I'd go through all the routines we had worked on together. It didn't make me remember Jocko better; it kept me from remembering him.

The Mexicans were saying I was real loco, but they laughed when they said it. Except once in a while when I was practicing a fast draw and double shift, one of them would stand up and mutter something to the others and they would all go through that crossing of themselves. Strange people, the Mexicans. Very godlike, though.

And then one day the foreman said we were in Texas and would be at the ranch in a week more or less. I don't know why but the first thing I thought of when he said that was fried eggs. I think I'd have given up one of my guns for a fried egg. I'd stopped thinking about taking a bath about three weeks before. But I'd never stopped thinking about fried eggs.

★ 15 ★

Texas didn't look any different from the rest of the country we'd passed through, but the whole crew was as excited as a bunch of crazy colts. They couldn't wait to get going in the morning and they hated to bed down at night. The singing started up again at the fire, and the old songs sounded brand new the way they were singing them. They complimented the cook about the beans and didn't try to get off their watches early and were awful polite to each other. The grass was the same grass, the trees were the same trees, and the damn dust was dusty as ever, but they acted like we were in heaven or someplace good.

They almost had me doing crazy things, but on the third day it all changed. We were riding through this little valley when all of a sudden the right outrider gave a whoop and a holler. I was near enough to hear him and I looked where he pointed. Up on a hillock looking down on us were five Indians. I'll admit it here and now. I got scared just looking at them. You would swear they were made out of stone the way they sat there, never twitching or blinking once. The only way you could tell they were live people was that every once in a while one of the horses would roll a muscle and the Indian swayed a hair as the weight shifted.

Their faces were all covered with streaks of bright paint, and three of them were holding rifles and the other two had long spears. While I was looking at them, my horse had been moving towards them, and if I hadn't heard a shout from the foreman and stopped the horse dead, I would have moved right in with them.

"Come back here," he yelled, and I turned around and rode down to him. The hands had the horses milling by this time, and the men without guns were scooting to the chuck wagon to dig them out.

"You fellows fixing to have another woman?" I asked the foreman.

"No woman with this crew," he said. "These bucks are out for fun and games."

"What happens now?" I asked him.

"I guess I better go find out," he said. "Cover me."

He loosened his gun in his holster and started moving slowly toward the Indians. My guns were always loose so I just followed after him. I don't think he knew I was there, he was concentrating so hard on the five ahead of him. They watched him coming towards them and then at the same moment, just like with a flock of birds, they wheeled and galloped out of sight over the hill.

He turned his horse right around and bumped into my horse.

"What the hell you doing here?" he wanted to know.

"You told me to cover you," I said.

"That didn't mean you had to get so close up," he yelled.

"It's easier to cover close up than far away," I answered, and he started laughing.

"You sure are a caution for a stableboy," he said.

Just then the most godawful screaming started up on the other side of the herd, and the horses came boiling at me. Somebody began shooting, and shooting busted out all over the place. The foreman wheeled and started riding through the herd to where the screaming had come from and I followed after as fast as I could, what with horses coming at me and dust billowing and me not knowing what was going on.

Just then an Indian came tearing by me and as he went by he tried to stab me with a long spear. I leaned over just enough for the point to miss me and dropped him as he went by. These savages were up to no good and I got two more in the near vicinity. I could see maybe twenty Indians working their way through the herd, and the Mexicans were weaving in and out and I couldn't see the Texan anywhere.

I had bust through to the other side and came on the

chuck wagon tipped over and smoke curling out of the inside. I jumped off my horse and ran over to the wagon. Some of the old sacks were on fire and I pulled them out of the back and stomped the flame out. The cook was nowhere around and by this time the horses and the whole bloody match had moved up on the hillside where the Indians had been spotted in the first place. They all disappeared over the hill and I couldn't even see any dust from them.

There I was all alone with the wagon. Out on the grass were the three Indians I had dropped but not another living soul. I didn't know what to do. I hated to leave the wagon because that held the rest of my guns and the food and everybody's packs. Which reminded me and I reloaded the three bullets I had used.

My people were in trouble over there sure enough, but I tried to think through what the foreman would want me to do. I stayed with the wagon. I got on my horse, who had been standing there eating grass since I'd first jumped off him, and rode over to where the Indians were laying.

They were all cold dead all right, but they still gave me the jeebers with all that paint on their faces. One of them looked like that Indian whose squaw we had used out on the prairie. I squatted down by him and studied his face. You couldn't be sure about Indians because they all looked so much alike. The three of them laying there on the ground looked real natural, nothing like Mr. Evans with his red eyes and stinking whiskey breath or Jack with that terrible softness through him.

That Indian wasn't the one that had been with the squaw, just looked like him. I was sure glad. Bad enough to kill somebody, even an Indian, but I wouldn't have wanted to kill that other one. Don't know why but I wouldn't.

Quite a bit of time had gone by with me squatting there looking into that face, and the sun started to drop near the horizon. I figured it might be quite a while before they all came back so I made a little fire and cooked some beans. Then I took me a shovel from the wagon and walked off a ways and dug a hole deep enough to lay down in. It didn't take too long because the dirt was soft out there.

I hauled my chest of guns to the hole along with my own pack and somebody else's. I lined the hole with the canvas

from the other pack and opened mine up for a cover. My
horse had been tied to the wagon so I moved him over to
the other side on a longer rope so he could have new grass
to work on. Then I took the pot of beans and crawled into
the hole. I went to work on them and as it got dark I
finished them off. I took a drink of water from the canteen
and then stood up and pissed as softly as I could on the
grass. I fingered my belt and found I had three cartridges
which gave me fifteen counting the ones in the guns. Then I
sat down in the hole to wait out the morning.

It was a long night. What with the tarp under me and my
own blanket over me, it was snug and cozy in the hole and I
kept dozing off. I could hear my horse grazing time and
again, and there were other noises, but nothing that would
make even a girl skittish. All kinds of things go through
your mind in the dark, and at one point I figured out that
one of those Indians was shamming and right now he was
crawling towards me with a knife in his teeth. Except that I
had rolled all three of them over a couple of times and
taken their knives off them. I'd found two spears near them
but nothing else. It was a long night.

I must have been sound asleep when the false dawn came
because first thing I knew the sun was peeking its head over
the hill. The wagon was still laying on its side and my horse
was grazing beyond the wagon and the three dead Indians
had company. Two live ones. They were standing by their
horses and looking down at the bodies. I lifted both my
guns to the rim of the hole and tried to breathe real soft.
Injuns can hear a man fart twenty miles away, Jocko had
told me once. I didn't intend to put them to the test.

They looked to be arguing about something. One of them
was waving his hands at the other and I could almost hear
his howls way over to where I was. The other one kept
turning his back on the wavy one and then turning back
again and waving his arms once or twice. The real excited
one finally jumped on his horse and started yelling from up
there. The other one walked over to the wagon and started
poking around inside. He crawled out carrying something
and climbed up on his horse. Neither of them paid no
attention to my horse grazing out beyond them.

"Go the other way, Injun," I heard myself saying over

and over again. I knew I was saying it out loud, but there wasn't nothing I could do about stopping saying it. I'd killed me enough Indians. I'd killed me enough everybody. "Go away," I said, "go away."

They didn't go the other way. They came right towards me, arguing and yelling at each other and not paying the slightest bit of attention. These two were carrying guns instead of spears, and I knew I couldn't fool with them. So when they came within sure distance, I dropped the both of them, the one on the right with my right-hand gun and the one on my left with my left-hand gun. It was good shooting because they were yelling and moving around and making their horses nervous.

They both flew back over the rumps of their horses and landed every which way. Their horses just stopped still and didn't move at all. Those were sure steady animals.

I was just about to stand up and look them over when the one on the left, the quieter one of the two, sat straight up and looked around. I snapped another bullet into him and he flopped right back again. I lay there another minute or so deciding whether or not to put another one in him to play it safe and maybe to give the other one a little more to think about.

They looked permanently quiet so I stood up slowly and ambled toward them, keeping both guns pointed right at the two of them. They were gone all right this time. The one that had sat up had a hole in his chest and a hole in his head. I had aimed the first shot at his chest and the second at his head so I figured there hadn't been nothing wrong with the shooting. The problem had been with the Indian.

I picked up all the gear there was, my own from the hole and the Indians' from the grass, and brought it over to the wagon. I tied my horse and the Indian horses to the spokes of three wheels and started a little fire to cook some beans. The Indian rifles were beat-up and rusty but I piled them alongside the spears from the day before.

The sun had moved up a ways by this time, so I moved over on the west side of the wagon. It was a real comfort to be able to eat in the shade because there wasn't any chance of that while we were on the move.

It was nice and peaceful sitting there with a belly full of

beans, just resting with my back against the side of the wagon and the blue sky and bright sunlight just outside the shadow. It was so restful that I could feel myself drifting off even though I knew it wasn't very smart and I guess I was just about going under when I heard the Texan say, "What the hell you think you're doing, boy?"

Even though I knew that voice as well as I knew my pa's, I was on my feet with both guns on him before he finished the "What." He was shook by my jump and lifted his gun straight out at me. I guess he'd come around the wagon with his gun out, not knowing what to expect, and had dropped it down when he saw it was me.

I slipped the guns back in the holster as fast as a man can. He put his away almost as quick. It's bad manners to hold a gun on a friend.

I walked around the wagon to him, and out beyond were the Mexicans with the horses. Everybody looked real beat, especially the horses. The cook came scrambling off a horse and running towards us.

"Is he there?" he was yelling. "Is he there?"

"You seen the boy?" the Texan asked me.

"No, I ain't seen him," I told him.

The cook came running up to me and grabbed me by the arm.

"He is with you? No?" he said.

"No, I ain't seen him," I told him.

"Madre Dios," he said, and sat down and started to cry.

I don't like to see a man cry. Every once in a while when I dragged my pa home from one of the saloons he would break down and start to cry and beg me to forgive him and promise to give up drinking and call to my mother in heaven to be witness to what he was saying. I could put up with my pa drinking and all because he couldn't do otherwise, but no man should ever cry.

"What will I tell her?" he kept saying over and over.

The Texan came over to me and pulled me off to the side a bit.

"What happened here?" he wanted to know.

I told him the whole story from the time I bust through on the other side till he came walking over me in my sleep.

"You got all those five out there?" he wanted to know.

I nodded at him.

"That's five more than we got," he said. "And the only one of us missing is the boy. And three horses. But you picked up five horses all together, if we can corral the three strays out there. So we're two horses ahead and one boy behind."

I asked him what happened after they all rode over the hill and he said nothing much. There was a lot of yelling and shooting and scattering, but the Indians rode right on through and kept going, and they had most of the horses rounded up by dark and the rest in the morning.

"They must have ridden right on through with the boy," he said, "and he's either lying by the trail cut up into little pieces or he's going to get pulled to pieces by the squaws in one of their fun and games sessions or he's going to be worked to death or he's going to grow up a big brave buck, the adopted son of somebody or other. In any case, there's nothing much we can do about it one way or another."

He went over and gave the cook a little kick in the arm.

"Get up, old sport," he said, "and let's get this wagon in business again."

A couple of the Mexicans rode over and we all heaved on the wagon until it was righted. We cleaned things up a bit, and the cook started crying when we found a few of the boy's things, but by a little after noon we were ready for the trail again.

The Texan asked me what I wanted to do with the spears and the guns and I told him, "Nothing." So he busted them all up over the wagon wheel and threw a couple of the pieces over to where the Indians were laying. The three first ones were starting to swell a bit and the birds were flying low around them. I was wondering if we ought to give them a Christian burial but nobody said nothing about it so I decided I better not either. I guess only Christians get Christian burials.

We only rode a couple of hours before it was time to bed down for the night. The Texan had the cook dish up supper first thing and then douse the fire before the light was gone. He doubled the men on each watch but told me I could sleep the night through. I told him I could do my job but he said I already had. I didn't know what he was talking about but I was so sleepy I didn't much care.

So I unrolled my pack near where the fire had been, which was right in the center of where the men had their packs. Those on second watch were already settling into their blankets, and I heard the Texan say he didn't want nobody smoking from then on. I couldn't make up my mind whether to take my boots off or leave them on. You feel awfully foolish stumbling around in the dark with your bare feet. But my feet felt so hot I was afeared they would catch fire in the boots. So I tugged and tugged and finally slipped them off. They were full of sand and little stones and my stockings were wet enough to drown in. I stretched the toes over and over again till they felt human.

Then I crawled into the blankets and wiggled my bones. I could hear the Mexicans settling down for the night and I could see the Texan in the little light that was left sitting against the wheel of the wagon. I knew he was dying for a smoke, but it was past time to light one now. He looked like he intended to sit there all night.

It felt good to have him there by that wagon, and it felt double good to be in the middle of all those Mexicans. I was as safe as in that bedroom at the Jordans' and could sleep easy. Except I couldn't sleep. The face of that one Indian kept sticking in my belly. That's right, in my belly. It felt all cold and clammy down there, like I might be getting sick. It couldn't have been that Indian we gave all that food to. It would be terrible to kill anybody's pa. Mr. Evans, he didn't have no kinfolk anybody knew about, and I'm sure that Jack didn't have any wife and kids, I was plain sure about that. But that man out there on the plain had kids; I saw them myself. And maybe those five other Indians had wives and children and they were all sitting in their tents right now waiting for them to get back, not knowing who was going to take care of them or how they were going to eat. Mr. Evans had done away with just one pa and I had maybe done in five. It was the guns, the guns; it was so easy with the guns. And that Indian's face was laying there cold in my belly.

I slipped my hand under the raincoat roll and grabbed hold of the gun handle, letting my finger move easy onto the trigger. I couldn't remember whether I had a dead load under the trigger, and I almost pulled to find out. That would have been something to have a round go off in the middle of the whole kit and kaboodle. Those Mexes would have scattered to Jesus. The handle had been cold at first touch but now it was nice and warm, like it had a little fire of its own in there. I could feel my eyes getting too heavy to hold and me slipping off nice and easy. My belly was now as warm as my hand and all I could feel all over me was the handle of that gun, that was all I could feel and all I could see and all I could know as I drifted off into a nice easy sleep.

★ 16 ★

If it hadn't been for the look on the cook's face, you never could have told we'd been through anything when we took off the next morning. Everybody told the cook how sorry they were, including me, but it's not the same as losing one of your own kin. That had been a good boy, that Mexican boy, and once I let him shoot one of my guns at a rock, but he was just gone as far as I was concerned and that was the end of it. Other people must have felt the same way when my pa went, even the Jordans. They were sorry and all that, but I was the only one who really cared, who really had a big hole in his day. It's funny, my pa's been gone all this time, and to me it's like it was yesterday.

Two days later the foreman announced that we were on Barron land and I thought how nice it would be to sleep indoors that night. I should have known better by that time, but I couldn't help asking when dark started coming on and we drew up for the night.

"Ain't we going right on to the ranch house?" I asked the foreman.

He laughed and translated what I had said to the Mexicans. They laughed too. I didn't like being laughed at once and I didn't like having that laugh repeated eleven times.

"I asked you a civil question and I don't expect a laugh for an answer," I told him.

"Boy," he said, "we're three days from the main house. We've got a laughable amount of distance yet to travel."

He didn't know it but I was standing there scared, about as scared as I've ever been in my life. Because I had been about to move with my hands when he laughed at me. I was all ready to use the guns. I was so used to thinking in gun terms lately that I had almost drawn on my friend. My pa used to say that too many men thought with their guns instead of their heads. He didn't like that. He wouldn't have liked what I had been about to do. When we got to the ranch I was going to get rid of all those guns and use my head for a change. It was as simple as that. Just get rid of the guns and then you had to use your head.

Those next three days went mighty slow even though we moved out before dawn and didn't bed down till it was pitch black. But there it finally was on the fourth day as we came over a rise and looked down on a pretty valley that had a nice-sized stream meandering through it.

It was sure and definitely the biggest house I had ever seen. It stretched out every little which way in all directions, and there were various kinds of little huts clustered around it. Parts of it were log and parts were dobe and some was clapboard and some was a bit of each. There were patches of grass on some sides and plain dirt around others. There was even a little flower garden on one end.

Horses were tied up all over the place and chickens were wandering around and ducks and geese and some pigs and ever which all. And people. There were cowboys and Mexicans and women and babies and big kids and all sizes and shapes going back and forth, in and out and around. It looked just like a town that had everybody living in one building.

There were barns and corrals off to the sides and we headed down to one of the big circles. The Mexicans were yelling and whooping and carrying on something fierce, but the horses were too beat to get skittish and just ran down to the bottom of the hill and right into the corral. They shut the gate on the last of them and then galloped off to the closest big barn, where they jumped off and started to hug and kiss every Mexican who came running up. I never saw so many people in my life.

The foreman had slid off his horse and handed the reins to one of the Mexicans. He started to walk off toward the house but then remembered something and turned around and came back. He looked around a bit and then walked over to where the cook was saying something to this woman standing there. I couldn't hear what was being said, but all of a sudden she started tearing her hair and beating herself on the chest and she fell right down on the ground and started rolling around in the dust.

The foreman went over and squatted down beside her and held her kind of tight so she couldn't do herself more damage. He was trying to tell her something but she wasn't listening to anybody. She just screamed and pulled her hair as best she could and it was pretty bad to watch. Finally, a couple of the Mexican men lifted her up and carried her off followed by about a dozen women.

The foreman stood up and started back around and saw me sitting there on my horse.

"What you doing there?" he wanted to know.

"I don't know anybody or anything so I'm just sitting up here till I find out," I told him.

He called over one of the Mexicans and told him to take the horse. I slid off and came over beside him.

"Better come up to the house and meet the boss," he said and started off.

It was quite a walk from the corral to the big house and my legs really ached by the time I got there. I couldn't reason why until I remembered that I hadn't done any walking in weeks. We rode everywhere on the trail, and at night we just danced a few steps around the campfire. My rump was plenty tough, but my legs were weak.

The big house was a mite beat-up when you got close to it, but it was still the dangedest thing I had ever seen. People were running in and out of it like there was a fire both on the inside and the outside and they were trying to get away from it. The foreman knew right where he was going, and we walked right in through the front door into a big hall that had stone on the floor and our spurs clanged away as we walked over it. One of the Mexicans had sold me the spurs for two dollars when we were about a week on the trail, and I sure got my money's worth as we walked over that stone floor.

From the hall we walked into one of the biggest rooms I had ever seen in my life. The ceiling was as high as a house and the walls were all decorated with the heads of beasts from all over. There was even a tiger head up on that wall, so help me Hannah. He had the biggest, longest fangs I had ever seen, and my butt gave a twitch as I thought on those two things closing in on you.

There was all kinds of furniture in the room, so much that you had to keep walking around things in order to keep going in a straight line. I swear I'd of got trapped in there if I'd been alone, and I was so interested in looking at the chairs of so many colors and the rugs scattered over the floor that I almost bumped right into the man.

I might have bumped into him but I wouldn't have knocked him down because he was about the biggest man I had ever seen. He was older than my pa, but he looked like he could clean out any saloon without getting up too much sweat. He was standing there wearing some kind of velvety red robe and he had slippers on and was smoking a cigar that fitted his size. The smoke curled up between his big gray handlebar mustache and he squinted his eyes down at us.

I put out my hands to keep from bumping into him, but he never even made a motion. He was right because my fingers ended about five inches from him. I dropped my hands and just stood there.

The Texan took off his hat and I did likewise. The Texan didn't say anything and I didn't either.

"You finally got here, eh, Roy?" the man said, and I was so surprised to hear that the foreman had a name that I didn't catch what he answered.

"Jimmy and Alan bugged out on me so I picked up this one to take up slack," said the foreman. "I told him if he did a good job I would recommend you take him on regular."

"Did he do a good job?" asked the man.

"I recommend you take him on regular," said the foreman.

"You're on," said the boss. "Where's Jocko?"

"He got hisself killed," said the foreman.

"Horse, gun or Indian?" asked the boss.

"Gun," said the foreman.

"What else?" asked the boss.

So the foreman told him about the rest, about the Indians and losing the boy and how the horses were a might beat-up from the trip.

"Long as you all got back," said the boss. "You always have to lose something along the way."

"How are things here?" asked the foreman.

"Trouble," said the boss. "We got big trouble."

"Them?" asked the foreman.

"Them," said the boss.

"Bad?" asked the foreman.

"Bad," said the boss.

"How bad?" asked the foreman.

"Bad enough so that I forget my manners," said the boss, and he walked over to a big cabinet and took out a bottle of whiskey. He poured three glassfuls and pushed two of them over the table at us.

"I don't drink," I told him.

"Maybe I took you on too fast," he said. "What the hell do you mean you don't drink?"

"It's all right for them as wants it, but I don't want it," I told him.

"He's got reasons," the foreman said.

"He damn well better," said the boss.

Can anybody give me one reason why men make such a fuss about whiskey? It done my pa in, both for his own needing it and Mr. Evans' having too much of it that day. It was responsible for the killing of Jocko, and it hadn't done Jack any good either. I never saw whiskey make anybody real happy. They're either puking or crying or whining or making a big hoopla over nothing when they've got it in them. I'd had enough. If he didn't want me because I didn't drink whiskey, then I'd just go on back to where I came from.

"There's something female about men who don't drink," said the boss.

"That there female killed five Injuns by hisself," said the foreman.

"Who did?" asked the boss.

"The boy did," said the Texan.

So then he had Roy go over the Injun fight again and tell how they had found the five dead Injuns around me.

'Why didn't you tell me that before?" asked the boss.

"You weren't doubting him before," said Roy.

"You're good with a gun, eh?" said the boss.

"Jocko taught me some," I told him.

"He'll do," said Roy. "He'll do and then some."

"Tell me about yourself," said the boss. "Where you from?"

"I was born in Philadelphia," I told him, "but I don't remember anything about that. My ma died and my pa brought me out to Kansas where he practiced law for a bit but I don't really remember that either. Then he worked in a freight office and I remember a little bit about that and then he worked in a dry goods store and then he worked in some saloons as a bartender but that never lasted long and then he worked in a livery stable when he—" and I stopped talking because I didn't want to say it. The Texan didn't say nothing, nor the boss neither. They just pulled away at their whiskey, waiting, and I knew they would drink whiskey till doomsday while they waited for me to finish.

"When he died," I said, "and then I worked in the livery stable until I came here."

They still didn't say nothing.

"I've lived in a lot of towns," I said, "a lot of places, but I don't rightly have a home."

"That settles it," said the boss, slapping his leg hard enough to make me hurt. "He's Amy's watchdog."

"Things that rough, eh?" said Roy.

"They're stealing my cattle and my horses, they're killing my Mexicans and they're ready to hit wherever I hurt," said the boss. "They'd just love to catch her out somewhere."

"He'll do fine for that," said Roy.

"Okay, son," said the boss, "move your gear up here and settle yourself in. From now on you're one of the family."

And that's how an hour later I had me a big old bedroom with a big old soft bed on the second floor of that big old house, and how I was sitting in the kitchen with twenty Mexican women running around me while I ate a half dozen fried eggs. I was eating with my guns strapped right on. They had gotten me the room and the bed and the fried eggs. Best friends I ever had.

★ 17 ★

I wasn't too sure about being a bodyguard because I had never guarded any bodies before, but I wasn't going to slam the door on fried eggs and soft beds. I ate so many eggs and tortillas that I thought I was going to fall out of the chair, but I was too itchy from bug bites and such to sit still long, and I asked the cook where I could get a bath. She gave me a big grin, yelled to three or four of the girls and shoved me out the back door. The girls came right after and started running around collecting buckets and laughing and pushing me into a shed that was right close by.

There was a big, round wooden tub up on a platform in the middle of the shed. There were four steps leading up to the platform and a big trough coming out of the side of the tub. One of the girls mounted the steps with a wooden mallet in her hands and banged a plug into the side of the tub where the trough came. Then the girls started running in and out with buckets of hot water until the danged thing was near full.

I was standing there watching them, and it took me a bit to realize that none of them had been in for a minute. I figured it was time to mount up so I walked up the steps and peeled off my duds, laying my guns on top of my clothes. The water felt just right to my hand but damned hot to my body, but I felt so itchy that I just went right in, head under and all. I came up blowing water and it sure felt fine.

Just then one of the younger girls came busting in all red-faced and chattering and ran up the stairs, handed me a big chunk of greasy soap and took off again like a frightened bird. I soaped my hair all sudsy and ducked under till it felt right. Then I stood up and soaped me all over and under and in between. I don't know when I'd felt so good in my life, what with a belly full of fried eggs and a clean belly to boot, and I was sure grateful to the Texan and Mr. Barron for setting me up so fancy. I'd walk a long way for those two, I kept telling myself.

Right then one of the older Mexican ladies walked in very dignified and such and slowly climbed up the steps and put down some big, dry cloths near my clothes. She sort of bowed in my direction and I nodded back at her. Then she turned and just as slow as she came in she went out. She was showing that filly how a woman handles such a situation.

It was a great day for company because just then the Texan strolled in to pass the time of day.

"What you doing there, boy?" he wanted to know.

"I'm cooking a chicken for supper," I told him.

"Oh, aren't we the fancy, sassy one now that we're living in the big house and sleeping in beds and squiring the missy around," he said, and he kicked the plug out of the tub with his boot.

I wasn't finished with my bath and I told him so.

"You going to be bathing in dry air," he said. "The water is now at ass level."

I climbed out of the tub and started to wipe myself down. Just then the young Mexican girl came dancing in again, giggling and screaming and carrying on something awful. She ran up the steps, dropped some clean clothes on the floor and turned to run.

The Texan whipped the cloth from in front of me with one hand and caught hold of her with the other.

"You've seen what a man looks like, Chita," he said. "Now see how little a boy has to offer."

I swear if I hadn't needed my hands to cover myself, I would have gone for my irons. But Chita was sneaking looks under her hands and I was so nervous that it was all I could to to keep from setting down and bawling like a baby.

Instead I gave the Texan a big shove and he went right over backwards onto the floor and didn't move. I grabbed hold of my clothes and tried to put on some pants, but the Mexican girl started screaming and I looked over the edge to see blood coming out of the Texan's nose and even out of his ears. I jumped down and leaned over him, and he was breathing real funny, snorting like a colt breaking wind, and I feared he was done for.

I looked up and all sorts of people had crowded into the room, and the women were jabbering and the men were standing around muttering and the Texan snorting away.

All of a sudden in walked Mr. Barron and with him this young lady in a white blouse and purple skirt that was slit for riding. She was carrying one of them little whips and her cheeks had a flush under her tan like she'd been riding hard somewhere. Strange as it may seem, what with the Texan snorting his life away and the Mexicans jabbering, I took the time to look her over real good. She had nice straight features and real blond hair and big white even teeth that showed just a bit as she pulled back her lips at the sight in front of her.

Just then Mr. Barron started shouting orders and four of the men picked up the Texan and carted him off. He shouted some more and the women scooted out of there as fast as their chunky legs would carry them.

Then he turned to me.

"Son," he said, "what happened here?"

I told him right from the start and how it was me as killed the Texan.

"We'll see," he said, "we'll see."

Then he turned to the girl. "Amy," he said, "this here is the young man I was telling you about."

"I'm pleased to meet you," she said.

"Likewise, ma'am," I said.

"Jory," said Mr. Barron, "I don't think you should be standing around here naked among the Mexicans and such. Put your clothes on."

So help me, I didn't have the strength to look down even though that was what I wanted to do more than anything in the world. So I checked another way. I turned around and looked at the platform and sure enough that's just where my clothes were. I was standing there naked as a jaybird in front of my employer and his daughter, whose body I was to guard. Well, I tell you I grabbed those clothes and ran right through that door as fast as I could and smack into all those

Mexican women who were standing outside there waiting to see what was going on inside. They screamed like it was the end of the world, and I went tearing up the path to the big house and inside where I scared the hell out of two maids on the stairs and into my room where the Texan was laying on the bed with a wet cloth on his head and three women standing around him. They started screaming worse than the ones outside, and the Texan sat up and said, "What the hell is all that noise about?"

I figured I couldn't lose anything more that day so I put the clothes down on the floor and put them on one by one, slow and easy like it was Sunday and I had a good hour till church. He sat there watching me with a little grin on his face.

"Boy," he said, "you sure take offense real easy."

"I'm glad you ain't dead," I told him. "I didn't mean for to push you over like that. To tell you the truth, I don't know what I intended."

"I had it coming," he said. "I get carried away with my funning sometimes."

He pushed himself off the bed and stood up and fell right down again. We got him back on the bed and the women stuck another cold rag on his head.

"Man," he said, "I landed square on the noggin."

The two older ladies went out, and I noticed that the one left was that Chita who'd been the cause of all the rumpus in the first place. She'd stick a rag on his head, then take it off and dip it into the pan of water, squeeze it out and put it right back. She looked like butter wouldn't melt in her mouth.

I'd lost one of my boots on the trip home so I limped out in just one to see where I'd dropped it. When I got to the bottom of the stairs, Miss Amy was standing there holding on to it.

"You looking for this?" she wanted to know.

"That's mine," I told her and sat down on the stair to slip it on. She sat right down beside me. Those stairs were wide enough for five people to sit on, but she sat so close that I had trouble getting enough elbow room to pull on the boot.

"They tell me you're good with a gun," she said.

"Jocko taught me a few things," I told her.

"The hands say you're better than Jocko ever was," she said.

"He was mighty good with his tricks," I told her.

"Well, don't think a fast gun impresses me any," she said.

"Guns is evil, my pa always said," I told her.

"Then why do you carry them?" she wanted to know.

"Evil is more evil than guns," I said.

She started to laugh. "You sure are a funny boy," she said.

I thought about that a minute. Nobody had ever told me I was funny before. I'd tried a couple of times to tell the jokes that people told me at the stable, but somehow they never came out right and nobody laughed. And I hadn't even been trying to tell her a joke.

"I've got to go now," I told her and went back up to my room. The Texan was still laying on the bed and Chita was leaning way over him. I figured maybe he'd died while I'd been gabbing away on the stairs and I felt real bad about the whole thing. He'd been nice to me and then I'd gone and killed him.

I walked around to the foot of the bed, and my heart gave a big jump as I realized he wasn't dead at all. He was laying there on his back with the cloth over his eyes and his hand was stuck deep down the front of Chita's dress. She had her eyes closed and he was rummaging around in there something fierce.

"You feeling better?" I asked him.

Doggone if she didn't give a scream to outdo all her others, and he sat up in bed so fast that he ripped her dress pulling his hand out, and one of her tits flopped out naked as sin and hers were even bigger than Linda Cooper's, but not as big as one of the fat ladies back at the Golden Spur when I went to find the Texan and Jocko.

Chita shoved her thing back inside her dress, pulled it closed and scooted out of there. The Texan threw the rag against the wall and got off the bed.

"Doggone," he said, "but you know more ways to kill a man out of growth than a tribe of 'Paches."

"You ever see any?" I asked him.

"Any what?" he wanted to know.

"Any of them 'Paches?"

"How the hell would I know?" he said and walked out of the room. He walked real straight and steady, just like I'd never pushed him in the first place.

I flipped my hat onto a chair and jumped backwards into the bed. It was better than going into a pile of hay and not even itchy. It had been a long day. Here I was with a mess of eggs in my belly, a clean body and clean clothes and a bed soft enough to be sinful, as Mrs. Jordan used to say. I wondered how they were doing. Long ways back there. And here I was. . . . You know what? I slept right through supper and everything and the next morning I woke up so hungry I thought I was going to die.

★ 18 ★

I slipped down the back stairs to the kitchen and told the cook to fill me up. She fried me some eggs and steak and beans and tortillas and kept pouring coffee into my cup. Her food wasn't as tasty as Mrs. Jordan's, but it was so much better than the trail cook's that I had to keep eating till I couldn't stand it anymore.

Mr. Barron came out in the kitchen and watched me for a few minutes and then went out shaking his head. I don't know what was bothering him, but he came back a little later and made believe that he was surprised at seeing me still eating.

"Son," he said, "there's only so much food in Texas."

I knew he was funning me so I just kept on eating.

"If you're through by noon," he said, "Amy wants to take a ride up on the mesa. She's finished up now so go down to the stable and have them saddle her black and come back up with it. You'll only be gone a couple of hours so I don't think you'll need sandwiches." Then he laughed like he'd said something funny, gave the cook a big whack on the rump and walked out.

I finished up what was left on the table and started out to get the horses. The cook had been standing there watching me, and when I got up, she grabbed me by the arm and squeezed hard and said something like *"Muy hombre"* or something. I told her I liked her cooking and went along for the horses.

One of the Mexicans showed me which was Miss Amy's horse so I snared him and threw a saddle on. He was a black

126

beauty all right, and I had to reach high to get on him. He threw me right off. I didn't figure a girl's horse would be that rough so I got right back on him, and he bucked me around that corral for a good five minutes before he realized I'd been on a horse before and wasn't going noplace no second time around. I picked me up my favorite horse from the trail herd, a little devil we called Tiger, and rode up to the house. Miss Amy wasn't noplace around so I went inside and found her still at the breakfast table. She was nibbling on a piece of toasted bread and drinking some coffee. I didn't see how a girl as big as her could go very far on a little piece of bread first thing in the morning, but it wasn't my place to give her advice about her health. She asked me if I wanted something to eat and I told her I had already eaten. If there'd been any real food on the table, I might have thought about it, but I couldn't see sitting down for a piece of bread and butter.

She finally wiped her mouth with a piece of cloth and said she was ready to go. She was wearing a right smart outfit that almost looked like a man's clothes, and on her head she had one of those flat Mexican black hats with the straight brim all around. She looked real clean and neat.

The big black didn't give her any trouble when she mounted on the Mex's hand, and we started off up the trail to what I figured would turn out to be the mesa. I let her lead the way because I didn't know anything about the country at all, and we just jogged along for about an hour before we came up this small hill and looked down over a grove of trees that had a small pond in the middle of it.

"Here we are," she said and took off down the hill like a bat out of hell.

By the time I caught up with her she was off her horse and had started to unbutton her shirt. I dropped down beside her and waited to see what was going on.

"I'm going for a swim," she said, "and you can stay with the horses."

"Wait a minute," I said. "I'm supposed to be your bodyguard, and I can't guard your body if you're swimming there and I'm watching the horses here. That makes me a horseguard, not a bodyguard."

"I don't care what you call it," she said. "I'm going swimming and I'm not going to have you looking at me while I'm in the water without any clothes on."

This gave me something to think about, and something I didn't know what to do about. Mr. Barron trusted me to guard his daughter's body, but I'm sure he didn't want me looking at it when it didn't have any clothes on.

"All right," I told her, "I'll stay here with the horses, but I want you to call out to me every few seconds so that I know your body is all right."

"My body is just fine, thank you," she said and flounced off into the underbrush. Flounce was one of my pa's favorite words. He used to always have some woman flouncing off somewheres. But until then I had never known what a real flounce was.

I hunkered down by the horses and waited. I could see where a man was better off smoking at a time like this with nothing else to do, but I had promised Mrs. Jordan faithfully that I would never smoke and I had let that poor woman down on enough things already.

"You all right?" I called out.

"Just fine," I heard her say from the other side of the brush. "Just fine."

And then I heard a big splash.

And then I heard something else. I heard the brush crackle over on the left of me somewhere. I acted like I didn't hear nothing.

"You better come on back out," I sent out.

"No, it's too good," she yelled. "Too bad you have to miss it."

And she went splashing and banging around in the water while some people were sneaking up on us somewheres.

I stayed hunkered down while I tried to figure out something to do. They could have been on all sides of us, and there could be a hundred of them for all anybody knew, least of all me. The best way would be to make them show their hand and then figure out how to play it.

I stood up real slow and easy and called out, "I know you're out there and you better come out and show yourself."

Two of them started to stand up and I fell off to the side

and blasted away. The hat flew off one of them before they dived down again and I rolled behind a tree to figure out the next move.

"Jory, you idiot, stop all that shooting," I heard Roy yelling from over where the two men had dropped down.

"Don't worry, Roy," I yelled back. "I'll get you out of there." And I rammed two slugs into the trees to keep them honest while I rolled over to a tree on the other side.

"Stop that damn shooting, you damn fool boy," I heard Mr. Barron yell, and he stood right up and started walking over towards me. Then Roy stood up and came along with him. I stayed where I was till I saw where the other people were. But no other people came. Only Miss Amy. And she didn't look like she'd been swimming. She was all dressed up. I guessed it was all right if I stood up.

"Put those guns away," said Mr. Barron, so I holstered my irons.

Roy's face was all red, and I thought to myself that maybe that bump on the head had done him more harm than anyone figured and he shouldn't be running around again as yet.

"Boy," said the Texan, "I didn't say nothing to you yesterday about trying to kill me because anyone can make a mistake. But this two times in two days is coming on a bit thick, you hear?"

"I got no quarrel with you," I told him. "I shot at a couple of people were trying to get near Miss Amy's body."

"That was us, you idiot," said Mr. Barron. "We were trying to sneak up on you."

The Texan pulled off his hat and stuck his fingers into the holes in it.

"Man," he said, "if you hadn't been a couple of inches high, that would have been it. It's a good thing you were going for my puny old head."

I'd been going for the stomach and had missed a couple of feet high, but I wasn't about to admit up to any nonsense like that so I just nodded a bit.

"What you two doing up here anyway?" I asked. "I just saw you down at the house and that's quite a ride away."

Miss Amy had sat down on a rock and was laughing away to beat the band.

"You two," she said and laughed so hard she couldn't hardly keep talking. "Oh, you two. If you could only see your faces when you were walking up to him." And she laughed and laughed and laughed.

They got redder in the face than they had been, and that was plenty red.

"You two," she said and went into a new laughing fit. "Let's just check him out once to see if he respects a woman. Throw the stones in the water and make a big splash. He respects her all right. Enough to kill off two old fools who come creeping up in the woods."

"Now, you listen here, young lady," said Mr. Barron. "We were just trying to make sure you had someone with you that you could trust under all circumstances and all temptations. You know the trouble we had with that other fool."

"But this one doesn't seem to care if I go dancing around the world without any clothes on," she said, "so now I can go dancing around the world without any clothes on."

"That's not what it is at all," her father yelled, "and you better not let me catch you going swimming plumb naked anytime anyplace with anybody. The boy is to protect you on your rides and on your trips to town and on your visits and suchlike. But I want no nonsense, no funny stuff."

I didn't know what all they were talking about so I just stood there and kept my mouth shut. I liked the work I was doing and I liked that food and the bed and the house and the people. I would guard that body on rides and in town and on visits and suchlike. And anytime she wanted to go swimming without any clothes on or go dancing naked around the world I would make sure that nobody bothered her while she went swimming or dancing. Every inch of that body would be guarded every minute.

"Well," yelled Mr. Barron to me, "what do you have to say about it?"

"Well," I said, "nobody got hurt and Miss Amy had her swim and if we don't hurry a bit we're all going to be late for lunch."

Mr. Barron's mouth opened a little and he turned to the side and looked at Roy, who just looked back at him. And he turned to Miss Amy, who all of a sudden sat down again on the rock and started laughing even louder than she had before. She laughed and she laughed and then she stopped.

And she stood up and walked over and took my hand and led me over to the horses.

"Come on, Jory," she said. "We sure don't want to be late to lunch."

★ 19 ★

Life was pretty quiet the next couple of weeks. Miss Amy seemed to spend all her time with a lady who had come on from St. Louis with a lot of cloth that she was going to make up into dresses. The few times I saw Miss Amy she was standing in the middle of a room with the lady and a couple of the Mexican women fussing around her with pins while she stuck her arm out or back or whirled around or suchlike. "Hiyo, Jory," she'd yell, and, "Hiyo, Miss Amy," I'd tell her back, and then she'd go back to sticking her arm out or sucking in her gut.

It was all fine with me, what with the three meals a day and the soft bed at night, but just working the ponies a little was kind of dull, and I began to wish I had one of the regular jobs on the ranch even if it meant sleeping and eating in the bunkhouse and riding fence all day.

But then one morning Miss Amy stuck her head in the door of the kitchen and said, "When you get through plowing through all that stuff, Jory, catch up a few horses and we'll go for a ride." I gobbled everything down as fast as I could, and I had the black and my pony in front of the house in no time at all.

"Let's go visit the scene of the crime," she said, and she rode off toward that mesa. It was a fine, clear day and the sun was already pouring it on hot, so it felt good to let the pony just run into the wind. We kept up a steady gallop nearly all the way, and by the time we reached the little wood with the pond we were all a little hot and dusty.

I'd let Miss Amy stay a bit ahead of me all the way, and

by the time I dropped down beside her, she had already unbuttoned three buttons on her shirt.

"Your daddy said no swimming," I told her.

"I say swimming," she said, "and you and my daddy can go to hell."

Man, I sure liked that girl. She had a way of talking that was a gentle version of her daddy, straightforward but nice at the same time. She was going swimming, there was no doubt about that, but she put it at you in a nice way.

"Well, you be careful," I told her, "and keep talking to me like last time."

"If you don't hear from me," she said, "come down and see where I'm at."

"You just keep talking," I told her.

She went off into the woods and after a few minutes I heard a big splash.

"Wow, it's cold," she yelled.

"That's a spring-fed pond," I yelled back at her.

"It's got me springing," she shouted, and I could hear her beating some heat out of that water.

Just then I heard a branch break somewhere off to my left. That riled me up a bit. It's all right to test a man out once, but to do it everytime he goes out is just a little too much. If they didn't trust me to guard that body as it should be guarded, then they could just let someone else do it and I'd be on my way.

"Come on, Roy," I yelled out to him. "I hear you out there with Mr. Barron, and you're lucky I don't shoot your hat off."

Just then somebody behind me said, "You ain't shooting nothing but your mouth off. Get your hands up in the air."

I looked around and there was this big fellow standing there with a rifle trained dead on me. Another fellow came walking out of the woods on my left. He had a handgun drawn down on me, and he was smiling just a little, like to himself over something.

I heard Miss Amy give a yell and then another yell and then nothing. About a minute later she came stumbling out of the woods without a stitch of clothes on and behind her came a third man who was carrying a handgun, too.

"Well, now," said the smiler, and he had a big grin on his

face this time. "Isn't this a scandalous thing to behold in the woods."

Miss Amy was standing there soaking wet and torn up a bit from the brambles and as naked as a human being can be. She didn't try to cover up anything with her hands, and I guess I was staring just as hard as the three strangers. But she looked everybody straight in the eye, and she was as far from crying as anybody could be. I could get real fond of a woman like Miss Amy.

"This is a mistake you'll regret," she said to the smiler.

"Mistake?" he said. "Me and the boys are riding through the woods peaceful-like and we come on this terrible scene. There is this beautiful young daughter of the area's second-leading rancher and she has just been raped several times by this cowhand who finally beats her to death but not before she has put a bullet in his stomach that will kill him before anyone comes on the scene. How does that sound for openers?"

"You haven't got the guts," she said.

"I haven't, eh?" he said. "Well, why don't I start off the proceedings personally?" And he started to walk towards her. She stumbled back, and I could tell then that she was scared in spite of the brave front she had been putting up. It wasn't right that these three strangers should see the naked body that I was sworn to protect.

I went into my roll and the one with the rifle was dead before I hit the ground. My jump had moved me about five feet to the right, and as I hit the ground and rolled, I caught the one in back of Miss Amy square in the chest just as a bullet splattered into the ground not three inches from my face. I put both guns on the smiler and dropped him before he got a second shot off. I stood up quick and ran over to the one I had hit in the chest. He was still breathing, but everytime he did a big gob of blood spouted through the hole in his shirt. I pointed my gun at his head, but I heard Miss Amy say, "No, Jory, no!"

"He saw you naked," I told her, and I finished him off.

She was laying back on the ground where she'd stumbled, and I pulled her to her feet and walked her over to where there was some soft grass.

"Where are your clothes?" I asked her and started to move off to the pond.

"No!" she yelled. "No! Don't leave me."

She grabbed onto my shirt and held on for dear life. She was shivering quite a bit so I put my arms around her and tried to give her what warmth I could. She smelled real nice from the cold pond water, and I couldn't help thinking that I'd like to have me a girl like this someday with those pert things pushing at you and nice skin and a pretty face to look at too.

"Miss Amy," I told her, "if your daddy and Roy come on us now, I sure am going to have a lot of explaining to do."

She started to shake real hard, and I was wondering how I could warm her up more when I realized she was laughing and not shaking from the cold.

"Oh, Jory," she said, "I'm sure you could explain it to everybody's satisfaction."

"I better get your clothes," I told her and scooted off into the woods and down to the pond. I found them right off as they were piled neatly on a big rock. The sun had warmed them up and I used the slip to rub her down good and stop the shivering. She insisted on putting the damp slip on under her dress, and in five minutes she was dressed like nothing had ever happened. She had pulled her hair tight under her Mexican hat and you couldn't even tell it was wet.

"Let's get the story straight," she said.

"I fell down on my duty," I said. "Three men saw your body."

"Forget all that body business," she said. "Nobody saw my body because there wasn't any body to see. We rode up here and sat down on that stump to rest the horses and those three came at us out of the woods. You went for them and got all three. They're Muller's men, and that's all Daddy will have to know."

"Miss Amy," I said.

"Yes," she said.

"I saw your body," I told her.

"We can just forget that," she said.

"I'll try," I told her, "but I just want you to know I'm proud to guard a body like yours and I'm sorry I let anybody else see it. It won't happen again."

She looked at me for a long time, and then she put a hand on my cheek.

"You're a strange boy," she said. "A strange boy."

"Aw, I am not," I told her.

"Just keep that story straight," she said, jumped up and ran to her horse and took out of there fast.

I wanted to check the three men but was afraid she'd get too far ahead so I just took off after her. That black could really go, and I had trouble keeping her in sight. By the time I hit the big house, she was standing there on the porch waiting for me. Her father was just coming out as I was walking up the steps.

"Nice ride?" he asked.

Miss Amy started to cry.

"Oh, Daddy," she wailed, "it was just too horrible."

Mr. Barron's face got so red I thought he would bust.

"What's going on here?" he yelled at me. "What did you do now?"

"We had a mite of trouble," I told him, "but it's all right now."

"Trouble!" he yelled. "What kind of trouble?"

"These three fellows tried to give us trouble," I told him, "but it's all right now."

"It was three of Muller's men," said Miss Amy between her sobs, "and they were going to kill us."

"But it's all right now," I told him.

"Muller's men," he yelled, and his face got even redder. "Where are they? Where are they?"

"They're back there," I told him, pointing out in the direction of the mesa, "and it's all right now. They got themselves dead."

Well, this kind of thing went back and forth for about five minutes before Roy was found and about twenty men went tearing off to the spot I told him about. Miss Amy went to her room to rest, and when she went by me, she gave me this big wink. I doubt to this day that she was really crying. What she was doing was softening her daddy up, that's what she was doing.

I went into the kitchen to get me some lunch, and none of the Mexicans said nothing to me while I was eating. They just stood around and whispered to each other and looked over at me with sad looks. Every once in a while a new one would come in and the whispering would start all over and then the long looks.

I finished lunch and was sitting on the porch letting some sun soak into me when the posse came tearing back with the dead men on three horses and three of the Barron hands riding double.

There must have been a hundred and fifty Mexicans crowding around the horses and talking and yelling and jumping up and down. Mr. Barron and Roy came running up to me all excited. Mr. Barron's face was as red as when he'd left, and even Roy seemed more het up than usual.

"Five shots," said Roy, "five shots. You got in five and only one of them got in one. You know who got in that one? You know who got in that one shot on you?"

"I didn't know any of them," I told him.

"That was Vinnie Mountain," said Roy, "and he's killed more men than you got years."

Mr. Barron was just standing there looking at me. His face wasn't as red as it had been, but he was breathing kind of heavy.

"Jory," he said, "I owe you the life of my daughter. And I'll never forget it." And he turned around and went into the house.

"Well," said Roy, "it looks like you ain't going to have no worries. What you looking so sad and reflective about?"

"Nothing," I told him, "just nothing," and I turned and went up to my room.

But I was feeling sad. Maybe not sad but somewhere off a way from happy. It wasn't killing those men. They were going to do us in and hurt Miss Amy real bad. I didn't know them before and I didn't know them now.

It was Miss Amy and her body. I could still feel her on the front of me, holding hard like there was just the two of us left in the world and nobody was going to split us up. I could still smell her wet hair and the clean feel of her was there in my hands, the soft skin and the muscle underneath and the bone underneath that. I could still feel it in my hands like she was still there.

I looked down at my hands and they were stark white like I'd been squeezing something hard. I rolled off the bed and got out my guns, all five of them. And I put down five different cloths on the floor planks and broke every one of them guns down, screws and all. And I cleaned and oiled every single part, screws and all. And I put them all together again. I put them all together and I checked them out one by one, testing each action just like Jocko had showed me, working them all until I was positive that each and every one of those five guns was working like it should and maybe a little bit better. There was nothing more you could do to those guns. But I still had the peculiar feeling.

So I got up from the floor, so stiff that I couldn't sense hardly nothing in my legs at first, and I strapped on the Navys. Then I practiced. I worked until all I could feel in my hands was the hard handles of the guns and the sweat was pouring off my forehead right into my eyes. I was hitting the butts harder than I should have for a good draw, hitting them way too hard. But I had to get the feel of the soft away from them, and this was the only way I knew how.

★ 20 ★

The sweetness of life, my pa used to say, is based on whether somebody is kicking or kissing your ass at that particular moment. Now don't get my pa wrong; he wasn't an obscene man. But life had not dealt kindly with him, and he was inclined to get moody.

Life was sweet to me after I dusted those three in the little woods. My first salary had eighty dollars in the wad instead of forty. Mr. Barron didn't let Miss Amy roam very far, and she seemed inclined to stick around the womenfolk, so I didn't have to do much bodyguarding for a spell. The Mexicans had oohed and aahed over the corpses until they had been carted off to town for delivery somewhere or other, and after that, every time I came near a Mexican man he took off his hat and the Mexican women sort of stooped a bit and looked down at the ground. Even the Mexes I had been out on the trail with acted this way and kept on doing it no matter how hard I tried to joke them off it.

For a while I tried taking off my hat when they took off their hats, but that didn't work so after a time I just sort of bent my head a little when they did their tipping or bowing. I tell you, we were the most dignified ranch in the world.

I rode around a bit by myself and practiced with the guns every day and burned up a lot of Mr. Barron's ammunition, but that grew tiresome. The cook kept piling so much food on me that I even grew tired of that, and once I didn't even come in for lunch.

I asked Mr. Barron if maybe I could do some work around the place, but he said there were plenty of people to do the work and I should just keep practicing with my guns and having a good time. Roy was too busy to spend much time with me, and I couldn't pal around with people who kept taking their hats off every time I came near, so I started thinking about maybe quitting the place and taking off for California and the goldfields.

One bright Monday morning I got up on my horse and said to myself that this was the day, this was the day I started riding out and maybe just kept on going. I had my favorite guns, and all my money was in my saddlebags. They could keep the rest.

I had never been to town since I had arrived at the ranch so I thought I would stop by there to pick up some edibles and a few necessaries. The town was located on Barron property, but it was a good five-hour ride, and I was plenty hot and dusty by the time I arrived there.

It wasn't a big town but it wasn't a small town either. There were two American and two Mexican saloons and two stores and pretty near twenty houses of one type or another.

My throat was all dry and prickly from the brush, and I decided to have me a beer even though I didn't like beer. At least it would be cool and wet. One saloon was called the Oasis and the other one had Max's Place hung over the door. I took a chance on Max.

It was almost chilly inside after the blaze of the sun, and I wondered if maybe I wasn't coming down with one of them grippes. My throat had never been this dry before, even on the trail. I walked inside the door and stepped quickly to the side just as Jocko had told me always to do when coming into a saloon from the bright outside. It was funny how all those things he had told me by the trail fire had stuck in my head. It's too bad Jocko hadn't had no education; he would of made a great teacher.

There were six men in the place besides the bartender, two standing at the bar and four at a table playing cards. I walked down to the end that had nobody at it and told the bartender beer when he came ambling over.

"Passing through?" he asked as he slid the glass in front of me.

"Might say that," I told him.

"Where you heading?" he wanted to know.

"California, maybe," I told him.

"Where you been?' he pushed again.

"Here and there," I told him.

Jocko had said that it was best to answer short when you were in a strange place and a man kept pushing you on what was none of his business in the first place. The two men down at the other end of the bar were pretty drunk, and I guess the bartender wanted an excuse to stay away from them, but that wasn't none of my affair. I just wanted to get that scratch out of my throat.

"I'll have another," I told him, and he went to fetch it.

"You looking for a job?" he asked as he came back with the beer.

I didn't feel like talking much so I just drained that glass down in one gulp and told him to get me another.

"Plenty of jobs around," he said when he came back with the third one. "Both Barron and the Mullers are looking for men, especially men who can handle a gun."

"Max, you're talking too much," said one of the poker players. I couldn't tell which one it was because nobody even raised his head. That voice just came out of the pack.

"I'm just passing the word on," said the bartender. "Ain't saying nothing everybody doesn't know already."

"I'll sing at your funeral, Max," said another voice from the table.

Two more men came in the door and walked up to the bar. They were halfway between me and the two drunks at the other end, and they ordered whiskey and beer in loud voices. Max hurried over to serve them and then came right back to me. From the look on his face I figured that he didn't like the two new ones any more than he did the drunks. I couldn't blame him in the least because they were big, ugly-looking men with stubbly beards on their faces and greasy clothes and double irons on both of them.

"You looking at me, kid?" one of them said.

I tell you I almost jumped out of my boots. I guess I had been looking at them kinda close and half asleep, and when he spoke to me real loud like that, I gave a start. My throat was still dry and I was feeling a mite lightheaded. I'd never had three beers in my life before. Come to think of it, I'd never had two beers before in my life, and I have a feeling it was the beer affecting my brain a bit. I couldn't help thinking for a second that maybe I had inherited my pa's curse. In any case, what with feeling bad and maybe a little bit drunk and disgusted with myself, I wasn't about to take no guff from any dirty, ugly middle-aged man.

"Yes, I was," I told him. "I most certainly was."

"I don't like people looking at me unless they got a special reason," he said. "You got a special reason?"

"It's just that I was thinking how dirty you looked," I told him.

The only sound in that place was of four chairs scraping back and footsteps moving over against the further wall.

There's going to be a shooting, I said to myself, and that man's going to get himself killed.

"You worked as hard as I do you'd look dirty, too," he said.

I couldn't think of nothing to say to that so I just kept still. He was looking at me like I was supposed to say something.

"Know what I work so hard at?' he asked me.

"No, I don't," I told him.

"I work hard at squashing punk kids like you," he said and started towards me.

I stepped away from the bar and faced him straight, letting my arms hang loose by the guns. He stopped dead in his tracks and looked at me kind of surprised, like he hadn't even noticed I was packing guns.

"Boy," he said, "all you were going to get was a slam in the mouth. Now you're dead."

His friend had moved away from the bar enough to come at me from an angle, and I could tell that this wasn't going to be no one for one deal. I didn't need to shift an inch to have them both right so I just stood there quietlike. There was plenty of time, plenty of time.

"The kid's got guts," said the man who had stepped back from the bar. "He ain't shading a hair."

"True enough," said the first. "How'd you like to work for the Mullers, kid? It will save you from getting dead."

"I already work for a man," I told him. "Mr. Barron."

"Well, he's one short then," said the first one and made

his move. I put a bullet in his shooting shoulder and tried the same for his partner. The second shot was a hurried one, however, and I missed the shoulder and drilled him right in the chest, shooting a little right for safety's sake. I put another shot in the left shoulder of the first one just to make sure he wasn't going to use his other gun. Jocko had told me that a lot of men carried two guns, but that very few could pull two at the same time or shoot straight with them. I was good proof of that. I had aimed at the man's shoulder and drilled him through the chest. Must have drilled through some vital organ because he was dead before he hit.

The other one just sank to the floor in a sitting position and stared straight at me. I'm not sure he was looking at me, but he was sure looking in my direction. He tried to talk but nothing came out of his mouth except for the spit that was running out of both corners. He looked real sad there with blood running out of his shoulders down his shirt and his eyes trying to pop out of his head.

I wondered why nobody was helping him, and then I realized that nobody was moving in the place. They were all standing there looking at the guns in my hands. I slipped them in the holsters and people started moving around. A couple went over and checked the dead man on the floor, and the bartender came out from behind the counter with a couple of wet rags that he put on the hurt man's shoulders.

I bust out in a cold sweat and felt a mite dizzy there in the place. I walked over to the bartender and asked him how much I owed him, but he just shook his head a little at me like I was crazy or something. I pulled a dollar out of my pocket and rang it down on the counter. I knew it was too much, but I didn't want to leave less than I owed, and he wasn't going to tell me.

I started to walk out of the place, but just as I reached the door, I turned around and walked back to the wounded man. He had big tears running out of his eyes even though he wasn't crying or anything.

"I ain't never had this many beers before," I told him.

Then I went out and headed back to the Barron place. I seemed to get there before I knew it, and the sun was just setting down. I walked into the kitchen where the cook scolded me for being so late. She put supper on the table and I ate and ate and ate, and all of a sudden I threw it all back up again. Everybody in the kitchen got awful excited and started running around and rubbing my face with cold towels, and finally Conchita put my arm over her shoulder and helped me up the stairs to my room. She pulled off my boots and lay me down on the bed and started kissing me all over the face while she was crying so hard that I could feel the tears falling on my face like raindrops.

I sat up in bed and grabbed her by the shoulders.

"You know," I said, "I ain't throwed up like that in a long time."

★ 21 ★

He was the biggest man I ever saw, maybe ten feet tall, and he was dressed all in black and his eyes glowed in his head so bright that they looked like diamonds in a bed of coal. He was so big you couldn't turn any way to get away from him and I keep walking closer and closer even though I wanted to turn around and run. But it wasn't no use because I just knew he was on the other side too, so I kept walking closer and closer, just waiting for him to reach out and squeeze and squeeze and squeeze. But the more I kept walking the more he stayed the same distance away so I started to walk a little faster and I could feel the sweat pouring down the groove in my back and then finally the two giant hands lifted out from all that black with the two eyes shining and they grabbed me by the shoulders and started to squeeze and I yelled, Pa, Pa, I yelled, Pa, Pa, Pa . . .

And Miss Amy was standing over me in the broad daylight shaking me by the shoulders and saying, "Jory, Jory, wake up now!"

I stopped yelling and looked around and I was soaking hot with my mouth so dry I couldn't have yelled more if I wanted. I could see Conchita standing there back of her, and her mouth was moving something fierce but I couldn't hear any sound coming out of it.

"Looks like my supper didn't agree with me," I said.

"That was two days ago, Jory," said Miss Amy, "and you've been burning up like a wheat field."

"You here to go riding?" I asked her. "I'll just get my clothes and we'll be on our way in a minute."

Her mouth dropped open a bit and then she started to laugh real hard.

"If you ain't just a caution," she said. "Sure I want to go riding. Hop out and we'll get cracking."

I rolled out to the side and slipped off the bed. Conchita gave a little scream and I looked over at her to find out what all the yelling was about, but nobody seemed to be attacking her. I felt real dizzy standing there so I dropped down to my knees to get better traction. Miss Amy stopped laughing and was trying to lift me back up to my feet, but she wasn't that strong. Just then the door bust open and in came Mr. Barron and Roy.

"What the hell's goin' on here?" yelled Mr. Barron.

Conchita still had her hand in front of her mouth and Miss Amy was still trying to lift me up and I was trying to decide what the hell I wanted to do, so nobody said much of anything.

"Amy," said Mr. Barron, "this is a mighty peculiar situation for a father to walk in on."

"We're going riding," I told him.

"You can't go riding when you're stark naked," he yelled, and I looked down and sure enough I was.

"You seem to spend half your time here running around bare-assed," yelled Mr. Barron, "and I say there's no need for it. You ain't got that much to be proud of."

Roy had come over and him and Miss Amy lifted me back on the bed and tucked me under.

"I'd like a drink of water," I told anybody who was listening. Miss Amy made a sign to Conchita, who scurried out of the room.

"Boy," said Mr. Barron, "what the hell you want to tear that town apart for? I knowed you was anxious for something to do, but killing two men . . ."

"I just killed one," I told him. "The other one was just nicked in the shoulders."

"He's dead, boy," said Mr. Barron. "Went into convulsions and gave up the ghost."

"That's too bad," I said.

"You funning me?" Mr. Barron asked. "Here I been complaining to the Mullers about the gunmen they been bringing in and all the trouble they been causing and you go into town and wipe out his foreman and his top gun just like that."

"I'd like to have seen that," said Roy. "They've spread the word that you're half bear and half antelope. You're gonna carry a rep with you now and all the tough boys will be looking to challenge you."

"I don't want any trouble," I told them. "It's just that I don't like people bothering me."

Miss Amy started to laugh again, and her father told her to get the hell out of the room and don't let him catch her with any naked men again.

She came over to the bed, leaned down and kissed me smack on the forehead right there in front of her father.

"Never you mind," she said. "We can go for our ride tomorrow."

"Look, boy," said Mr. Barron after she left the room, "I don't give a damn in hell how many of the Mullers' scum you kill, but I can't have you just going into town and gunning them down. I'm the one that's been screaming that we got to have law and order around here, that we ought to have a sheriff and everything, and you go around making me sound like I don't mean it."

"Do you mean it?" Roy asked him.

"Of course I don't mean it," said Mr. Barron, "but what the hell has that got to do with anything?"

I got up on my elbows and said, "Mr. Barron, just as soon as I can sit a horse, I will get my presence from yours and be out of the way."

"Don't talk nonsense," he snorted. "Long as you're here, the bastards will swing wide when they have to come this way. Don't you dare think of leaving. This is your home."

I sank back on the pillow and thought about that for a minute. I'd never had a real home in my life. I couldn't remember my ma, and sure the cheap boardinghouses and stables my pa and me lived in couldn't be called homes. And though the Jordans did their best to make their house my home, somehow it was always Mrs. Jordan's home and nobody else's. Not even Mr. Jordan. This big old building didn't feel like a home to me, but then as I thought about the room I was lying in and the meals in the kitchen and my own two horses and the Mexicans taking off their hats when I walked by, I thought that this sure would make a good home if you could get a home sometime.

"That's nice," I said and closed my eyes down. "That's real nice."

"Let the boy sleep," said Mr. Barron, and I heard them tiptoe out with their boots clunking and their spurs jangling.

I thought maybe I would get me some sleep, but I heard a noise like a little mouse scurrying and I opened my eyes to find Conchita tiptoeing into the room with a glass of water in her hand.

"Hey there," I said, "that sure looks good."

She brought it over and held my head as she tipped the glass in front of me. I keep on drinking until I drained the whole glass and she let my head lean back on the pillow. Then her eyes got all teary as she looked down on me and she started kissing me all over the face. She sure was the easiest woman to break down in tears that I ever did see.

I heard the glass clunk on the floor and Conchita was squeezing me tight and kissing me right on the lips and her hand slid under the blankets and took hold of me right where that woman had pinched me at the Golden Spur. But Conchita was rubbing soft and easy, saying, *"Muy hombre, muy hombre,"* over and over, while she licked my face with her red tongue, licking my lips and my cheeks and my chin and kissing me, kissing me.

I slid my hand into her dress just like I'd seen Roy do and I felt her soft tits warm and smooth with the big nipple on each one and Chita pulled right away from me fast and looked down on me for a second and then yanked her dress and slip right off standing there by the side of the bed. She wasn't wearing no underpants or nothing and she pulled back the covers and got right in with me and started all over with her licking my face and my chest and she put her hand on my pisser and I messed all over her hand and the bed and we both watched it as it came and came and came all over everything.

Chita looked up at me with her eyes big and round and her mouth open. *"Jesu!"* she said, *"Jesu, Jesu, Jesu!"* She was still holding on to me tight and I could feel my thing throbbing in her hand and she looked down again and said,*"Jesu, Jesu, muy hombre, muy hombre,"* and elbowed me aside and rolled me over her and pulled my hurtin' pisser into her all wet and soft and I didn't feel weak and I didn't feel sick. I didn't feel weak and sick at all.

★ 22 ★

It didn't take me long to get back on my feet, but somehow the spirit was gone from me. Those three beers had poisoned more than my stomach, and I was feared that my pa's curse had fallen on me. I vowed never to take another drop.

Miss Amy and I went riding up to the mesa, where she decided to take a swim and insisted that I come down to the shore with her in case any bad men were around. She made me turn my back while she undressed, but when she was in the water she kept standing up near shore and I could see her tits standing out on her chest. Hers weren't near as big as the others I had seen, and they looked a lot harder than Conchita's, but they were nice enough, I guess. Anyway, she kept on doing this, and I was feared someone might walk up on her and see her body, so I kept walking around in the woods and she kept yelling for me to come back and it was pretty noisy all in all.

When I finally did come back to tell her we ought to be getting back, she just stood up in the water and walked out to me. She picked up her slip and rubbed herself down with it and even asked me to wipe her back for her. While I was wiping it, she turned right around fast, and I was wiping her things before I knew she had done it. And she grabbed hold of my face and kissed me right on the lips, and I said, "Miss Amy, if your daddy comes walking out of those woods, I am going to walk into that water and keep going."

She laughed and kissed me again full on the lips, and I could taste the clean again, so strong it almost made me dizzy. Her lips were thinner than Conchita's and harder and she didn't stick her tongue in your mouth or slobber all over. I liked Chita doing that to me but this was nicer somehow, different and nicer. I tightened my arms around her just a bit and was thinking of moving my hands around front when I first thought of Mr. Barron and then of Roy and then of any goddamn cowboy who could stumble on us there, and I knew my ass would be fried and refried more than any beans in the history of Mexican cooking and I dropped my hands and stepped back.

Miss Amy looked at me for a second with her head tilted, nodded once or twice like I had just said something to her and then laughed again. She wrung out her slip and dressed up in her clothes.

"Jory," she said, "I hear any more about you and that Conchita and you're going to think drowning is an easy way out."

She had a strange little smile all the way home, and we never said one word to each other. When we reached the ranch, she just slipped off the horse as Juan grabbed the reins and she went into the house without even a good-bye. Juan looked up at me and shrugged his shoulders in that special way, and it gave me the idea he'd been hearing things about me and Conchita too.

That was the last I saw of Miss Amy for a while. A friend of hers named Betty Whitman came over for a visit from California and the women started making dresses again and giggling all over the place. Every time I came near that Betty Whitman she went into a case of the leaping hysterics, and it got so I looked around corners before making the turn. Miss Amy wasn't any help in the matter because she was always whispering things in that Betty's ear, and then the two of them would look at me and bust into that fit of giggling.

One morning Mr. Barron asked me to have breakfast with them because he wanted to talk about something, and the two girls just sat at the table and giggled away at everything we said. It got so bad that he told them to shut up, but that made them just go at it all the harder. At one point Miss Amy slipped her foot under the table and started rubbing it against mine. Miss Betty knew what she was doing and started laughing so hard she had to stuff her piece of cloth in her mouth. I'd had all I could so I just stood up and walked out of there.

"Where the hell you going?" Mr. Barron yelled after me.

"To hell out of here," I yelled right back.

I was so mad that I jumped on the first horse I saw with a saddle and galloped all the way to the mesa. I didn't hear or see anything till I got there, and then I heard that horse groaning like he was going out. It was the first time I noticed that someone had ridden him hard before I had taken him off, and I almost had killed the poor fellow with my meanness. I jumped right off and started to walk him cool.

I was so put out at having harmed the horse that I walked right into them without smelling a thing. As I came past a tree, a big fellow stepped out from behind it and whanged me over the head with a branch. I went right down to my knees and he whanged me again. I fell over on my left side so I had to go for my right gun, but he kicked my hand so hard I thought it was broke, and then he reached down and pulled the gun out of the holster, rolled me over and lifted the other one. By this time there were three others standing over me, all with guns pointing straight down.

The big one lifted up and kicked me a good one in the ribs.

"He ain't so tough," he said. "What's so tough about him?"

And then he kicked me again.

"Take it easy," said one of the others. "They said to bring him in undamaged."

The first one reached down and pulled me to my feet.

"He ain't damaged," he said. "He's in fine shape."

And then he slapped me across the face so hard that I could really hear bells ringing.

"Come on, friend," he said, "you're invited for a visit. The baron wants to see you."

"I work for Mr. Barron," I told him. "You made a mistake."

"Not Mr. Barron," he said. "The baron. Baron Muller."

I figured I was in trouble.

★ 23 ★

Sometimes when my pa was deep drunk he would go into this long-winded business about how important it was to die nobly. I wonder what he would of said about being kicked in the head by Ab Evans. Or how Jocko felt about the way he went. One thing I'd learned was that nobody goes pretty.

And on the way to the Muller spread the one thing I knew was that one way or another they meant for me to go. But the peculiar part about the whole thing is that I didn't care. I really didn't care. I'd seen and done a lot in my fifteen years, and there wasn't nobody who gave a real damn whether I went or stayed. Maybe the Jordans cared, but they had probably already put me aside as out of their lives. The Texan liked me about as much as he liked anybody, but I don't think he liked anybody too much. Mr. Barron liked me to guard his daughter's body, but there were plenty of other people who could do just as good a job. And I thought for a while that Miss Amy liked me, but she and that other giggler were more than my stomach could take.

Conchita liked me, that was for sure. But then again, according to what all the rancheros said, there wasn't hardly anybody that Conchita didn't like.

So I rode along with my hands tied behind my back and the big fellow making all kinds of remarks about how it took a man like him to tame a punk kid like me and giving me a clout on the head every once in a while to emphasize a special point. Inside myself I was feeling real tranquil, as my pa usually used to say after his fourth drink, real tranquil.

It was a long ride to the Muller ranch but my head was still ringing when we got there. We came up over a rise and there was the ranch sitting in a hollow just like the Barron spread. It looked almost as big as the Barron place with barns and dobe huts scattered around the big house like they'd been dropped there by a big wind. There were Mexicans and chickens and horses tied around just like at the Barron place. But there wasn't any grass or flowers or neatness to anything. No woman had a say in how that place was kept up.

We rode down toward the big house and stopped in a little grove of trees about a hundred yards in front of it. They were the only trees in that whole area and they stood out there like a naked woman. There was one big tree and three smaller ones grouped together and they weren't such treesy-looking trees in the first place, what with their leaves browned up like they was dying and dust over everything.

We rode up to the biggest tree, where there was a pile of rags on the ground with a chain hanging from the biggest limb of the tree right down into the rags. And just as I discovered that there was some kind of human being in those rags, the big fellow rode over beside me and knocked me off my horse. I should have known better than to have taken my eyes off him, what with the way he'd been banging me, but it's a strange thing to suddenly discover that a pile of rags has a body inside them. I came crashing off the horse onto my left shoulder and if I hadn't done a little gun roll when I hit I swear I would have broken something. As it was, what with my hands tied and my head ringing from the whacks, I hit a lot harder than I would have liked. Hard enough to get jolted right through the teeth and then some.

I landed right next to that thing in the rags and my head was lying right flat in the dust by his ass. I lay there a bit until the dust settled and then I raised up enough to look him over. There was a mess, sure enough. This skinny little Mexican had been whipped so hard that about all that was left of his shirt was his collar, and the red, raw, bloody stripes down his back looked like cut-up cow meat. The blood had dried black in a lot of the places, and the flies were sitting there on top of the blood getting their nourishment.

There was a chain padlocked around one of the little man's legs and it ran up over the big limb and came down again to where it was padlocked over his other leg. There was enough chain so that he could have moved around quite a bit and you could see by the puddles of dried blood that he had. Somebody had chained this little man up and then whipped him around that tree until he couldn't move no more. My sweat turned cold on me and I shivered in the heat of that baked dust. I had fear inside me.

The three men who had brought me in were dancing their horses around me for fun, and the horses were as scared as I was. They tried to keep from stepping on me, but every time they shied off they got a spur in the flank and in their confusion I knew they were going to make a mistake and I was going to be trampled. A bunch of Mexes had drifted over to watch, and they stood in a big circle around the trees. They weren't laughing or hollering like the three *hombres* on the horses. It was like it was their duty to watch somebody trampled and scared half to death.

It wouldn't have done any good to have scurried around to get out of the way of those three crazy men so I just lay there and tried to close my mind off the way my pa said those old men in India can do. I did better than expected because I suddenly noticed that those horses weren't dancing around me anymore and I didn't know exactly when they had stopped. I was so caked with dust that it was hard for me to make out much so I moved my head slowly around the circle. There were three sets of horses' legs and two pairs of men's legs.

The men's legs were mighty interesting. They were wearing boots that came up to their knees, and the boots were so shiny that the sun glared off them something fierce. They were so bright and shiny that the dust didn't dare settle on them, and I knew these were boss men standing there, men who don't get dusty in the sun or wet in the rain or hot in the heat or cold in the cold.

"Stand him up," said the pair of legs on the left, and the big fellow slid off his horse and pulled me up with one jerk. I fell right down again.

"Stand him up," said the voice again, and I ain't never heard anybody repeat something that sounded so exactly like what he had said before. It was like I was hearing the same thing twice in once. The big fellow gave me a clout in the head and pulled me up again. I sure took a dislike to that big man, and I could feel my fingers tingle where I wanted a gun in them and the chance to pull a trigger again and again and again.

I looked over at the boots and there were the Mullers standing in them. It couldn't have been nobody else. You could be from the moon and know that these were the Muller brothers, the ones who made Mr. Barron get so red in the face when somebody just mentioned their name.

They sure were a strange-looking pair. They were men of good size, each one standing a bit over six feet. And they had heft to them, filling out every nook and cranny of their clothes. They were wearing cavalry-style pants, stuff that looked like soft doeskin and that flared out over the boots before tucking in again at the waist. Their shirts looked silk, shiny, shiny silk like Mrs. Jordan's best dress, and they had white silk neckerchiefs around their throats. Both of them was sporting beards, trim-cut things that tapered down to a point, and the older one had flecks of gray in his. Both of them had half a pair of spectacles screwed into their right eyes, with black silk ribbons running from the glasses to a button on their shirts. And on their heads they had the dangedest hats I ever saw in my whole life. They were white, pure white, and they were shaped like hummocks, with a big round button on the top and dividing lines like pieces of pie all around. They must have been made special for hot places because neither man had a drop of sweat on his face and their eyes were shaded like cool twilight.

Both men had quirts hanging from their wrists and the older one raised his and pointed it at me.

"Bring him closer," he said. He spoke English as good as anybody I ever heard, but it was a peculiar kind of English that had a whine to it, like the zing of a bullet across a canyon.

The big fellow gave me a shove that almost drove me into the baron, and he lifted his stick to stop me short. He poked the stick into my chest just hard enough to stand me up straight and stood looking at me long and careful. Nobody made a sound or even shuffled his feet while this was going on. The Mexicans were still in their circle like they were going to take root, and the three beauties who had brought me in weren't jangling their spurs either.

"So you are the terrible one, eh?" said the baron, talking like to himself but talking loud enough to hear quite a ways. "You are the one who is killing my men and frightening the peasants in the night. You are just a boy, a very young boy. How old are you, boy?"

I was so busy listening to him talk to himself that I didn't realize he was asking me a question until I noticed him looking at me like he was waiting for an answer. Then I had to go back over in my mind what I'd heard him say in the first place till I came to the part where he had asked me the question.

"Old enough," I told him.

The quirt flicked across my face before the word "enough" was hardly out of my mouth. It wasn't a hard flick and it didn't draw any blood, but it was hard enough to tell me that it could be harder and that it would be harder.

"When I ask you a direct question," the baron said, "I want a direct answer each time. Otherwise you will be punished." And then he whacked me one across the face hard enough to draw blood and the tears came to my eyes as fast as the blood and I could feel blood and tears working their way down the dust on my face. I wasn't crying, mind you, it was just that the sharpness of the cut brought that water out of my eyes the same way the blood was pulled out of the skin. I could tell from his eyes that I hadn't even really annoyed him, just disobeyed a simple order. That pile of rags behind me had annoyed him one way or another, and it didn't pay, it didn't pay at all.

"Send the people back to their work," said the baron, and one of the Mexicans standing behind him said, *"Vamos, muchachos,"* and that circle melted into nobody quick as the flick of the whip. "You three get something to eat and then go back out on the mission," said the baron.

"We need some rest," said the big one. "We were out three days to get him and the others ought to do something on their own."

"Everyone stays out until the mission is completed," said the baron, "and that means everyone."

But the big one wasn't satisfied. He had to get one more lick in. "You sure you can handle him alone?" he said, meaning me. "He scares the milk right out of the cows, you know," and he gave me a clout on the top of the head that smashed my hat right down on me and drove me to my knees. Things were moving funny in front of my eyes, with everything blurred and the blood dripping off my face into the sand with a sound like my pounding heart. Even though everything seemed to be moving slow as molasses I could hear my heart pounding fast like a horse galloping past in the night. I sure must have been a sorry sight.

"You are a man who invites death continually, Petersen," said the baron, "and one of these days I will accommodate you." His eyes never changed while he was saying that, and Petersen turned around on his heel and walked off toward the big house. His two friends followed. The only ones left behind were me, the baron, his brother, the Mexican who had told the other Mexicans to go back to work and that bag of bones lying in chains behind me. I got up on my feet again and waited for what was coming. Dying wasn't going to be as easy as I figured. I wasn't really scared, but there was something cold poking at my guts, and I just hoped I wouldn't make too much of a mess of it before they finished me off.

"I have forty-three white men working for me," said the baron, "all of whom wear guns on their hips and carry rifles on their horses. They like to shoot at animals and snakes and cans on top of rocks. But when it comes to putting their sights on the body of a man and pulling the trigger and making him dead, there are maybe seven out of the forty-three who have that special something inside them that makes them pull the trigger. That one there"—and he pointed his stick at the back of the big man—"enjoys doing it. Therefore, I pay him well and allow him little liberties.

"You are obviously another," he said, "who enjoys killing people in a simple and uncomplicated manner. I need men like you to fulfill my plan for this area. But right now you are more important as a pigeon than a hawk, and so it would be fruitless to discuss what might have been."

"Carlos," he said, "remove that piece of carrion."

The baron stepped back to where his brother was standing, and the Mexican moved past me to the pile of rags. I turned to watch him take a key of of his pocket and unlock the padlocks that were holding the chains to the legs of that poor little man.

He reached under his arms and hauled him to his feet. And he stood there, that little pile of bones and blood and rags stood there all by himself. I had figured myself as dead and gone as that thing lying on the ground, and here he was standing straight up into the sky with his eyes half open and his look directed straight at the baron. I'll swear he wasn't afraid, that little man, just interested. He was looking straight at the baron because he was interested in what was going to happen to him.

"I have been here two years," the baron said, and this fellow Carlos translated into Mexican, like it was something he did without being told when to do it. "And in that two years," said the baron, "it has been necessary to have you whipped three times. You never seem to learn that this is now my land, that your people have no rights to it no matter how many documents you have that supposedly came from the king of Spain. I have kept you alive as a lesson to the rest. Death can be too easy. But you are not a cat, you are a man, and three times is your limit. The next time there is a breath of dissension, no matter from what source, the whipping will not stop until you are cut in two. You are dismissed."

The little man turned and walked towards where the Mexicans were working around the big house. They had stopped everything when the little man had been lifted to his feet and had watched the proceedings from a distance, like scarecrows in a field.

He walked slow but firm towards them and stopped just as he came up to the first bunch. He looked them over careful, moving his head slowly from left to right and then back to the left again. Nobody moved toward him but they opened up a path for him to enter and then they gradually formed a line between us and him so that he disappeared behind a wall of people, and when they opened up again he was gone. They hadn't done anything to make their big boss mad, but they hadn't turned away from the little man either. These Mexicans must have been from the same people as worked on the Barron ranch, but it was like day and night to see how they acted. The Barron spread was always full of animals screeching and women trying to match them and men laughing and lots of action and color and good feeling. These people were like a candle flame, burning, burning, but quietly, quietly.

"Put our goat in the blind," the baron said to Carlos, and the Mexican looked at him. "The chains, the chains," said the baron, and he pushed me toward the Mexican with his stick. He had right fine black leather gloves on his hands, but you could tell he never touched people with anything closer than that stick.

The Mexican snapped the chains around both my ankles, tried them out and stepped back. "Cut him loose," said the baron, and the Mexican's knife made a quick slice between my hands.

"Come," said the baron, "we still have work to do." He stepped off without looking back and his brother followed right after. He hadn't said one word the whole time I had been there, just stood like a statue with that glass screwed into his eye. The Mexican followed along behind the two brothers and I was left alone.

I tested the padlocks holding the chains to my legs and they were working just fine. I looked up at the limb the chain was looped over and that worked just fine, too. It was a big old limb about the size of a man's thigh and it went straight out about four feet before soaring straight up into the sky. All the branches under it had been sawed off, and the trunk of the tree was too big around and too smooth to be climbed. You were pinned by that tree as fierce as if you were in the strongest jail in the world, and I could tell by the way the bark was worn off the top of that limb that it had held more than me and the little Mexican in its time.

I moved around to the shade of the tree trunk and pondered my predicament. The baron wasn't keeping me alive because he liked the color of my eyes. He'd of squashed me like a bug if I wasn't going to be of some use to him. It was for damn sure something to do with Mr. Barron, and it was for damn sure going to happen pretty soon, so there wasn't no use trying to figure it out beforehand. My part in it had to do with hanging from a tree in chains and that was all I could do about it.

I saw men with rifles standing around the corners of all the buildings on the ranch, looking every which way. They didn't want to be taken by surprise on any account. And I saw the three who had brought me in ride off in the direction from which they had brought me. The big one turned around in his saddle and looked at me from the distance. I know he was thinking how nice it would be to come back and give me a few clouts before he left. But he'd pushed the baron as far as he was going to that day, and I'm sure he figured he was going to get another chance to clout me anyway. They disappeared over the hill.

The Mexicans were working off by the house but not one of them ever looked over at me. I was about as alone as a man could be. And I was as thirsty as a man could be. But there was as much chance of getting water as there was conversation. So I made myself as comfortable as I could in the soft dirt and hunkered back against the trunk of that big tree. I reached down to adjust my guns so I could set back easy and it came as a surprise to find they were gone. I was so used to being with them that I could hardly believe I was without them. That man Petersen had them. He had banged me on the head and taken them away. And I didn't know what to do without them. I was nothing without those guns. When those three men had jumped me and Miss Amy up on the mesa, I'd almost got us killed because my thumbs hadn't moved fast enough to stop that third one from getting in his shot. If he hadn't been off those three inches, we'd have been done sure enough. And when that Petersen had banged me on the head, I was too slow getting the iron out to do anything about him. I'd let the guns down. And now they were working for him. All that was left was plain old me. Whatever was going to happen would have to happen without me doing anything about it. And I pressed down a little more against that great big tree.

★ 24 ★

The Mexicans all disappeared just as the sun was fooling around with the tops of the hills. Even though I couldn't smell no cooking in the air, my belly told me where everyone had gone, and I suddenly turned as hungry as I was thirsty. Men with rifles came out and relieved the ones that had been skulking around the buildings all afternoon. There was about twelve of them scattered over the place and what with the twelve that came out to spell them and the forty the baron had mentioned on the road, I figured this spread was almost as big as Mr. Barron's.

There was a little stone house set between my tree and the hill I'd first been brought over, and the two men who came from the big house towards that place looked me over real careful when they went by. They didn't say anything or do more than look, but they looked real careful. The two men coming back did the same thing, only this time one of them started to say something but shut his mouth when the other one squeezed his arm. Somebody had told them they could look but not touch, and I figured I was four clouts to the head to the good. None of them was specially mean-looking, but none of them looked too kindly neither.

Just as the sun was sinking its edge into the hill, an old, old Mexican man came trudging out from the house toward me with a plate and a cup in his hand. I didn't hardly believe it even when he shoved the whole business at me. The plate was heaped way high with beans and the cup was steaming coffee at me. I put the plate on the ground and took a big swallow of the coffee. Which almost finished me off right there because that was the hottest coffee I ever encountered in my whole life. It burned going down and it burned when it got there and it stayed burning for what seemed a night and a day. My eyes were so full of tears I couldn't see which way and by the time I could see where I was and take a breath without having it turn to steam, the little old man was practically back to the house. My mouth felt all funny, but I was so hungry I pulled that big spoon out of the tin and started to shove beans down my throat. I couldn't taste nothing but it felt good to have solid matter going through. And I blew as hard as I could on the coffee and swallowed that right down too. They weren't planning to starve me to death because that plate had more than a good helping on it, and I cleaned it up so that the tin shone and I drank the coffee down to the last drop.

It was getting real dusky around then, and out from the house stepped the baron's brother and the fellow they called Carlos. They walked right up to me and the brother bent over and tested the chains on my legs. He was right thorough about the whole business, testing the padlocks and pulling the links. He never said a word the whole time and neither did the Mexican. They made a circle of all the outbuildings and then walked into the main house just as dark dropped over the place.

There wasn't a light stirring anywhere in any of the buildings or the main house. Every once in a while a match would flare up and you could see someone take a long drag on a cigarette, but there wasn't nobody moving about. The ranch was locked in tight.

I stood up to stretch my bones and kicked over the coffee cup onto the tin plate. It sounded like one of God's thunderclaps in all that stillness and I froze tight in my tracks. I don't know what I expected but I sure expected more than I got. Because nothing moved out there. You couldn't hear nothing or see nothing. I walked around in the chains as far as the length would allow me. You could move quite a bit in all directions, but when you came to the end, that was it. One more step and you fell over. I walked as far as I could to the other side of the trunk and pissed in the sand. I wondered how many people had walked to the end of these chains and pissed their hope away at this spot. The way that limb was worn there sure had been a lot of customers in the past few years.

I grabbed up the ends of the chains and tried swinging with all my weight, but I didn't even make that limb sag. I tried shinnying up the trunk, but you couldn't get a hold with your hands or your feet, and I didn't have no spurs to dig in with.

A chill had come into the air when the sun had been down awhile, and all that sweat laying on my body was cold and greasy. I knew I was going to live through the night and that made it out to be a long night. I leaned my back against the trunk and slid down on my butt. I reached down and dug out a bit of dirt to make a round spot for my rear and leaned back against the tree. I slid down lower again until my back was on the ground and jammed my hat down to make a pillow. It was going to be too cold to sleep but I figured I might as well be comfortable as I could. And I dozed right off and slept solid till sunup.

First light pulled my eyes wide open. I hadn't moved an inch in the night so I'd had as much rest as if I'd been back in my bed at the ranch. Except that I felt terrible. My head and bones ached and big pieces of skin were hanging loose in my mouth. Things had been better for me in the past.

My bladder was filled to bursting and I got up and went over to my outdoors outhouse of the night before. I had just started going real solid when I heard a noise behind me and turned my head to find a good looking young Mexican gal standing there with a plate of beans and a cup of coffee. You know, no matter how long I live among these people I can't get used to the idea of heeding nature's call in front of a woman. A Mexican man and a woman will be talking and if one of them has to go, he or she turns away a little and goes. Never stops the conversation, just keeps on talking while he's going. Now this girl didn't give a damn in hell about my water running out, but it sure did bother me. I wasn't likely to have many enjoyable events that day, and she was spoiling my relief. However, I knew if I waited till she went away, a hundred others might show up, so I just went and went and went.

When I finished and straightened myself up and clanked back to where she was standing, she said, *"Mucho gusto, hombre,"* handed me the plate and the cup, went over and picked up the plate and cup from the night before, handed me the spoon and walked off with the dirty utensils.

The coffee was set down to cool while I worked on the beans, and strange as it may sound, it was kind of pleasant to be sitting there while the day grew up around me. A few

Mexicans straggled out as I was polishing off the plate, but they never even looked at me as they fed the chickens and swept around and saddled horses and suchlike.

The day guards came out of the bunkhouse to bang their tins off and then headed to the buildings to relieve the night crew. The same pair from the day before went past me on the way out, and then the other two came past me on the way in. They all looked me over real careful again, but this time nobody tried to say anything. I could tell they were talking about me coming and going, but whatever it was they kept to themselves.

The coffee was plenty cool by the time I got to it and I drank it down real slow and easy because I figured there weren't any treats like water around that place during the day. I polished up the utensils in the dirt and stacked them nicely by the tree. Mrs. Jordan would have been proud of me.

When the sun had reached near ten o'clock, the baron and his brother stepped out of the big house with that Mexican fellow after them. They disappeared around behind one of the buildings and I saw them come out the other side and go around another building and after a little while they walked out to where I was. The baron tipped his stick at me a little like he was saying good morning. I didn't say nothing. His brother walked over and tested the ankle locks again, pulling each one hard enough to force a grunt out of him. I just stood there saying nothing because you couldn't tell what might draw you a clout on the head or a whip in the face around that ranch.

The baron turned and walked toward the little house that was between me and the knoll. The two guards came outside to meet him and he spent some time with them, pointing at the knoll and sweeping his whip around in a wide circle and pointing back at the main house and then pointing off to the left again. Nobody else did any talking, not the guards or the brother or the Mexican. It was the baron gave all the orders around there and you damn well better mind them.

At high noon the little old Mexican came shuffling out to me with a big plate of beans and a cup of coffee. He put down the plate and cup, handed over the spoon from the other outfit and carried them back with him. I sure would have liked to chaw on a chunk of beef, but those beans were plenty tasty, tastier even than the Barron cook could make, and I wasn't complaining. It was sure a surprise when I dug into them to find that there were enchiladas buried under the beans and underneath these were three tortillas piled one on another. The taste was as good as the surprise and I cleaned it all out till the tin sparkled. When I went to pick up the coffee, I found it was water instead of coffee and that made a nice change too.

It was getting spooky being chained to that tree in the bright day with Mexicans working away at their jobs and the guards holed up in the buildings and nobody paying much attention to me. I stood up and walked around and around that tree, back and forth as far as I could go each way, and it reached a point where I just wanted to grab hold of those chains and pull that tree right out of the ground and pick it up and smash everything down, the buildings, the people, the animals, everything. I wanted out.

But the tree didn't pull out that easy, and I was held tight. Was he going to whip me to death or shoot me or just keep me on show till I was an old man, till I died from eating too many beans? I could feel them working in my stomach and the pressure was uncomfortable. I'd sweat when I sat in the sun and get a chill when I moved into the shade. I was too tired to stand and too uneasy to sit. I tell you, I'd seen better times.

And then they came riding over the hill, the three men and the two girls. At first, I just saw the bunch of them coming over the brow, with maybe me the first one to spot them. You couldn't tell much with the sun in your eyes, and it wasn't till they passed the little house that I could make out that there were three men and one girl riding straight up and one girl slung over a saddle. The two guards came out of the house and followed the horses right up to where I was.

They stopped square in front of where I was standing. The girl sitting up on the horse, the big black, was Miss Amy, and the other, the one slung over the saddle, was her friend the giggler, that Betty Whitman. She looked awful still and her hair was all undone, hanging down and dragging in the dust.

Miss Amy looked all right, but scared, plenty scared. She was looking at me like she wasn't seeing me and her face was white under her sun-darkened skin and her cheeks were bright red. None of those colors seemed to go right together and it made her look strange, mighty strange.

I'd been so busy looking at the women that I hadn't noticed the men at all till the big one got off his horse and walked towards me. He loomed over me all of a sudden and I felt him before I saw him, and it was like a big shadow had come up over me and was going to crush me right down into the ground. He stopped about six paces in front of me and even then his shadow covered me over. That little tickling I'd been feeling in my belly ever since they had chained me up turned to cold stone and I threw up all those beans and enchiladas and tortillas right on the ground. They kept coming up and coming up and coming up and my eyes were so full of tears that I couldn't see, and I was afraid to move lest I get the stuff over him. I didn't want to do that.

It finally stopped. And I untied my kerchief and wiped my eyes and my mouth and looked ahead. They were all still standing there just like they had before, all of them. Miss Amy's face was the same as when I had first seen her and she hadn't moved. She hadn't moved a muscle.

I looked at him again. He was the biggest man I had ever seen, maybe not taller than Mr. Barron, but bigger all round, with hands that could crush a steer's skull. He was dressed all in black with even a black kerchief. There was about an inch of stubble on his face and he had thick black hair on the back of his hands. He was about as fearsome a man as was ever put on God's earth, and nobody had to tell me that the man who handled the whippings for the baron had come home.

"Go get the baron," he said, and his voice was high-pitched, almost like a girl's. It was strange God should put a squeaky voice in a man like that.

One of the guards from the little house took off for the ranch at a run.

Nobody said nothing while we were waiting for the baron, and nobody moved around much. The two other men with the big one just sat their horses and watched Miss Amy and watched me. They looked tired and dirty, like they'd been making cold camp for a few days, but they were paying attention to their job, they weren't slacking up any. I didn't look at Miss Amy again, just kept my eyes on the man as he looked me up and down real careful.

He walked around to get closer to me and I turned to keep facing him. He came up real close and I could feel his bigness around me, squeezing like he was pressing me between his hands, but he never even touched me. He was wearing one gun, slung real low and so tight to his thigh that it bit in a way, which showed he had some extra meat on him. I couldn't help wondering how much he weighed, and I wouldn't have bet against three hundred pounds give or take a few. His horse wasn't all that big but he didn't look all that happy either.

We might have been standing there till doomsday if the baron hadn't come stepping right out of the main house and over to us. He was followed by his brother and the Mexican, and the guard walked careful behind them. Everybody made damn sure nobody stepped on anybody's feet around there.

"My instructions were that these people were not to be abused," he said, "that they were to be kept intact until the completion of the mission."

"Nobody touched nobody," said the big man.

"And what about that one?" said the baron, pointing his whip at that Betty Whitman, who was hanging there dead.

"She had an accident," said the man. "Fell down and hurt her head when she tried to get away."

"That's a lie," screamed Miss Amy, with tears busting out of her eyes and her voice rising to a pitch that scared the birds in the trees.

She jumped off her horse and ran over to her friend. Nobody did nothing to stop her. She pointed at the big man.

"He said that since she wasn't part of the original deal, it wouldn't make any difference if he used her for a minute," Miss Amy yelled, "and he started to drag her off in the bushes and she hit him in the nose and he clouted her in the neck and killed her."

Miss Amy reached down with her two hands and pulled Betty Whitman's head up and and there on the side of her neck was a big purple mark bigger than a man's fist. Maybe it was just a fluke that anybody hit there would fall down dead, but that purple mark looked death enough, death enough for anybody.

"Dealing with you, Baum," said the baron, "is a complicated procedure. You are paid to do simple things simply, which is all that could be expected of you. And yet, each time you add a factor that complicates the situation. I am not a man of infinite patience, Baum, and one day you will find that your bother has exceeded your worth."

The big man just looked at him while the baron was telling him all this. Nothing changed on his face, and I couldn't tell whether he was going to reach out and belt the baron on the side of his throat and make him dead or say he was sorry or say nothing. He said nothing.

The baron turned and walked away for a few steps with his head bent down and his forehead puckered. He was really thinking, that boy. He turned and came back.

"The illusion must be maintained," he said. "Above all, the illusion must be maintained."

He turned to his Mexican and said, "Get the leg chains for the live one and some thin rope for the dead one." The Mexican took off fast. The baron went over to his brother and started talking to him in their own language. He was explaining something to him and every once in a while the brother would grunt and say "Yah" and nod his head. The baron would point his stick out at the knoll and then move it in a circle and the brother would grunt. It was just like when the baron was telling those men out at the little house towards the knoll.

The Mexican came running back with some chains clanking over his shoulder and a length of thin rope hanging from his arm. The baron motioned for him to put the chains on Miss Amy. The Mexican put an ankle lock around Miss Amy's left ankle and then walked the length of the chain around the tree trunk, not over the limb like for me, and then clinked the other lock over her right ankle. The only ways to get her out of there was to split her in half or cut down the tree.

"Put the body against the other side of the tree," said the baron. He spoke out to everybody who was listening, but nobody made a move toward that Betty Whitman. I wouldn't have wanted to touch her.

The big man looked at everybody with a little bit of a grin on his face. It wasn't a sneer or a smile or anything like that, it was a happy kind of grin like Mrs. Jordan used to have when she'd bring the pie to the table and plop it down for us to look at.

He walked over to the horse and pulled the knot that was holding the body tight. Three pulls and the rope dropped down and the body stayed there. He gave the legs a little shove and that Betty Whitman slid off the horse on her head into the dirt and her body folded at the neck and she went plop on her back into the dust. There was just this little plop as she folded into the ground, and I looked over at Miss Amy who was standing right there by the body, and her face was tight again and not moving a muscle. I wasn't doing too well at protecting her body, but it didn't bother me because we were going to be dead soon and I wouldn't have to give no explanation to her daddy. I owed him to see to it that Miss Amy didn't die messy and I vowed to do something about that if I could, but messy or not, we were dead, just like we were already laying in the holes with Pa or Jocko.

The big man reached down and flipped Betty Whitman over. He slid one hand under her crotch and the other under her chest and lifted her up like she was a piece of mesquite. No strain on his face, no pulling of the muscles. He had his hand open flat on her chest and he kept moving it to rub her soft things as he carried her over to the tree. He made sure that everybody knew what he was doing, especially Miss Amy, and he turned to give her a bigger grin as he leaned Betty Whitman in a sitting position against the trunk of the tree.

"That's good, that's good," said the baron, "but more around toward the casa so they can only see her sideways from the woods."

Betty Whitman was moved about another four inches around the trunk by the big man and then he stepped away from her. Her head plunked forward onto her lap.

"Tie her in a sitting position to the trunk," the baron said to the Mexican. "I want her to look natural."

The Mexican moved over to the tree and uncoiled his rope. He cut it into short lengths with his knife and then tied her to the trunk around the chest and the belly. Her head flopped forward, so he tied a piece around her throat and he made it tight so her head stood straight up. The rope was cutting into her throat real bad, but we cared more about that than she did.

"Fix her hair," said the baron, and the Mexican cut a short piece of rope and gathered it around her hair in the back. When he pulled it tight and tied it, it looked real neat. From close up she looked pretty bad, what with the rope cutting into her neck and the purple bruise and the dirt all over her and flies buzzing around her head, but I'll bet she looked fine from a distance, which is what that man had in mind.

The baron's brother walked over and tested the ropes holding Betty Whitman. He turned her head just a bit to the right and stepped back to look at her just as that European man did who came to town and painted some pictures and gave one to Mr. Jordan in trade for some supplies. It was a picture of the Trail End saloon with a dog sitting in front of the door and Mrs. Jordan wouldn't let Mr. Jordan hang it up anywhere and I'll bet it's still in the back storeroom. Anyways, that's how the brother looked at Betty Whitman.

Then the brother walked over and tested the ankle locks on Miss Amy and then he came over and tested mine. He looked up at the baron and nodded.

"Fine," said the baron. "Now maybe we can start making preparations. I want messengers sent out to every man we have out looking for the girl and I want everybody back immediately. It will take them at least a day to discover that she is not lost somewhere and maybe another day to figure out that she is here. Then they will come riding here in true Texas fashion and we will rid ourselves of the pestilence forever. However, we must leave nothing to chance, so there is much work to do."

He turned to head back to the ranch house and then all of a sudden stopped dead. He looked over at the two men who had come in from the little dobe building.

"What are you two doing here?" he asked.

They looked down at their feet and didn't say anything.

"Look at me when I talk to you," said the baron.

They looked up from their feet and pointed their eyes at him like they were guns.

"Whenever I ask a question," said the baron, "I expect an immediate answer. I am going to ask you once more. What are you two doing here?"

"Well," said the one who had almost talked to me the day before, "we saw Baum here bring in the girl and just followed along."

"You were supposed to stay at your post until relieved," said the baron. "Your post is now exposed to the enemy, who could be moving in on us at this very moment."

Everybody but the big man, Baum, turned to look at the little dobe house. I turned right along with the rest of them, and I wouldn't have been surprised to see Roy and a swaggle of cow chasers coming at us with guns all blazing. There wasn't anybody, of course, just like you would know if you thought about it for a minute. No one at the Barron spread probably even knew the girls were missing yet. You couldn't always tell what Miss Amy might be up to, and she often was up to quite a lot.

"Hell, baron," said the one who hadn't said anything.

The baron held up his whip, which meant shut up right now and that man shut up right then.

"The penalty for deserting one's post in time of war, and believe me, my man," said the baron, "to me this is a time of war, is death. You people know by now that I do not play games, that I mean what I say, and that I expect each man to do his duty as I order it. I should turn you over to Mr. Baum and thus end the matter once and for all."

Neither of those men was a young kid, and you could tell by looking at them that their rifles felt easier in their hands than a hole digger or a branding iron. They were holding on to their rifles so tight that you could see the white spots on their fingernails. All they had to do was to turn those rifles out and there wasn't a man in the place would have lived more than a few seconds. Baum was looking at them kind of expectant, like he was hoping they'd make a move. But you could see from their faces that they weren't thinking of any move, they were just thinking about dying and how they weren't going to like it.

"However," said the baron, "this has been a very exciting day, we have attained our major objective, and I am in a charitable mood."

I could see those hands loosen up on those rifles and the two of them looked just about ready to turn and run back to that little house as fast as their long legs would go.

"Come here," said the baron.

The two men looked surprised at the baron and then surprised at each other. But they moved right up to him as soon as it sank in that he'd said come here.

"No misdeed must go completely unpunished," said the baron, and he rapped the man on the left across the face with his whip and then he raked him back on the other side. He didn't rare back and swing all his might with that thing, but you don't have to get up much working space and he slashed that face enough so that blood poured out of both sides. That man was caught by surprise as much as I had been, but he stood there holding on to that rifle for all he was worth.

We all turned to look at the fellow that was standing next to him because we all knew he was next. He knew it worse than we did but he didn't do no more about it than we did. The baron turned to look at him a good few seconds after we did. Then he looked him over real careful-like, studying him like you would a fly with one wing already pulled off. The baron raised up his whip and held it there a second. Then he raked him across one side of his face and then across the other. The blood poured out just as fast as it had on the other one, and I saw that fellow's knees wobble before he caught onto himself and held tight.

"To your posts," said the baron, and those people lit out of there like there was Indians after them. The baron didn't even watch them go.

He turned to the Mexican and said, "I ordered messengers sent after the men in the field. It is most important and yet you stand here to watch simple punishment inflicted. Why has my order not been carried out?"

"You have not yet dismissed me, senor," said the Mexican.

The baron smiled. "Ah, Carlos," he said, "you are worth a thousand of these pigs. You are dismissed."

The Mexican turned and went into the big house, going fast enough but not going that fast. He was a lot of man, that old man.

The baron turned to the big man.

"Baum," he said, "send your men for food and rest, and come into the casa for refreshment. You must be thirsty after your long vigil and journey."

Baum looked at his two men and they took off for one of the barns. He looked at me and then at Miss Amy and then at that Betty Whitman tied down at that tree. He pointed at Miss Amy.

"I want that one when you are through with her," he said.

"And you shall have her," said the baron. "*When* I am through with her."

"As long as we understand each other," said Baum, "as long as we understand each other."

He walked over and picked up the reins of his horse. The baron and his brother started toward the ranch house and Baum followed after. None of them looked back at us.

Miss Amy and I were there all alone under that tree, except for that Betty Whitman and she didn't count anymore. The Mexicans had disappeared again and you couldn't see no humans except when one of the guards came out around a corner once in a while to check on the outside of his building. It was like we were chained to a tree in the middle of nowhere, like maybe in the Garden of Eden or some faraway place like that.

Miss Amy was just standing there. She hadn't even looked when those two men had taken off her big black with them. I walked over towards her with my chains clanking and stopped right up close to her. She was dirty and sweaty and she was crying. You couldn't hear any sound, but you could see the tracks of wet working down her face.

"Oh, Jory," she said, "what is going to happen to us?"

"Nothing we can do anything about," I told her.

And as I said it I was looking her over real careful to try and figure out how I was going to kill her with the least amount of pain possible.

★ 26 ★

Miss Amy didn't want to sit anywhere near that Betty Whitman so we moved as far over as our chains would allow and humped down in the sand right in the sun. There was enough breeze to keep the flies off, but it was still hot enough to pull the sweat out of our skin and as I looked at Miss Amy I couldn't help thinking how I should have gone swimming with her when she asked me.

Miss Amy was sitting there telling me how she and Betty Whitman had gone riding and were up in the foothills when the big man, Baum . . . and I was hardly listening to her as she went on about what happened. I could hear her and knew what she was saying but it was like from a far distance, and I was sitting there thinking about when Pa and I ran the livery stable and eating Sunday dinner at the Jordans' and stuff I'd read in Pa's law books and how close the stars looked sometimes when you were sleeping out on the trail and crazy things like that.

"Do you think they'll find us?" Miss Amy asked.

"Oh, yes," I told her. "They'll find us all right."

"He's planning on them to find us, isn't he?" Miss Amy said.

"He's planning on them to come riding right in here for us and he's planning to cut them into little pieces," I said. "And he's got a damn good chance of having his plans work out."

"That's terrible," said Miss Amy.

"It's terrible that your daddy didn't plan on it first," I said.

"My daddy would never do a thing like this," she said.

Three men came riding down the knoll and as they rode by the little dobe house, the two guards came out and had a word with them. One of the guards pointed at us with his rifle and then they all talked some more. The three men wheeled their horses and came riding by us, looking us over real careful but not saying a word to us or each other. They lookcd like they'd been making cold camp a few days, with the tight look on their faces that comes from cold rations and squatting without a fire. They rode on by and went past the big house to the bunkhouse. One of them led off the horses while the other two came back and went into the big house.

Eleven more men came in before the sun touched the horizon and they all stopped for a few words at the little dobe house and they all rode by us without saying a word. It got so that Miss Amy and I didn't do much talking, just sat there staring at the knoll waiting for the next pair or three to come riding over.

My stomach started grumbling and I looked up at the sun to see it was way past suppertime. Maybe they figured they didn't have to feed us no more now that the plan was working, but I figured the baron wrong on that. He was going to keep us in as good shape as possible.

The little old Mexican came shuffling out of thc long dobe house with two plates and two cups clutched in his hands. I don't know how he managed to keep all that beans and coffee going in only two hands without spilling any, but that's just what he did. One plate was piled high as a mountain and the other had just a fair amount of beans in it. He stuck the big one in front of me and I motioned for him to give it to Miss Amy, figuring that was the polite thing to do. He stuck the big plate in front of me again. I motioned for him to pass it on to her, and he said, "No, senor, no," in such a strange voice that I looked up quick and darned if it wasn't the Mex that had been almost beaten to death under this tree. I was so surprised that I just took the plate he handed me and the cup of coffee.

Miss Amy hadn't really noticed any of this. She had started staring over to where Betty Whitman was tied to the tree and she looked as dead as the dead girl. Miss Amy had been too young to know what was going on when her mama had died, and her daddy had seen to it that nobody died around her since. Her mind had been protected as well as her body, and she didn't know what to do about what was going on. I hadn't been much help. Her friend was dead and she was alive. So she looked at her friend.

The Mexican stuck the pan of beans in her hand and put the coffee down beside her. He went over to the tree and picked up the empty plate and cup and brought my spoon over to me. Then he went back to the long dobe house.

"Miss Amy," I told her, "you better eat something."

She started eating the beans without taking her eyes off that Betty Whitman.

I was hungry so I dug right in, spooning off the top where they had cooled a little and saving the enchiladas underneath for dessert. It was beans all the way down and I was feeling disappointed when all of a sudden my spoon went clunk against something that wasn't tin. I pushed the beans aside and there lying on the bottom of the pan was a knife that just fit into the bottom of the tin. It was a very narrow blade with a tip like a needle and a fairly long crossbar between the blade and the handle.

I was so busy looking at the knife that the three horsemen were almost on us before I noticed them. Miss Amy had stopped eating her beans and was just staring away at Betty Whitman, holding her plate in one hand and her spoon in the other and her coffee on the ground untouched.

The three men had come much closer to us than any of the others had and one of them was edging up close to where Miss Amy sat.

"Come on, Charlie," one of the other riders said. "You want to get your face whipped up?"

"Nobody whips up my face," said the close one, but he turned his horse right around and went on riding towards the houses. He'd been close enough to see but those two faces out there by the little dobe house were what he was seeing instead of my plate.

I took my cup of coffee and worked over towards the tree. While I was drinking the coffee I was digging a hole in the soft dirt with my heel, and then I moved my back to the ranch house and slid the knife and some beans along with it into the flat hole and shoved dirt over it with my boot. I couldn't make it too neat or tidy but I got it covered just as the baron, his brother and that Mexican walked out of the house and started towards us. I tossed down the rest of the coffee and moved away from the trunk, not too far but far enough. I spooned the rest of the beans into my mouth and started washing out the plate with dirt.

The baron walked up briskly and looked us over, including Betty Whitman. "Look at this one," he said, pointing at me. "He eats. His world is coming to an end and he eats. I don't know whether that is good or bad." He talked to his brother for a bit in their own language and the brother came over and tested our locks and then checked the ropes on Betty Whitman.

While he was doing this the big one, Baum, came out of the bunkhouse and walked over. He had a stick in his mouth that he kept whirling between this teeth.

"We've got thirty-six in," he said to the baron, "and five to go."

"If there are thirty-six in," said the baron, "I know how many are yet to come in."

Baum walked over to where Miss Amy was sitting with her beans in one hand and spoon in the other. He reached down and picked up her coffee cup and drank it all down. Then he dropped it beside her. She'd sweat a lot that day and had nothing to drink but I wasn't going to make any complaints.

"The Barron ranch must have people out looking for the girl by this time," said the baron, "and they must be beginning to wonder what happened to this one"—and he pointed at me. "Tomorrow they will comb their own territory and tomorrow night they will think of us and the morning after that they will come riding."

"Suppose they come riding tomorrow?" said Baum.

"We are on the alert," said the baron. "We are ready for any eventuality. But they will not come tomorrow. They will come the day after."

He and his bunch walked out to the little dobe house and then all the other houses and then walked back through us to get back in the big house. The baron, his brother and the Mexican walked right by us, but Baum stopped to look at

Miss Amy a bit. He was moving that stick around in his mouth and looking her over like you would a horse that you might buy and then again you might not. She didn't look back at him, just sat there staring at that girl against the tree. But I could tell she knew he was looking at her because she was sitting tighter than she had before and she was holding those beans and that spoon like they were going to be bent in half. Then he turned and walked back and went into the big house instead of the bunkhouse. There weren't any lights lit on the place at all, and just as darkness fell I heard three more horses going by us from the hill. And as we sat there quiet, two more horses went by. That army was sure growing by leaps and bounds. And I moved back to the tree to find the knife.

★ 27 ★

You know how sometimes you know something's there but you're never sure even though you're sure. One time a drunken drummer gave me a real gold piece that I hid under a loose board in the livery stable, and I bet I looked under that board twenty times a day to make sure that little coin was still there. It always was. Until I gave it to my pa one day when he was real desperate for nourishment. And do you know the next day I went and looked under that board even though I knew that gold piece wasn't there anymore. And it wasn't.

Well, as I edged quietly toward the trunk of that tree, moving slow so my chains didn't clink and get Miss Amy out of her trance, I feared that knife wasn't there anymore. I knew I'd put it there and that nobody had been near it and that it still had to be there, but I feared that it wasn't. It was.

I took it up in my hands and used sand to rub the beans off it, and I could feel it come clean and bright as the dirt grated over it. I slid the knife under my belt. The moon wasn't up yet and you could just see the white of your hand and no more. Even the moon couldn't throw any light on the predicament. We had a knife, a nice thin sharp one. But we had these chains, strong tough hard ones. And a tree, a big fat slippery one. That knife couldn't cut those chains or the tree in two. Oh, you, Jory, I told myself, you've got to think, *hombre*, think.

I was just about to stand up so I could think on my feet

when horses went by the tree at a slow walk and a man said, "Look out for the damn branches."

"Are they tied up out here?" somebody asked.

"Never mind," said the first voice, "it's none of our business. Keep moving."

They went on by. I waited till I heard the horses stop by the bunkhouse. As the door opened somewhere, you could see a faint piece of light and then it was gone. Miss Amy didn't say anything or stir around. She was out of it and it was just as well. A noisy woman could have caused problems.

But she wasn't my problem. It was that goddamn tree. She had to help me with my problem. She had to help me get out of there—now, right away.

Something strange was going on inside me. That big man had scared me, scared me about as bad as anything that ever happened to me. The only other time I'd ever been scared this bad was when we'd first landed at the Jordan livery stable and my pa had gone right off with the money Mr. Jordan had advanced and he hadn't come back and I couldn't find him all that night.

The next day I finally came across him beside an old barn on the other side of town and when I was trying to drag him out of there a bunch of kids had come hollering down on us and they stood off and yelled things at me. I couldn't quite make out the words but they sounded like "drunky's son, drunky's son," and stones came flying in, big stones, and I was trying to keep my pa from getting hit and every time I would try to cover one place a stone would come in at another and one hit him in the nose and they were hitting me all over and I was scared, real, real scared. Until finally some lady came along and yelled at them and they run off. That's all it took, one lady yelling scat and they left us alone.

I was that scared again but I knew no lady was going to come along and yell that tree down and us out of there. I'd have to do all the yelling around there, so I was thinking before I was moving and I was moving real easy.

I felt the knife in my pants again and moved around to where Miss Amy ought to have been. She was still there and I could see her shadow looming against the sky. It wouldn't be good to startle her none and bring everybody running.

"Miss Amy," I whispered, "Miss Amy." That shadow didn't budge. "Miss Amy," I said a bit louder, "it's me, Jory." Nothing.

I crept over to where she was, soft as I could. You didn't make much noise in that sandy dirt. I moved right up to her and put my face near hers. Her eyes were closed tight and she wasn't hardly breathing. I was just about to shake a little life into her when I thought I heard horses and froze right where I was with my hands tight on her arms. I listened, oh, how I listened. Nothing. Maybe the wind.

We had to get out of there. Soon! "You're hurting my arms, Jory," said Miss Amy, natural as could be. Like we was resting our horses on the mesa and she was talking about something back at the ranch. I didn't drop hold altogether, just slackened up to comfortable.

"Miss Amy," I said, "we've got to get ourselves out of here before they trap your daddy and kill us all." She was listening. You could tell she was listening.

"What's stopping us from getting out of here," I told her, "is that tree, that big old tree. We've got to outsmart that tree." And I was thinking at that tree, thinking, thinking, thinking. We weren't going to cut through it with my little knife, that was for sure. We'd have to go up over it.

"Miss Amy," I said. "I'm going to brace myself out along the ground and pull my chains tight as all get out, and I want you to climb up those chains till you get to the limb." I showed her just what I wanted her to do and then I laid down on the ground and tautened those chains till they were real stiff and just about eight inches apart on the bottom. She walked up behind me and climbed on my back and grabbed hold of the chains and started to pull herself up a little at a time, inching up, inching up. She was a good strong girl and I held the chains at a nice easy angle for her with the strain biting into my hands and my ankles and it had gone past the part where I could still hold on when all of a sudden the strain slackened and I heard her say, still in that natural voice, "I'm on the limb."

I looked up but couldn't see her up in the branches.

"You on tight?" I asked her.

"No trouble," she said, "no trouble at all. Now what do I do?"

I hadn't even thought ahead to that part. She was up on the limb and I was down on the ground. Best thing would be to get me up there with her. I'd tried pulling myself up the night before when I was swinging on the damn chain, but my hands had kept slipping and the ankle locks were so heavy I couldn't keep going up, kept sliding down until I cut myself up and had to stop.

"Miss Amy," I said, "I'm going to give myself a good run and go up the trunk of this tree as far as I can. You take hold of your near side chain and when I say 'Go,' you drop out of that tree on the far side, holding that chain just as firm as you can. Maybe that will pull me up to where I can grab that limb and get on top. Then I'll pull you back up on the limb and we'll go on from there."

She wasn't quite sure what I was talking about and neither was I, but as I explained it to her again and once again it all made sense. I slipped off my boots.

"You ready?" I asked her.

"I'm ready," she said, and I couldn't get over how easy and natural she sounded.

"Well, here I go," I said, and took a run from the end of my chain right up the trunk of that tree and, as I felt my foot begin to slip, said "Go!" and found myself quick as a wink upside down and banging my head against the tree a good enough one to see extra stars in the world. But I was sliding up, up, swinging and sliding and moving up and I felt my foot hit the side of the limb and reached up to take hold as I began to slide down again, down, and could feel Miss Amy's body right beside me as she was being pulled up again and she let go and fell as I went head first right in that sand.

I knew I wasn't dead because the pain in my head and my ankle were powerful enough to bring the water out of my eyes. And ears and nose, too, I thought, as well, until the salty taste showed me it was blood. I thought of Roy laying there when I pushed him off the bath scaffold and I wished he was there to help us. 'Cause I couldn't do anything about it. Couldn't even move.

"Miss Amy," I said, "you all right?"

"I'm all right," she said but the way she said it I knew she'd gone back into her mood. I felt down to my ankle and it was all sticky there. I could wiggle it all right and it didn't feel broken, but it was sure tore up on the outside.

Just then there was a big bump and somebody said something that sounded like "Ocktooleeb her."

"Who's there?" I said, worrying that Baum had come to have some fun.

"Sh!" somebody said. "Sh!" The moon broke through then from wherever it was and I could see a man getting up from the ground and when he came over to me, I could see it was the baron's brother. He walked over and bent down and tested the ankle locks. He grunted twice over my ankle locks and then went over and tested Miss Amy's. Then he went over and checked the ropes around Betty Whitman. Then he turned and headed back towards the ranch house. He never said a word to any of us. I was pretty sure he couldn't speak English the way the baron could. The baron only seemed to know a couple of words of Spanish so he had to talk English to the Mexicans. And the brother didn't seem able to speak English or Spanish so he just spoke his own language and grunted at everybody else.

I got up and limped over to where Miss Amy was sitting. Her eyes were open but she didn't seem really awake. I shook her a bit and then a bit harder. She'd gone back inside herself. I could tell she knew I was shaking her but she didn't acknowledge it none.

"Miss Amy," I said, "you should go over there and relieve yourself now because it's dark and there are a lot of people around in the daytime hours and I know you wouldn't want to do it then." She didn't answer. So I went over and took care of myself, which had come on real urgent when the baron's brother bumped the ground.

I went over to the trunk of the tree and buried the knife again.

Then I went back and pulled Miss Amy over on her side and lay down beside her and held her tight so the wind wouldn't get at her too hard. It would have been a lot warmer by the tree, but I figured she didn't want to get any closer to that Betty Whitman than she had to.

I sat up again and moved Miss Amy a little and dug her a hole for her hipbone and dug me one and lay down again. It was getting real chill and she felt nice to be wrapped around.

I even thought for a minute of putting my hand inside her dress, but I figured that wouldn't be right. I was her only protector such as it was and it wouldn't be decent to do that. Besides, her father would kill me if he ever found out.

The next day was going to be a long one, a real long one, and I was trying to think of something to do to get us out of this mess but I fell asleep before anything could come to my mind.

★ 28 ★

At first I thought it was the pounding of horses' hooves, but when I woke up enough to know where I was, I realized it was the beating of Miss Amy's heart. It was going awful fast, and every once in a while it would just stop dead for a second before going on again. It was still black but you could feel light on the way. We hadn't moved at all during the night, and my hip was still snug in the little hole. But I couldn't feel nothing in my left arm, which was under Miss Amy, and though I knew it must just be asleep, you can't help but feel a little worried when you don't feel nothing from the shoulder down. I was pinned just like it was branding time.

"Miss Amy," I said. "Miss Amy."

"Yes, Jory," she said, just as natural.

"Miss Amy, my arm's gone asleep under you and I can't move," I told her.

She sat up and turned around and started rubbing my arm all over. I still couldn't feel anything, though I could hear her rubbing and pounding away for all she was worth.

"All right now?" she asked.

"Miss Amy," I said, "I cannot feel one blessed thing and I fear the arm is dead, dead away and will rot in the sun."

"Nonsense," she said and commenced to pound and batter and rub all over again. And then I felt it. First I felt a tiny pricking and then it got harder and then I went through the damnedest pain I ever had in my life. That arm ached so that the sweat poured out on my face in that chill air and I thought I was going to faint right down in the dirt. She kept rubbing away all the time, and finally I could clench my fist back and forth and the arm felt all hot and itchy. Miss Amy insisted on keeping up the rubbing even though I told her it was all better, and she looked so anxious for something to do that I just let her. It almost felt like she was rubbing the sun up along with my arm and it got lighter and lighter by the minute.

And then I did hear horses' hooves pounding, and across the flat they came riding, about a dozen of them separated into twos and threes. They were riding so easy that I never did once think it might be Mr. Barron or Tex come to get us. That would be tomorrow, according to the baron's plan, and he hadn't been wrong yet.

Miss Amy stayed sat down but I stood up as the horsemen came together into one bunch just before they reached us and galloped past with hard looks at us except for one Mexican who swept off his big sombrero to Miss Amy and gave her a big smile. I knew he didn't really mean to be friendly but it was pleasant just the same.

They swept on past the big house and disappeared behind one of the buildings and you couldn't even hear what became of them. We were all alone out there with the sun starting to rise and the wind sighing the trees.

"I have to go, Jory," said Miss Amy, and I knew right away what she meant.

"You walk out to the other side of the tree," I said, "and I'll turn my back. Ain't nobody else out here."

She walked and I turned, but you could hear her all right in that clear air. I gave her a minute after the noise stopped and when I turned around she was already almost back to where we had slept. She was very careful not to look at the tree where Betty Whitman was tied. I couldn't much blame her. The body had smelled something awful when I was burying the knife the night before. It was like when you break the crust of hen manure that's been sitting in the open a couple of years. There's nothing and then all of a sudden there's enough to make you forget your name. The face was bloating up quite a bit, too, and you couldn't hardly recognize her like she was Betty Whitman anymore. She was just a thing rotting in the sun. And all those black flies setting on her mouth and nose and eyes. I wished now I had closed her eyes when I had the chance.

Miss Amy was like the old Miss Amy. I mean she was still dirty and tore up and unhappy-looking, but she was part of what was going on again, not that thing sitting in the dark with her eyes closed.

"I'm hungry, Jory," she said, "strange as that may sound." And just then a Mexican woman came shuffling out with two cups of coffee and two big chunks of fresh bread. No beans. She didn't bother picking up any of the used utensils, just turned around and got out of there.

It felt good to bite into that fresh white bread, and somebody had put sugar in the coffee. It was almost like having a picnic out there in the sun except that every time one of us moved a leg the clink of the chain let us know that it wasn't no picnic we were on.

We were sitting back to back so we would have each other to lean on, so she was the first one to see the baron coming.

"The German's coming with his bunch," she said.

I put down my cup and stood up, and Miss Amy stood up with me. The baron came rolling along with his brother and Baum and the Mexican and two hands I had never seen before. The baron nodded at me and touched his whip to his hat towards Miss Amy.

"Right here, gentlemen," said the baron, "will be the focal point of the action. They will come sweeping down from the hillock"—and he pointed over to the knoll—"and will head directly here to release the prisoners. This afternoon we will add six more men there"—and he pointed to the little dobe house at the foot of the knoll—"and this will give us great firepower from the rear. Your men"—and he pointed the whip at one of the strangers—"will be firing from the main house. You"—and he pointed to the other stranger—"will be situated over there"—and he pointed off to the left somewhere—"with your twenty horsemen and will ride in to cut down what is left."

"What if those Barron people all don't do according to your plan?" said Baum.

"I have studied these people," said the baron. "I know exactly what they will do. They will do it this way because their minds can work in only one way and I know in which way their minds work. Including yours, Mr. Baum, including yours." And he looked at Baum as though he was asking him a question, but whatever it was, Baum didn't answer, just looked over at Miss Amy and showed his teeth.

"I want all men stationed in their positions after the midday meal," said the baron. "Give them enough food and water for tonight and tomorrow morning and tomorrow noon. No man is to stir once he is in position, under penalty of death. We will all hold our positions. That means you"—and he pointed to Baum—"and you"—and he pointed to his brother—"and you and you and even me. Any man who leaves his position for whatever reason will be executed. You are to remain concealed and alert. Each of you is responsible for seeing that his men remain in position and on the alert. There will be no fires and no light shown and no noise. Every man is to remain alert upon pain of death."

The baron's brother came over and checked our chains when the baron and his crew moved off to tour the buildings. Then he moved off to follow his brother.

Just before noon a Mexican man and a woman came out with big plates that had beef and beans and bread and enchiladas on them. There was coffee and they also brought a big gourd that had water in it. The man kept looking at me like he was expecting me to say something. But I didn't have nothing to say to him and finally they went off.

I dug into my beans real careful, not quite knowing what I would find, and I didn't find nothing but more beans. So I took Miss Amy's plate and poked around in there but she only had a lot of beans too. Our plates were the same so I ate hers and she ate mine rather than trade back again. She didn't ask me why I had taken hers in the first place, just ate when I told her to.

While we were sitting there sipping up the rest of our coffee, a whole passel of hands drifted out of the bunkhouse and started to scatter around. They were all carrying rifles and they all had handguns and some of them had sacks slung over their shoulders. They moved in on all the dobe houses and disappeared inside. And then there was nothing. Just me and Miss Amy and a whole big ranch with nothing. I don't know what they all did with the Mexicans, but they were gone like they'd been stuck in a hole somewhere. Just then the twenty horsemen came riding out from the bunkhouse, all of them with gunnysacks slung over their saddles, and they moved out to the left and disappeared. We were alone again, the three of us. And Miss Amy started to cry a little.

"Miss Amy," I told her, "don't you cry. I'm here to protect your body and this is just what I am going to do."

"Oh, Jory," she said, and she started to laugh. She was laughing and crying at the same time and I hadn't seen anybody do that since Mrs. Jordan used to do it all the time, and I almost sat down and busted out crying with her.

"Oh, Jory," she said, "you are so good and so brave and so ridiculous. My daddy is going to come riding in here and they are going to shoot him right down in the dirt and everybody with him, and then that man is going to come out and get me."

I knew what man she was talking about.

"Miss Amy," I said, "buried over there in the dirt by that tree is a knife. When it gets dark, I am going to bust open these chains and get us out of here."

I could tell she didn't believe me, that she thought I was trying to jolly up her spirits. She looked over at the tree.

"The Mexican brought it out to me yesterday," I said. "Buried under the beans."

"Why didn't we run away last night?" she said. She still didn't believe me but she wanted to believe me.

"You've got to try a lot of plans before you find one that works," I told her.

She looked at me real quietlike. "How's your foot?" she asked.

"Fine, just fine," I told her. It might have been. It might have been. My boot was puffed out a little around the ankle but you couldn't see anything wrong from outside that boot. I couldn't see it but I sure could feel it.

"Then how are you going to get us out of here?" she asked. "Tell me your plan."

I stood there and looked at her. I wanted to say something, I tried to say something. But there wasn't anything to say. All I could do was just stand there and look at her.

"Oh, Jory," she said and sat down on the ground.

I sat down too. The sky had clouded up and the sun was hid somewhere and the wind was blowing enough to put sand in your eyes. It would have been better to sit behind the tree to break the wind, but Miss Amy wouldn't have gone near that tree for nothing, and I couldn't leave her out there alone.

So we sat there in the wind, taking a drink out of the water jug every once in a while. It seemed to me that nobody was going to bring us supper. The baron had us fat enough. The water was just to keep us sassy.

Miss Amy didn't seem to feel much like talking so I didn't bother to try and cheer her up. And besides, I was trying to think of how I was going to get her loose. I thought and thought all afternoon. Well, not really all afternoon. I would find myself falling into an awake-sleep in which I would just sit there and stare at the horizon and be like a blank. Once in a while my head would nod and that would snap me awake and I would say to myself, Think of how you're going to get Miss Amy free and loose and out of here, boy. But nothing would come and I would sink into that sleep again.

★ 29 ★

There was still enough light to make out shadows when Miss Amy came over and sat down beside me.

"Jory," she said, "how do you feel about me?"

"Why, I like you fine, Miss Amy," I said.

"Is that all?" she said. "Is that all you feel about me? That you like me just fine?"

"You know what I mean," I told her. "You know it ain't easy to put into words."

"You've got to," she said. "You've got to put it into words. Do you love me?"

Nobody had ever asked me that. Do you love me? Tell the truth, I'd thought about that word once or twice in relation to Miss Amy. Sometimes when we were riding and yelling and whooping through the wind, I would look over at her with her body edged forward in the saddle and her lips pulled thin and the sweet clear tan skin on her face flushed in the sun and I would get this strange feeling in my stomach and my chest and the word love would come out somewhere in there.

And when I saw her all naked and she kissed me and hugged me tight, I had another strange feeling but it was kind of mixed in with the feeling I had in the first place and the word love came out somewhere in there. I loved my pa, I guess, except that he had me so upset most of the time that it was hard to tell what I was feeling. And I loved the Jordans, I guess, though that was all so mixed up with grateful that I didn't know which was exactly which. And I loved Miss Amy, I guess, not like my pa, not like the

Jordans, not like anything I knew about. I never would have told her because her pa, much as he might like the way I could handle a gun, never would think me fit for the likes of her. But she wasn't asking me like she was expecting no for an answer. She needed a yes.

"Miss Amy," I said, "I love you."

"Then you must promise me something," she said. "You must promise me that that man will never get me."

Here I'd been thinking along those lines right along, but when she put it out in the open like that, it still gave me a start. Wasn't any sense in making out like I didn't know what she was talking about. We were a long way from home.

"I promise you," I said. "I promise you for sure."

That didn't make her none the happier-looking but it did seem to give her some kind of relief. She sat back on her heels and closed her eyes for a second and the light disappeared and her face along with it. We were in the dark. Just like I was that time when all those Indians were around. And right then I knew one thing we were going to do. It might help some and at least it would keep Miss Amy busy and not thinking about our problems.

But where and how? The best place would be near the tree, but I knew Miss Amy wouldn't be able to work there even if I moved Betty Whitman away as far as my chain would reach. The most danger would be from the side and from the back where the ranch house was. I started to move over to the tree and stepped bang on my tin bean plate. I dropped down quick and searched around until I found the spoon and the cup.

"Miss Amy," I said, "have you got your spoon and cup to hand?"

"They're right here somewhere," she said. "I've got them."

"Hang on tight to them," I told her. "We're going to need them."

I moved over to where the tree loomed up and tried to figure out the best spot to give us the most protection. It was hard to do in the dark even though I'd been sitting around staring at everything for I wasn't sure how long anymore. I made the decision as best I could and called

Miss Amy over. She clanked up to me and stood there waiting to be told what to do.

"Miss Amy," I said, "the baron is counting on wiping out your daddy and his riders when they come whooping in here tomorrow. Now there is just a chance he may be wrong, that your daddy and his riders are going to wipe the baron out. It don't seem hardly possible but then again it ain't impossible. So we're going to dig us a hole here tonight and make ourselves a place to hide."

"But what good will that do?" said Miss Amy. "They'll just walk out here in the morning and pull us out of the hole."

"Not if your daddy hits around first light," I said, "when everybody's sitting still like the baron said and waiting for him. It ain't a good chance but it's one of our only chances."

"What are we going to dig with?" she wanted to know.

"Spoons and cups," I told her. "The dirt is soft and it's all we got."

She dropped down to her knees and started digging. Didn't say another word, just started digging away like she was going to China before sunup.

I found my way back to the tree and dug out the knife. The stink from Betty Whitman was pretty bad, hanging over everything like a cover you couldn't throw off on a hot night. I slid the knife under my belt and went back to Miss Amy, who was moving right along in that soft dirt. She was using the cup to scoop up and was throwing the dirt around with right abandon.

"No," I told her, "we have to pile it up around the hole to give us a barrier." And as I held her hand still to show her, I heard a noise coming from in back where the ranch house was. I gave her a squeeze to tell her not to move and then soft as I could I moved away from the hole. Didn't want nobody finding that offhand. I couldn't move too far because whatever it was was coming up fast. I ducked down low and saw it. From the shape against the horizon I could tell right off who it was. And he was alone again.

I stood up and said, "Who's there?"

"Sh!" he said. "Sh!"

He bent down in front of me to feel the ankle locks, and I pulled the knife out of my belt and drove it down into the back of his neck as hard as I could. The point struck something halfway down and slid off a bit but stayed in all the way as I drove and drove and drove. He made a noise that wasn't too loud and went flat down on his face. I fell down with my knees as hard as I could and landed on his shoulders and back. The air went out of him with a soft whoosh and then there was nothing, nothing at all.

"Jory?" said Miss Amy, real soft.

"Right here," I told her, just as soft. "Everything's fine."

She didn't ask another thing, just started digging again. I reached around and felt the baron's brother's face. There didn't seem to be no air going in and out of his nose and I reached under and felt his chest and there wasn't nothing working in there either.

I got off and felt down to his waist for his gun. I needed a gun. Real bad. My right hand was working its fingers, feeling out for a gun. I didn't like that knife, didn't like it at all. I wanted a gun. There wasn't no gun on his waist or under his arm or in his sleeve, and I thought back and couldn't remember him ever wearing a gun. A couple of times he'd carried a little whip like the baron, but he hadn't ever seemed to carry a gun. Nor the baron either. We had to have a gun.

I moved my hands over him again, feeling careful everywhere, because my gambler friend had told me once that men hid weapons in peculiar places, even under their balls. There wasn't nothing but a hard small lump in one of his pockets, and when I fished it out I could feel it was a metal ring. With four keys on it. I sat down sudden.

Because I knew, I knew. It just had to be. I carefully took the first key and tried it on my ankle lock. You couldn't see a thing in the dark so I had to do it by feel, but the key was way too big for the hole. So I tried the next one and the next one and the next one. But I couldn't get none of them to fit. So I moved over to where Miss Amy was digging and sat her down and tried them on her, and none of them would fit her locks either.

She started digging again without me saying anything to her. I held the keys in my hand so hard that the metal was digging in and I could feel the sweat all greasy in the palm. We had to have a gun. God owed me a gun.

I took the first key in my right hand again and tried it. Too big for the hole. Same with the second one. Third one fit right in and I heard the click as I turned it and the collar fell right off my foot. Same with the other one. Went right in, clicked and the thing was off. Do you think I might have mixed up those keys in the dark the first time and used the same wrong one twice while the right one was sitting there? I didn't wish that key from a wrong one to a right one. I knew things like that didn't happen. Unless God all of a sudden reached down and handed me a gun. Tell the truth, I sat still for a few seconds.

I went back to Miss Amy's ankles and tried the good key. Didn't work. And none of the others either. Tried them all. Over and over. They wouldn't work in those locks. "Come on," I said, sweat pouring over my eyes and drying in the wind while Miss Amy sat there patient and quiet. I finally quit with a grunt and sat back. She didn't say a word, just started digging again, placing the dirt real careful around the hole.

I went back to where the baron's brother was laying and went over him again real careful. Real careful. Nothing else. Nothing. He was just carrying those four keys. It took quite a bit of pulling to get the knife out of his neck, and it made a grating noise, louder even that the sound he'd made when I'd drove it in. Didn't like that knife, didn't like it at all.

I wondered if somebody would be coming out soon to find out where he was. But then again, I had the feeling that nobody knew where he was, that this was something he did on his own. That man sure had his mind set on checking out locks and ropes and suchlike. It was something he had to do. The baron had pointed his whip right at him when he said that nobody was to move from his post no matter what happened. But he had to come out and check those ankles. He probably would have gone over and pulled on that Betty Whitman's ropes if I'd let him be. He sure was a strange one.

But what about the baron? How strange was he? Would he stick to his rule and let nobody move in that dark even though his brother was missing? I wouldn't have. I'd have lit the lanterns and come out searching. So would Mr. Barron and Roy and Mr. Jordan and even my pa. But the baron, the baron he was different. Different or not, we'd have to take the chance. I wiped the knife off as careful as I could on his jacket and moved back to Miss Amy.

"Miss Amy," I said, "we're going to need a gun real bad if we have to hold off people until your daddy gets here. I'm going over to one of the buildings and see if I can get us one."

"Who was that out there?" she said, and she kept on digging while she was talking.

"That was the baron's brother," I told her.

"Is he dead?" she wanted to know.

"He's dead." She kept on digging, carefully putting the dirt where I had told her, a cupful at a time.

"Will you be gone long?" she asked.

"I don't know," I told her. "I don't really know what's out there."

"I'll be all right," she said. "You go do what you have to."

I squeezed her arm and moved over to the tree, where I sat down and tried to slip off my boots. Easier said than done. Hardly done at all. Both legs had taken a beating from the ankle chains, but the one I had hung from when I slipped upside down was a real mess, all puffy and gooey around the ankle when I finally got that boot off. It was a painful process.

I straightened my legs right out while I thought for a minute on the best thing to do and then I decided to go for the little dobe house at the foot of the knoll because that was the one I had watched the most and knew the most about. I knew where the door was and the window slits and how many men were there.

It was real strange crossing that open space to get to the house. There was no moon at all and lots of wind, and it whooshed over the ground in spurts and jumps that made it seem more like a person than wind. I started out real slow and careful, moving easy and quiet, but I kept going faster and faster until by the time I reached where the house was I almost ran into it. It was so unexpected that I dropped down flat on the ground and knocked the wind out of myself. It sounded real noisy but nobody came out to ask who was making all that racket out there. I lay still for a while and when that didn't seem to get me anywhere, I moved up to a crouch and worked my way next to the house, right smack up against its wall.

I felt up with my hand to what I considered the right distance and moved along till I found a slit. I stood up and put my ear to it. I could hear voices in there and smell tobacco and there was a clinking now and then that said whiskey was being poured. Every once in a while a voice would get loud or someone would laugh loud and then I'd hear someone make a big shsh noise, but right after that somebody would talk loud again.

I became so busy trying to find out what they were saying that the opening of the door almost made me yell out in fear.

"Close that door," somebody hollered, and the man said, "Shit!" as he pulled the door shut with a bang. My eyes were pretty used to the dark, and I could tell that the fellow wasn't too big as he moved out away from the house. I followed maybe three steps behind him quiet as I could. He didn't go too far before he dropped his rifle on the ground, opened up his pants and started to water like a horse in pain. You could hear that stream even over the wind, and it sounded like it was never going to stop until the end of the world.

One time back on the trail the Mexicans had been talking about how to kill a man quiet with a knife. They lived with knives the way white men live with guns and they were always talking about this or that with a knife. To kill quiet, one had said, you must jam the weapon as hard as possible into the kidney, and he had pointed to a spot on his back. It constricts the throat, he had said.

I moved up those three steps and drove that knife as hard as I could right into that man's back. It was so hard that when the hilt hit his back, my hand kept going and knocked into him so fierce that my wrist was bent almost in two. He fell forward right on his face and started to make a gargling sound in the dark. I fell on him with my knees just like I had done with the baron's brother and the air went out of him hard. I jumped up a little and came down on him hard again. He didn't make any more noise. I reached back and found the rifle and started to reach down to take off his gun belt.

It only takes a man so long to piss and I was feared those people might come out of that house looking for him. So I pulled him up to a sitting position and worked him over my back. Then I picked up the rifle, looked back at the house to get my bearings as best as possible and started back to where the tree and Miss Amy was. It was easier walking not quite straight up with him on my back, but it wasn't that easy altogether. The man was heavy, real heavy, and I had to keep the rifle from banging on the ground and my feet was getting cut up from all kinds of sharp things that you never know are there until you walk around without any boots on.

I had to stop to rest a little ways out and then I had to rest about every ten steps. Once I fell down flat on my face when I stopped to rest and I wasn't sure as I was laying there whether or not I could carry that man anymore. I didn't know whether he was dead or alive. The knife was still in him because I knew if I pulled it out he would start bleeding all over the place. I worked my way up to my knees and then up enough to get moving again. And finally, there it was, the tree, the big tree.

I went right to the tree until I felt my boots and then slid him off my back. I fell down right alongside him and just lay there, sweat pouring off me and a lump in my throat that almost kep me from breathing.

"Jory?" I heard Miss Amy call. "Jory?"

I couldn't answer her. I didn't even want to answer her. I just wanted to breathe.

"Jory?" she said again. "Is that you, Jory?"

"Yes," I got out. "Yes."

She didn't say another word and I could hear her digging.

I reached around to where I'd dropped him and undid his gun belt. The belt was loaded with cartridges, every hole filled. I checked the gun and it too was loaded right up. I strapped it on me. The fit was a little tight, but it would do. I felt in his pockets and they were loaded with rifle shells, maybe twenty altogether. Sometimes things work out better than you hope.

I took the rifle and moved over to Miss Amy. "We've got

a rifle and a gun and some shells," I told her. I felt down to where she had been digging. She'd made quite a bit of progress so I must have been gone quite a while. Which meant we didn't have all that much time left to make the hole deep as we'd need.

I laid the rifle down at the head of the hole and went over to where I'd left the baron's brother. I reached under his arms and hauled him over to the hole. I went back to the tree and pulled the other one over to the hole.

"Miss Amy," I said, "even with both of us digging we're not going to have this hole as deep as I'd like to protect us till your daddy gets here. So we're going to put these people alongside the hole and throw dirt over them and they'll be part of the barricade."

She didn't say anything. So I pulled the baron's brother along one side and the other fellow along the other side. And then I found my cup and got in the hole with Miss Amy and started digging along with her. Every once in a while there would be a small root, so I took my knife out of the other one and cut the root and then I'd dig in hard with the knife to soften up the dirt for our scooping. And as the first small light came up, I saw that we had ourselves a fair little fort there in the middle of nowhere.

★ 30 ★

It looked like a shallow grave and that thought was in my mind as I crawled in beside Miss Amy. She had just enough chain and a touch to spare when she lay down flat in it. We weren't deep as I would have liked but we were down far enough for protection from straightaway fire. There was one spot I wasn't sure of, so I slipped out of the hole quick and moved over to the tree where I cut Betty Whitman down and dragged her up close enough to the hole to block that line of fire from the left. It was pretty bad to drag her over in the dirt what with the way she smelled and felt, and I didn't dare look at Miss Amy while I was doing it, but it was needed and had to be done.

Just as I got her set where I wanted her, I heard a shout from the ranch and without looking I took a dive right in that hole, landing partly on Miss Amy but hurting neither of us. I took off my hat and peeked over the hillock that was made up partly of dirt and partly of the baron's brother. The Mexican who was always with the baron was running towards us from the ranch house. He was carrying a rifle and he had a funny look on his face and he was yelling as he was coming.

I hit him in the chest with a rifle bullet and he flopped right over backwards and lay still. I was pondering on whether or not to run over and get his rifle when two more men came boiling out of the ranch house and started on a run for us. I dropped one with the rifle but missed the other as he turned and pounded back behind the wall.

Just then I heard a rifle bang on the left and a bullet

whacked into the body of the one I'd dragged from the dobe house. I figured we were there to stay.

Since there wasn't any more sense to keeping quiet, I took out the handgun and shot through the chain holding Miss Amy to the tree. I pulled the end all the way around and then had her hold her other leg up in the air a bit and shot the chain right off her. It was a ticklish thing to do but it worked just fine. She had about a foot of chain hanging off the lock on each leg, but I hadn't dared work any closer what with a chance for pieces of metal flying or a richochet or something.

It didn't take long to do the business with the chains but by the time I had finished and peeked out, a line of men was coming at us from every one of the houses. The baron and the Baum fellow were coming from the main house and there were quite a few from all of the others, even the little dobe house. The baron was making hand signals to all of them and they were moving slow and easy as they came, spreading out as far as possible with lots of space between each man. I pulled the two dead casings from the handgun and reloaded. What with the repeating rifle and all, I figured I could finish off twelve or fifteen before making sure Miss Amy went easy. The baron and Baum had to go first, and I was just about to set the sights on Baum when a thousand rifles started going off to the right of me. There was just the rifle shots and no screaming of bullets, and I swiveled around fast to see what was going on.

My pa used to say that there were things in the world too wondrous for the naked eye, and one of the reasons he drank was to dim his vision in case he ever encountered one. My pa was perpetually prepared, as he used to say, and he would have needed a bellyful of whiskey to shade his eyes from what I was seeing.

For coming down that knoll lickety-split was a drover's wagon with the wheels tied straight, no horses in front and no people on top, heading right for the little dobe house.

Behind it came charging maybe twenty men on horses, and I could have sworn even at that distance, and it was a far piece, that it was Roy and Mr. Barron leading the pack. You could hear their yelling and hollering and wahooing all the way to where we were, and they were shooting their rifles and guns to beat the band. The men at the dobe house were shooting up at them, but I didn't see anybody fall off his horse.

Miss Amy and I got up on our knees to see better and just then the wagon hit the dobe house and the world blew up. Well, it didn't really blow up, but it got shook up quite a bit. Our side of the dobe house stayed solid, but the other side seemed to jump up in the air and scatter around for miles. The noise was like the crack of doom, and men came spilling out of that dobe house like matches out of a box. They could have been cut down easy as they scampered for the next house closest them except that the Barron people had problems of their own. Noise is a two-way thing and it must have hit back as hard at them as it banged forward toward us. Anyways, there they were with their horses milling around and falling down and the baron's men had all the time they wanted to mosey over to the next house. Except they wasn't moseying; they was pounding for salvation.

The baron's men in the closer house were shooting away like fury, but our people managed to get behind the wall that was left after the blast and I could see spurts where they were shooting back.

Which reminded me of what was going on and I grabbed Miss Amy and pulled her down with me into the hole. I squivered around as fast as I could and peeked over the top at the ranch house. There was nobody there. You couldn't see any of the men at any of the other houses either except for two men who were behind the walls of a house straight across from me and they were taking turns peeking around the corner of their house at what was left of the dobe. They weren't paying any attention to us at all. I dropped one of them and was about to get the other when a whole bunch of bullets tore into the dirt around me. I dropped down to reconsider.

"Miss Amy," I said, able to spare a moment for the first time, "your daddy is here."

"I saw him," she said, "and Roy and Phil Miles and Ken Slater and some of the other hands. They're here to get us out."

"Well, they've still got a ways to come," I told her. "But

it looks a lot better for us than it did before. That baron ain't as smart as I thought."

"It's just that my daddy is smarter," said Miss Amy.

"Well, I ain't going to argue that point one way or another," I told her. "I think maybe that the baron didn't consider that your daddy had to fight a lot of Indians to set his ranch up proper, and they teach you tricks that white men don't ordinarily consider. Anyways, the main thing is for us to stay alive until they get to us."

"When will that be?" she asked.

You know, you can get mixed up in a conversation with a girl and you find yourself answering questions that nobody in his right mind would have asked in the first place. Her daddy had to fight his way over quite a stretch of ground before he was going to get near us, and there was a good chance he wouldn't even make it. But I couldn't go telling that girl that. And I couldn't go telling her that I didn't know when they might make it if they did make it.

"Pretty soon," I said. "It ought to be pretty soon."

That was all she wanted to hear. She settled back in the hole, pulled the water jug to her and took a drink. I wouldn't have been surprised if she had settled in for a nap. But before she had a chance, the shooting started up again something fierce. I peeked over the top and a whole slew of Barron riders were pouring down that knoll to get behind the walls of what was left of that little dobe house. They had two wagons pulled by two horses each and the wagons looked cram full of things. Probably ammunition and grub and suchlike, I figured, and it reminded me of how empty my belly was. Here I hadn't had a chance to relieve myself for about three days now, and still my belly felt empty. I took a pull out of the water bottle and made myself comfortable.

It was a cloudy, windy day but every once in a while you could see the sun pale and ghostlike through a break in one of the layers. Rain had been trying to come in for two days now and it would have its way sooner or later, but right now the winds were fighting over it, first this way and then the other.

Every once in a while a bullet would bang into our little hillock from one side or another, and I made myself little peek holes in between things so I wouldn't have to stick my head up over the top. I would see one of the baron's men running this way or that between a building, and once I raised up fast to take a shot at one of them, but I almost got hit myself so I didn't try that again. Besides, I wanted to save my bullets.

Shortly after the sun skimmed past the noon mark there was another big explosion and I sneaked a look in time to see part of the building that was closest to the little dobe house go up in the air. Mr. Barron's men must have been working their way up with dynamite and were going to blast their way all the way to the ranch house. Every once in a while another bunch of Barron men would come streaking down the hill, and once they came down with another loaded wagon. The odds were evening out fast. I was trying to think of a way I could tell Mr. Barron about those horsemen hidden off somewhere, but we were pinned down too tight for any fancy stuff. I was hoping they would reach us before dark because it was hard to tell what would happen if we were alone out there in the night again. The baron must have been pretty mad at me for killing his brother and spoiling his plans a bit. I didn't care.

"Jory," said Miss Amy, "where were you going when they caught you?"

"I don't know," I told her. "Just away."

"How far away?" she said.

"I don't know," I said. "Far as I could."

"Jory," said Miss Amy. "I don't want you to go away. I want you to stay and marry me."

Married, that's just what she said. But that was for grownups, people near twenty. I felt tired enough to be that old. Here I was laying on my belly in a shallow grave somewhere in Texas, peeking this way and that way and this way again to see if I could kill somebody before he killed us. My eyes saw men running and shooting and falling and buildings blowing up and fires burning, and my eyes saw Ab Evans' boot pulling back to kick my pa in the head. And my ears heard rifles going off and handguns and dynamite and men yelling and my ears heard that clunk sound when the boot hit that head. My nose smelled gunpowder and things burning and my nose smelled sawdust and my own puke. I took both my hands and put them on the cheeks of Miss Amy's face and held her tight and easy at the same time. And I put my lips on her lips, that were cracked and scabbed up in spots where she'd been bleeding. And she felt good and she tasted so good.

"Miss Amy," I said, "I'd like to be married with you. I'd truly like that."

Just then a great rush of yelling broke out and I peeked through to see the baron's horse cavalry swinging in between one of the buildings where our men had been shooting from. They were a beautiful sight to see, coming in a straight line, each man spread out about five feet from the next one, pretty as a picture. According to the baron's plan, they had been supposed to come on to ride down what was left of our crew, but nobody was following the baron's plan much that day and there wasn't nobody out in the open to be cut down.

The shooting was something fierce but those cowpokes tore right through that space between the houses, flashed across the open spot right by our tree and disappeared to the south just as pretty as you please. There was something about the way they was riding that convinced me they wasn't coming back, that they realized that the cutting down was a two-way business and they was going out of business.

Our men were now established in the second house on their way and had a place with four solid walls and a roof to cover them. I wondered if the baron was planning a new plan and I wondered if Mr. Barron had a plan of his own and how their plans might affect our plans. Not that we had any special plans other than to stay alive until they reached us.

About a half hour later we saw that our side did have a plan. A wagon poked its head out from behind the second house with four men pushing it inch by inch towards us. They came about twenty inches when the guns in the ranch house put up such a how-de-do that those four men dropped everything and scampered back behind the wall. One of them staggered like he was hit, but he made it all right. The wagon was just left sitting there. If they could have pushed it to us and turned it on its side, we would have had some nice protection and a few hands to help us. But we were still alone. And it was dark.

Everybody must have been just as surprised as we was because the shooting stopped. Completely. Not a shot. The insides of some of the houses was burning, but there wasn't enough light to shoot at anything.

"Jory," said Miss Amy, "let's run for it."

"They'll shoot at anything they hear," I said. "We best sit still till we see what's going to happen."

An arrow with a burning rag on the end arched up in the sky from the closest house held by the Barron spread, and by the light I could see two men running out towards us from the ranch house. They were closer than I like to think of, and I dropped them both with the handgun just before the arrow hit the ground and the light went out.

"Miss Amy," I whispered, "you mustn't talk or move or make any noise. We have to listen to hear if anybody's coming out for us."

Another arrow went up in the sky and started its way down. The ground was empty except for the two men laying close to us and the one further back. They were feared to be caught in that light.

We listened. Quiet. Not moving. Nothing. Miss Amy put her hand on my back and I could feel both her heart and my heart beating through that hand. That's how still it was. And every once in a while a flaming arrow would zoom up in the air and whoosh down again into the sudden dark.

It got so we were just laying there waiting for the next arrow and watching it go up in the sky and then come down again. I wasn't hardly looking around to see if anybody was coming out to kill us or not. We were just watching the arrows.

Miss Amy had been hunching over my back and she moved up a little so her head was next to mine and she pulled my face around and started kissing me soft and easy on the lips and around my mouth. She was getting me stirred up but in a strange way because my heart started beating slower than usual. Whenever Conchita got going with me I could feel my heart start pounding like it was going to break out of my chest, and I couldn't wait to jump on her and finish it off.

But this was slow and steady like we had all the time in the world and no place to go and nothing else to do. I pulled her over to where she was facing me and slid my hand inside her shirt where she was pushing out at me to take her. She pulled my shirt out of my pants and moved her hand up on my chest and was rubbing me like I was rubbing her.

"Jory," she whispered, "Jory, Jory, show me, show me."

I could hear bullets whanging in the dark, some of them whining right over us, and the arrows would come every once in a while to break the dark and I could see her face so sweet and pretty looking at me like I had never seen a woman look at a man, never, never, and I didn't think to look around to see if anybody was skulking up and I didn't hear those bullets close like they were. It was like that hole was somewhere off in an ocean all by itself.

I reached down and pulled up her skirt. She was wearing men's long johns underneath and I unbuttoned the front and felt of her, the soft hair like fine wire and I tried working my finger in there but I couldn't seem to get it. With Conchita it was like folding your hand into a pitcher of warm milk, all open and ready and go ahead and do it.

I unbuckled my gun belt and let it fall off and unbuttoned my pants and moved against her but it wouldn't work no-how, what with us all scrunched in that hole and her so tight down there I couldn't figure which way was up and me feared to raise my ass above the horizon. But I pulled her all the way underneath and widened her legs as far as each side of the hole would allow and all the while she was kissing me on the lips, kissing and kissing and kissing with her eyes closed which I could see whenever another arrow arched up and I was bound and determined when all of a sudden the earth moved underneath enough to throw me to the side and I came down in the dirt hard enough to near break my tool in half.

The pain hit me as hard as the noise that went booming all around us. Our men must have been planting explosives all the time we were fooling around, and the baron's men surely had been out on their own cussedness. Because when those dynamite sticks started going off, all the rifles and handguns started up again, and the flashes were every which way. Fires busted out in all the houses, including the ranch house, and you could see men running back and forth and falling and getting up and falling and not getting up.

I fastened my clothes and buckled on the gun belt while Miss Amy fixed herself up. Her face was all red in the reflection of the fires. You couldn't see much of what was going on, just shapes flitting here and there and muzzle blasts going off everywhere. It was pretty in a way, the red flames and the pink and gray smoke and all that noise whamming around from dynamite and guns. Every once in a while a horse would bust past without a rider, and a couple of times men on horses breezed by, getting out of there as best they could. You couldn't tell who was who or what so I didn't try to shoot anybody or ask questions. It was everybody for himself.

"Miss Amy," I yelled, "it's time we got out of here," and I pulled her to her feet and off to the left out in the dark away from the houses and everybody in them. She couldn't run too fast because of the ankle locks, but we made out pretty good until we were far enough away from the burning buildings so that they looked like a soft glow in the night.

We ran and ran until she said, "Jory," and fell down. I had left the rifle behind because I needed one hand to hold my gun and the other to pull Miss Amy along. I could have put the gun in the holster and took her on my back, but I didn't even think about that for more than a moment. I was just too tired. She was too heavy and the rifle was too heavy.

I fell down beside her and we just looked at those glows in the night. I didn't know where we were, probably out in the stark open where we'd be sitting birds come morning. But that girl couldn't move and neither could I.

And there we sat for I don't know how long. The shots sounded real clear in the night air and the shooting kept up something fierce. There were a few more explosions but then they stopped and there was just the guns shooting.

We could have gotten up and moved off some more but we didn't. I had my gun and I had Miss Amy; that was my piece of the world. But a piece of the world was no good, we both knew that. We had to know what was happening there, whether it was us or them. Because if it was them, we couldn't run far enough.

Without saying a word, the two of us stood up and started back towards the ranch. As we got closer, the fires looked brighter and you could see almost like it was day. Most of the shooting was going on around the biggest dobe house near the ranch house, but there was shots being fired all over the place and men riding here and there and jumping off horses and jumping on horses.

I was running in a crouch with my gun in my right hand and holding on to Miss Amy with my left. She was running like me, keep up as best she could but stumbling now and then as her chains caught somewhere or the ankle locks banged against each other. I had to find the keys for those blasted things before she stumbled us into something we couldn't run away from.

We ducked down whenever anybody came near us because you couldn't tell friend from devil in that crazy light, and these people were shooting first and asking who you were afterwards. I worked our way over to the ranch house because I figured that's where the keys had to be.

The front doors were gone and I guessed someone had put a stick of dynamite to them. You could see flames shooting inside but not burning fierce and we passed right in to the damnedest mess you ever saw. It looked like the fight had been through there and then gone on. There wasn't a stick of furniture that was more than a stick and everything else was smashed, smashed flat. Little fires were burning here and there but nothing big, nothing too hot to go near.

I don't know why we went in there; to get the key, I thought. All I could think about was that key and freeing Miss Amy of her chains. It was a foolish thing to do, to go in there, but you don't think too unfoolish when you've been chained up to a tree for three days and buildings are being blown up all around you and guns are going off like it is Fourth of July and everything's smashed and burning and the girl you're sworn to protect is weighed down by two heavy ankle locks and a length of chain off each foot. We had to have that key.

It's a good thing we went in there, too, because there was Mr. Barron leaning against the far wall with blood running out of his chest and there was the baron over against the other wall with blood running out of all of him and at his feet the little Mexican who'd given me the knife. He'd given me the little one and kept the big one for himself because in his hand was about as wicked a pig sticker as I have ever seen. I knew it was the Mexican who gave me the knife because the back of his shirt was ripped and I'd never have forgotten those scars. Someone had bashed the back of his head in but not before he'd sliced up the baron for dinner and leftovers. That man's plan had gone wrong.

Miss Amy had run over to her pa and took his head up in her arms and was crooning over him while she tried to hold back with her hand the blood that was streaming out of him. I was moving over to help her when I felt something behind me. Didn't hear nothing, just felt it.

I turned around and coming out of the corridor was Baum, brushing the top of the door with his head. He looked ten feet tall standing there, and his black clothes were covered all over with blood, like someone had poured bucketfuls on him. There was blood on his hair and on his beard and his hands were all blood.

He saw me at the same time I saw him, and his eyes got bigger as he was looking at me, red, red eyes that looked right through me to I don't know where. He was so big and black and bloody that I wanted to turn and run out of there. He was breathing hard, snorting like a horse in pain and he was working those hands open and shut, open and shut. His holster was empty and there wasn't no gun in his hand and he started moving over towards me, snorting away and working those hands, and I tasted something in my mouth that I had never tasted before and I could hardly see with the sweat in my eyes and the fires burning crazy all around and this Baum coming at me out of the flames and I knew who he was, I knew who he was, and I yelled, "Pa, Pa," and I could hear someone else yelling, and it was Miss Amy and she was yelling, "Jory, Jory, Jory," and I knew what that man was going to do to her after he crushed me with those hands that were reaching out and I raised my gun and shot him and he stopped. He stopped dead still and looked down at his chest where the bullet had gone in and he fell right down, backwards, not towards me, backwards.

I dropped the gun on the floor. I knew that man was dead and I wanted done with killing. I dropped that gun because I didn't have the strength to hold it in my hand anymore. It had all gone into that bullet that had knocked Baum down, all my strength was there inside his chest.

Why did I have to go around killing people? It was carrying the gun that did it. If you didn't have a gun, you figured out some other way of doing things. My pa had never carried a gun. He carried a bottle. And that bottle . . .

"Jory," said Miss Amy. "Jory!"

I turned and she was looking up at me like my pony looked at me sometimes, pushing her head up and at me like there was nothing else in the world. "Jory," she said, "help me."

And I bent down just as Mr. Barron opened his eyes and blinked away real hard, tears coming out of his eyes in a steady stream. "Jesus Herman Christ," he said, "we all made it, we all made it."

And in busted Roy with three of the Mexican hands, then with their guns out and fanning all around looking for people to shoot and nobody to oblige them. Roy rushed over and bent down over Mr. Barron trying to get at where the wound was. He jumped up and looked around, then rushed over to the dead little Mexican and pried the knife out of his hand. He cut open Mr. Barron's jacket and then his shirt and his underwear and said, "It's in the shoulder, just inside the shoulder. Miss Amy," he said, "tear me off a piece of your slip so I can cut off this bleeding."

"She ain't wearing a slip," I said. "She's got on long johns."

And Mr. Barron raised up from his pain and give me a look that scared the living jeebers out of me. Roy didn't take no notice. "Then scout around, Jory," he said, "and see what you can come up with."

I was only too happy to get away from there right then, and as I headed into the corridor, I heard Roy tell Mr. Barron how the baron's men had scattered and what was he doing in the ranch house this way with a bullet in his shoulder.

All of the rooms was tore up awful bad but I finally came

on a little one that had a bed in it with a sheet over it. Standing in a corner was a table with five bottles of whiskey on it. There in the midst of all that destruction was five bottles of whiskey without even a crack in them. I picked one up and brought it back with the sheet.

When Mr. Barron saw the whiskey he almost cried for real. I took the top off and handed it to him while Roy was making a tight bandage, and that grateful man took several long swallows. "Here," he said, handing me the bottle, "Amy's been telling me about your doings. You're a real man now and big enough to drink."

I was about to tell him no but the bottle felt warm in my hand; it fit like the gun had. So I held it up and took a long swallow. It went down easy, warm and easy right in the belly. And I took another swallow and a third, and they all fit nicely, warm and snug.

"Hey," said Roy, jumping up and taking it away. "Other men have put in a hard night around here." And he and Mr. Barron swallowed in turn while the dawn broke around us. One of the Mexicans came in to say they had a wagon ready, and we carried Mr. Barron out to the wagon and laid him down in the back. Miss Amy clanked alongside and we lifted her up in the wagon next to him. One of the Mexicans pulled a saddle off a horse and they put that under Mr. Barron's head.

"Get in, Jory," said Miss Amy. "Come along home."

"I'm going to find my horse," I told her. "Then I'll be along."

"Come with us now," she said. "They'll bring your horse."

"No," I said. "I'll find him, then I'll come."

She was going to argue some more but the horse started up, and I could see she was thinking about jumping out of the wagon but she still had those leg irons on and she just plumb didn't have the strength. She kept her eyes on me all the time until the wagon turned behind a burned-down house, and it was that pony look, that little pony look.

I went right back into the house and to the room where the whiskey was. I sat down on the bed and drank me a bottle, drank it in long, easy swallows that went down warm and nice until I felt that cold go out of my stomach, felt it melt under that warm whiskey. I thought the baron and

Baum had put that cold there for good, that I was never going to be shut of it. Miss Amy hadn't known nor Mr. Barron nor Roy nor anybody that those people had put the cold in my belly. I hadn't even talked about it with myself, but it had been there all right, it had been there. That's what whiskey did, it warmed that cold.

I stood up feeling a bit lightheaded but able to move straight. I took me another bottle off that table and carried it down the corridor to the front room where the baron was laying over there in the corner and Baum in the middle. I looked down at Baum and at the gun I had dropped beside him and went out the door.

Juan was standing there with my very own horse, just as if we were home and I was going out riding with Miss Amy. He smiled. Not a real smile. The old-timer had been through too much to get up a big smile, but there was something in his face to show that nothing was changed, that the sun had come up.

I slipped the bottle into my saddlebag and mounted up. If that horse had given even one of his warmup bucks, I would have gone flying and dead as I hit. But I guess he was smiling a little bit, too, 'cause he just shook his head twice, turned right around and headed for home.

★ 31 ★

Somehow I expected everything to be different, and it came as a surprise to find the Barron ranch exactly as I'd left it three days before. Thirty miles away, the houses were still burning and there were some dead men starting to bloat and the baron's plan was dead along with him. We hadn't even found one wounded man; they'd all faded away into nowhere.

Here everything was the same with women running around and screeching along with the chickens and the men riding out on fence or rounding up calves or bringing in horses and laughing and joking and bragging on what great fighters they were. We'd only lost one killed, a vaquero named Jorge who didn't have no relatives, and maybe a few of the senoritas missed him, but he didn't cause no hole in the community.

It was impossible to tell how many was wounded because everybody claimed they was wounded someplace or other. They were all limping or holding their arms or making painful faces whenever they had to do anything. And they all took to wearing handguns, tying them down tight and making a big show about putting them on or taking them off. Me, I couldn't wear my guns. I tried strapping them on the day after we got back, but they felt so heavy that I had to take them off. I knew they weren't no heavier than they'd been before, but they didn't feel right and there wasn't no use to wearing them for anything, so I just didn't. Besides, my ankle had swelled up so bad that I couldn't even wear a boot, just a moccasin, and it didn't make sense to weigh myself down any.

The Mexicans changed towards me, too. They didn't step aside and take off their hats or bow their heads anymore but gave me a wave or a smile or a *"Buenas dias"* when they passed. We were all one, a family like. They were still respectful more than I would have liked, like I was as old as Mr. Barron or something, but it was better than it had been before.

I hadn't talked to Miss Amy since we'd got back, other than to greet her when we passed. She was terrible busy taking care of her pa the first couple of days, but it didn't take him long to get back on his feet and go roaring around with his arm in a sling. But something had happened between me and Miss Amy that had made her stand off, and when I thought back on what I had tried to do to her in that hole, I could sure understand it. That had been a crazy three days and if she thought I was going to go around telling everybody what she'd said and done in those three days, she was wrong. I wanted to tell her that I wouldn't ever tell nobody and that she had nothing to fear from me, but it's a hard subject to bring up, especially when she never stopped flitting whenever I came near her.

Conchita came slipping up to my bedroom every chance she got, and once I pushed my hand down the front of her dress but it didn't feel right and I told her to stay away from me. I was sorry I said it as soon as I said it, but I couldn't change it even though the tears came right to her eyes. Every time she was around me after that she looked at me like I had beat her with a whip, but I couldn't do anything about it, I just couldn't.

Roy was busy getting things going again at the ranch, and he had his troubles convincing the Mexes that they were ranch hands and not warriors anymore. "Goddamn fools," he said to me. "They wanna go off on a rampage somewheres."

He rampaged at them until they settled down to work again, and inside the week they weren't bothering with their guns too much anymore.

One morning, the first day I had been able to get both my boots on, I was sitting in the kitchen eating flapjacks with honey on them, and Mr. Barron walked in and asked me if I'd care to take a stroll with him. He hadn't said much to me since he'd been walking around and I figured maybe Miss Amy had told him something about what had gone on in that hole and he was getting ready to send me off. Didn't need me for anything anyways. With the Germans gone Miss Amy could ride all over to her heart's content and just worry about maybe getting a bee-sting. Bodyguarding was no longer a necessity around that ranch.

We went outside and walked down the field to the track where they held races every once in a while. Mr. Barron had brought in some horses from the East and was trying to breed some racers. It was fun to get on one of them long-legged things and let him go all out. Almost like flying through the air.

We stopped by the fence and he leaned over it and stared at the hills in the distance.

"How old are you, boy?" he asked. "Nineteen?"

Wasn't no point in telling him I wasn't.

"Amy's twenty-two," he said. "Pretty near twenty-three.

"But the boy's big for his age," he said, almost as much to himself as to me, "and he's going to get a lot bigger. When they're both in their twenties, nobody's's going to think on it. Amy tells me," he said, "that she not only can't live without you but that she damn well won't. She's talking about marriage. How do you feel about it?"

I looked away over those rolling acres, knowing that all around me there was enough land to ride forever if I wanted to and still call it mine. And I thought of Miss Amy who smelled so good in the dark and looked so good in the day. It made me feel real old to have to give up those two years out of my life forever. I wouldn't never know what it was like to be seventeen or eighteen. I was about to tell him yes when he said, "Don't have to make up your mind this minute. There's all this"—and he pointed around him—"and God knows how many steers and people to worry about and those goddamn Athertons pushing into our range from the north and the town to straighten out and the schools to get started," and his face was getting redder and redder till he sputtered out.

"There's responsibility," he said, "responsibility. Some men don't like it. Some men can't take it. You think on it." And he walked off.

I stood there staring way over to the hills. Nothing was ever as simple as you'd like it to be. Conchita was simple. Miss Amy was not.

I walked down by the barn and told Juan to saddle my horse and bring him up to the house. I went up to my room, passing Miss Amy on the way, and she gave me a little smile and scurried off. Girls were really something.

The bottle of whiskey was still on my dresser right where I'd left it. I'd been tempted a couple of times to see whether it still went down easy and warm but I'd never made the move. I opened the door to the wardrobe and pulled one of the guns from the holster. Didn't strap on the belt or anything, just took one of the guns. Then I picked up the bottle of whiskey and went downstairs where Juan was waiting with the horse. I put the bottle of whiskey in one saddlebag and the gun in the other. Then I mounted up and took off for the mesa.

It was a sweet day with the sun shining hot but just enough breeze to keep the sweat from rising. We galloped along easy and my ankle felt fine in the stirrup, about as strong as ever. I kept looking around, looking around, because so many things had happened to me on this piece of property, but everything was still. I rode down to the little pond and dropped off at the rock I had sat on while Miss Amy was swimming. I could almost feel her pressing against me and smell her wet hair, and I put both my hands on my chest and pushed in as hard as I could. The only way I knew I had closed my eyes was when I opened them again and saw the clouds riding on the water, fuzzy from the wind moving over it.

I walked over to where my pony was grazing and pulled the gun and the whiskey from the saddle bags. I put them both on the big rock, squatted down and looked them over real careful. I'd lugged them out there for a purpose, that was for sure, but I didn't know what the purpose was, that was for even more sure. It was something Mr. Barron had said. Responsibilities. That's what he'd said, responsibilities.

My pa's only responsibility had been me. But whiskey meant more to him. I had met my responsibilities. To my pa, to Jocko, to Mr. Barron and Miss Amy. But that had always meant killing people. I didn't want to kill anybody anymore. Responsibility meant killing people sometimes. But I wanted Miss Amy and I wanted the ranch. And with them came responsibilities. You could ride away from them. Or with whiskey you could stay and forget about them.

I picked up the gun and walked right down to the edge of the water, close enough to feel the cool damp working through my boot. The gun was weighing heavy in my hand and I turned it so that I was holding it by the barrel, the cold slimness fitting snug in my palm, and the strength moved through me as I raised the gun on high. As I looked out at the water rippling in the wind, I thought on that night, that black night when I had raised up and threw Jocko's guns our there forever so that Jack wouldn't have the last say, and I thought on Mr. Evans and the baron and Baum, and I flipped the gun in the air, caught it firm by the butt and went into my twisting roll. The sky and trees and rocks all blurred as I moved through the air and just as I hit the ground I squeezed off a bullet toward that bottle of whiskey on the rock and came up on my feet with the gun fanning all around while the echo cracked through the hills.

The bottle of whiskey was still sitting there, straight and tall, on the rock. I looked down at the gun in my hand. It felt all right, tight and easy in the palm, but I'd missed clean. I raised it up straight out, closed my left eye and started to squeeze off when I stopped sudden. That's how Miss Amy did it when we fooled around with targets. That's how most people did it when they played with guns. I slipped the gun back in my belt. My hands were hanging by my sides, a little bit tight. I turned the palms over and looked down at them. There were the calluses on the thumbs where more times than I could count I had slapped the weapons into full cock, and there were the calluses in the palm where those butts had hit right exactly in the same place over and over and over again. Nobody else I knew had hands like that. Just me. I was the only one. I held them up in front of my eyes, almost straight out, then made the move, pulling and shooting in one quick motion, and the echo cracked again while glass flew in all directions, flashing as the sun caught the pieces and whiskey trickled down that stone, making it wet and dark.

The noise was still sounding in my ears and whiskey

soaking into the dirt while I mounted the pony and turned towards the ranch. The saddle was hot and I could feel the warm move into my belly. I thought of Miss Amy and how cold and tight she was down there compared to Conchita's warm softness, and I wondered how it was with other girls, which ones was like Miss Amy and which like Conchita. I thought on Betty Whitman and how she might have been when she was alive and how Baum had rubbed her dead things when he carried her across to the tree. Was it only Miss Amy and Conchita I was going to know about? Was it only going to be Miss Amy? That solid softness of her and the thin lips that tasted so clean?

I took hold of the butt of the gun sticking out of my belt. It was cool and hard like always. It had been so long since I had missed what I was shooting at that I had to check the feel of the butt. All those days without practice had dulled my aim, put off the draw just enough to miss the bottle. If it had been a man, any one of the men I had faced, I'd be dead back there by the rock, my blood soaking into the dirt just like my pa's whiskey. Then there would have been no more responsibilities.

But if I did what Mr. Barron wanted, and there wasn't no two ways about people doing what Mr. Barron wanted, I would be spending my time like he did, worrying about the cattle and the ranch hands and the women and the kids or about opening up a school. He didn't understand the feel of that butt, he didn't have time to practice. Nor Roy neither. He spent his whole day worrying about lost steers and drunk Mexes and horses with bad legs so that his worries weren't that much different from Mr. Barron or even Mr. Jordan and his dry goods store. He didn't even tie his gun down right.

And Miss Amy, that girl would take attention. She wasn't that much unlike her pa when it came to deciding how people were going to spend their time. I squeezed the butt again, hard, and again. I knew right then, knew for certain and forever, that once I let go that butt, once I gave up my practicing, I was just a boy who let people drip cold coffee over his ass.

I knew about responsibility. You could ask my pa or the Jordans or the people who used the livery stable or Jocko or

Miss Amy. They had all been my responsibility. But what about me? Me, Jory? What was my responsibility to me?

I pulled the gun from my waist and sighted down on a rock to my right, a bush to the left, a buzzard up above, just like when I was on the trail with Jocko, riding on down to Texas, to places I'd never seen. I liked Miss Amy, liked her, loved her, liked her a lot. But I didn't want a ranch any more than I had wanted a dry goods store. I knew right then that I'd run away from that as much as I had run away from going to St. Louis.

I'd wanted to see Texas. And I'd seen Texas. Now I wanted to see California. And Dodge City. I'd never seen Dodge City. And as I pulled and sighted, pulled and sighted, at rocks and trees and rabbits jumping out of the brush, I thought maybe I would go see Dodge City even before I went to California. I slipped the gun back into my waist. It felt nice and cool resting on my belly, and it made me feel easier about what I was going to do.

About the Author

Milton Bass lives in the hills of western Massachusetts with his wife and youngest offspring. He is a columnist for the *Berkshire Eagle* and an avid vegetable gardener. His Benny Freedman novels and the three other novels in the Jory series, *Sherrf Jory* and the upcoming *Mistr Jory* and *Gunfighter Jory*, are available in Signet editions.